Inspired from a true story

Sona

One Woman, Many Lives

Sona

One Woman, Many Lives

Ihina D. Basu
Sudipta Mukherjee

BLACK EAGLE BOOKS
Dublin, USA | Bhubaneswar, India

Black Eagle Books
USA address:
7464 Wisdom Lane
Dublin, OH 43016

India address:
E/312, Trident Galaxy, Kalinga Nagar,
Bhubaneswar-751003, Odisha, India

E-mail: info@blackeaglebooks.org
Website: www.blackeaglebooks.org

First International Edition Published by
Black Eagle Books, 2023

SONA
by **Ihina D. Basu** | **Sudipta Mukherjee**

Cover & Interior Design: Ezy's Publication

ISBN- 978-1-64560-461-7 (Paperback)
Library of Congress Control Number: 2023949072

Printed in the United States of America

DEDICATION

In loving memory of
my beloved friend Sona.

Ihina D. Basu

For Amit,
in gratitude for all that he has given me.

Sudipta Mukherjee

Prologue

This is not the story of a prisoner who had served sentences in prisons of three continents... America, Europe and Australia. This could not be called the story of a peddler, who had transported marijuana, heroin, and opium from one continent to another, under varied pretexts and at different junctures of her life. Neither is this, the chronicle of a drug addict or an alcoholic, although, she was crazily attached to both, enough to buy her those infamous accolades. This is not the story of a bar girl who had filled and re-filled glasses of drunkards for a greater number of years than she'd care to remember. This is not the story of a tarot reader, even though tarot reading had fed her for many years.

This is not exactly the story of a monk, who had taken reclusive bliss in the caves of meditative silence. Nor is it the story of a traveler who had embraced all the agonies and ecstasies of a voyager's life. This could not be sighted as the story of a mother, who had given birth to and nurtured multiple children, only to abandon them in the end.

If anything, this is the story of a woman, no more extra-ordinary than you, or the lady sitting next to you, full of folly – desire – frustration – hatred – anger – love – forgiveness – gratitude – and perhaps a million other emotions that claim a rightful stake in the constitution of human minds. A wild and inconsistent mash up of an inordinate number of elements, too numerous and, too spread out to be enlisted here and now. More so when the story itself has not yet begun, in its real sense of the meaning.

I don't claim to be too different from the woman who boards an early morning flight from San Diego, to attend a conference on drug abuse in AMA Conference Center, New York, in full knowledge of the purpose of her travel. Or the drug addict who sits aimlessly in a rehab in Astoria, looking at its bare wall with spectacular absentmindedness. Or even the woman who enters the Kentucky Correctional Institute for Women with charges as solemn as the murder of her abusive husband. I am not too removed from the journalist who travels from one city to another with nothing more than a duffle bag strapped to her shoulders. Or the volunteer who willingly enters a war zone to tend to people's injuries and care for them.

I have wrestled with death so many times in my one life that now it scares me no more. Just the reverse. I sniff a faint fragrance of familiarity in the idea; a light attachment towards it, however morbid it appears to an onlooker. I have spent extended moments of frightful intoxication and insane delusion, when I could not spot the difference between a hair and a hat. I have identified myself totally with that lame beggar who sits outside the VT Station, Bombay, looking at the passing crowds, anticipating a coin that could help her survive for the night.

So that's that.

Survive! That word defines the story of my life.

At its best, it is a chronicle of one woman's incessant efforts to survive, from the harrowing clutches of poverty, drugs and sex through the complex matrix of love, loss, and separation.

I cannot exactly tell you, what guides us in life. What it is that compels us to take that first step, which eventually leads us into a journey of a thousand miles? What plays in a traveler's mind, when he chooses one path over the other? As for me, it must have been a whim of the moment, or else, how do I elucidate this incredible journey that I now reckon as my life. I have lived my life, from moment to moment, not knowing most of the time, where my next meal would come from, if at all. Or what my next day would look like? If I would wake up hale and hearty and enjoy the sharp Santa Anna wind and mild Californian sun? Or I would discover myself sweating profusely in the impossible heat and sultry air of a mid-May Bombay afternoon? If I could be free, enough to decide for myself what my next step would be like? Or I would open my eyes and discover myself inside a harrowingly dark pit, the horrors of which would be beyond me.

The only certitude that accompanied me like a consistent companion was uncertainty. That I was aware of - uncertainty of an extreme kind. A variety of uncertainty that defies all logic and comprehension. And yet, I have lived. Survived. More number of years than I desired to. In my one life, I have lived one hundred lives, if not more, each one as enthusiastically as if it was the only one; as if it was the last one.

Chapter 1

II You are not my mother!" I yelled at Mama in a fit of rage that was adolescent and impossible.

Mama was lying on the couch, her belly swollen yet another time. She was to become a mother for the fourth time. Mama sprang up like a spring toy, her eyes flaring with anger.

"And from where does that come?" Mama said, deliberately, in a sharp voice. I noticed her cheeks turning rouge. She looked spiteful. When Mama looked like that, I invariably looked away and spoke. That made communication easy.

"Someone said you picked me from a garbage bin," I heard myself say, looking at my feet, avoiding her glaring eyes.

A slap; straight, crisp and cruel landed on my left cheek. I felt my ears burning, turning hot.

"Not a word. You hear me! Not a word more," Mama screamed at the top of her lungs, although I wasn't hard of hearing and standing next to her.

Then, she turned silent.

In the television, Richard Nixon was giving his Checkers speech that suddenly overshadowed the shabby room we were in. Walls and ceiling echoed with his voice. Lola cried out in her sleep, somewhere in the background.

Tears ran down my cheeks. Mama could have very well said that without the slap, I grumbled silently. There was no reason to hit.

I ran into the washroom and cried. Sitting inside the bathtub and crying was comforting. It suited me. Nobody could see my tears. Nobody knew that I was capable of crying. Wetness of the washroom felt like a cold comforter against the arid Santa Ana winds.

So that was Mama, my mother, Elizabeth Palmer. No Elizabeth Parker. No Elizabeth Palmer Parker. Well, I wasn't too sure. because, under different circumstances Mama used different surnames. Exactly like the shades of her lipstick - red, mauve, magenta, maroon... whatever.

Mama was a voluptuous woman with deep blue eyes and a luxuriant mop of brunette curls for hair. That was her natural color. And she loved those curls more than her children. Her children! Were we? Of course, we were! Apparently, Mama had no visible talent other than producing sounds at nights and babies once a year. Every year. Well, almost every year. All through her child bearing age. Some of her children survived; many did not.

"Sona, open the door. I need to pee," Mama banged the washroom door, hysterically, as though the motel was on fire.

I pretended not to hear.

"Sona, I say open the damn door," she shouted again, more violently. She coughed.

The child inside her must be scared like hell, I thought.

"You idiot! Open the damn door."

Still no response.

"I am gonna kill you Sona, if you don't open the door this minute."

Silence.

I inhaled deeply, and then forcefully exhaled all the air residing inside my little lungs. Once, twice, thrice.

"I need to pee Sona. It's urgent. Open the door I say," she screamed yet again. Her voice reminded me of a slit flute.

I rubbed my eyes with the heels of my palm, splashed water on my face, opened the door and ran out of the room.

"Prepare supper," I heard from behind.

"Prepare supper… from what?" I thought but didn't say.

For a longtime I sat in the parking lot that overlooked a Seven Eleven. On my right, a bright neon board blinked. "Motel 6." If memory did not betray me, that was our 45th place of stay in my twelve years of existence. Every three months or so, my parents decided upon a new space to dwell in. The place we were now was a cheap looking motel on Pasadena drive.

Surprisingly, this perpetual shift never seemed to bother them. Both my parents took it in their stride as gracefully as if it was something natural.

Father was seldom at home and Mama was either filled up with a child or suckling one at her breasts. Sometimes, both. And when it was time to do a chore or prepare a meal for the family, she feigned tiredness. Or perhaps she really was. I would never know. I was responsible for the day to day running of the house, or motel or wherever we were.

"Sona, am hungry," Larry tugged my golden braid.

"Tell that to Mama," annoyed, I barked.

"Mama says you are cooking supper tonight," he replied innocently.

"Oh yea!"

I turned my face away. A part of me wanted to run away from the motel that very moment. But where? And do what? At least I had a roof above my head, here, however transitory. Like an adult I rationalized.

Ten minutes later, when anger seeped out of me, I returned to the room and cooked. Mama lay on the couch the entire time, sifting through an ancient magazine with seminude pictures of hungry looking bosomy women for the hundredth time.

There was no oil in the kitchenette, hence we had boiled potatoes and roasted chicken; all procured from shops investing my wit in lieu of money. Mama had no problem with that. Interestingly, she never asked me where food came from. Whose money? Which shop? She was content if she had coffee swigging down her throat, cigarette on her purple lips and baby inside her tummy. And of course, strange sounds after dark, if Father was up and around. She had no other urge.

After supper, Larry, Lola and I often went out for a walk. That was my favorite time of the day; my escape from the pigeon hole of a room with its non-stop hum of television, mixed odor of old carpet, over used bed linen, and Mama. Mainly it was Mama, from whom I wanted to escape. I enjoyed the free sky above my head, the strong wind that brushed past my face and the gentle rhythm of my body while I walked. Even the cramp in my calves was a welcome break to steer my attention to.

While walking past houses, I often imagined a house like that for us. One entire bedroom to myself, where I could lock myself in and be at peace, away from Father's spiteful gaze.

My father, Mason Palmer prided in calling himself a 7th generation Californian. We were unfortunately the 8th. Unfortunately, because we were Mason's children and not exclusively Californian.

Mason was a very inspiring man. He inspired nothing but intimidation. A kind of fear that landed deep inside me and chilled my spine, blood, bones, flesh and skin into icicles. There was something about his eyes, or his ways of looking at me that discomfited me to no ends. And I would invest all my resources to remain as far away from him, as was possible. Another galaxy, if that was feasible. Yet, with him around, there was no escape. He had one thousand tentacles to catch me wherever I would dig myself into.

For months Father would remain away. Where? I had no clue. I was sure Mama too had no particular idea, and was at a remarkable ease with it. As for me, I wasn't overtly unhappy with that kind of arrangement - Father out of sight, away from home for indefinite periods of time.

Father was a chronic alcoholic. Social security officials would often catch him and keep him in their custody for days together. What would happen during those confinements, I'd never know. Just the way I would never know or understand a million other aspects of him. When at home he would drink a dozen pints of vodka a day and claim that it was perfectly natural to drink oneself silly.

The only good thing about Father being at home was that he brought in money, however insufficient. And that eased out a bundle of my worries.

By the time we returned to the motel, Father was home. He and Mama were locked inside. All kinds of noises drifted outside. Thumping, screaming, moaning, a few slaps. The spring mattress squeaked like a caged bird in distress. I felt miserable.

"What's that awful noise?" Larry asked.

I shrugged.

By then I was old enough to understand what Mamas and Papas did, when they wore no clothes and made sounds like that. The noise made me sick, bred in me an irresistible desire to retch.

"Come, let's sit outside," I said. Larry followed me. Lola slept in the pram.

We went outside and sat in the parking lot. It was dark. The silence felt comforting.

A memory rose in my mind.

It was this one time while opening the door abruptly, I had discovered Father and Mama in some kind of act, unclothed. My jaws dropped seeing the nude spectacle. The scene was so animal like that it knocked the air out of my lungs. Later, Mia told me that parents often did that when left alone. She had also seen her parents in a similar kind of act, making sounds that reminded her of dogs.

"That's a game, parents play," she added knowledgeably.

"Game? For what?" I had asked her, appalled.

"Why do we play games?" she questioned.

"For fun," I replied.

"Exactly! For fun," she added. "Also, to make babies!"

"To make babies?" I nearly screamed. "But Mama is already filled up with one!"

A car zoomed in and put a sharp break somewhere down the road. The noise snapped me back to the present.

I looked at Lola, peaceful in her sleep. She was ten months old. Something inside me first stirred, then melted. At twelve, I had become a mother of two children. A third one was on the way. Perhaps that was the reason I was sticking to that hell of a hole. Perhaps that was the reason I was enduring that gypsy life.

"Sona!" I heard Father scream after some time.

I somersaulted into the room at once. Mama was already asleep, draped in a sheet. The room was littered with clothes and garbage. I put Lola into the cot. Larry crawled into his make shift bed. Head covered, he drifted into sleep right away. I envied his luxury of innocence. I envied his sex. I was certain, it was his sex that saved him the horror from which I had no escape.

Father was on the couch, sipping vodka, waiting for his prey as if. I trembled with fear.

"Come here," he commanded.

I obeyed, silent as a lamb. Was there a choice?

Deliberately, I sat a little away from him. My heart began to race.

"Come, sit here," he barked, suggesting his lap.

And I knew right away the place he had pointed meant cuddles of a different kind; something so disagreeable that I shuddered at the thought. Yet, I could not speak a word against it. Protest was not for me to raise. Hence, I obliged; followed his instruction. When Father had bottle in his hand, wisdom was in surrendering to his fanciful whims, however dirty. I could hear Mama's loud snores from the other room. Why had she remained so blissfully oblivious to everything? Or was it a deliberate choice? Was she even my real mother? Was that drunken man sitting with outstretched legs and hunger in his eyes my own father? I had no way of knowing. Is this a father-daughter game? Does every father play this game with his daughter? I wondered silently as I inched towards him. The drone of queries inside my head was so loud that I missed what Father was saying, in fact screaming.

"How long does it take to move your lazy ass?" he yelled menacingly.

More scared, I jumped on his legs at once. My heart pounded so loud that I feared it'd explode into pieces right away, and I would die that instant. It did not. Neither my heart splintered into pieces nor did I die. I endured. I survived. I smelled Vodka in his breath. I noticed lust in his eyes. The effect was so nauseating that for a while I lost grip of my mind.

Slowly Father ran his finger on my face, as though he was blind. He would bring me closer towards him, touching and squeezing my buttocks in the process. I felt a fat sausage throbbing below my bottom.

The thought was disgusting. It bred in me a strong loathing for him. On Mama, for her strange aloofness. On myself, for surrendering to him.

After some time, he dozed off. Perhaps exhausted from his days work, or from the effect of vodka. And I would cry myself to sleep.

That incident happened again and again, almost every night when Father was home. Sometimes in the evenings when Mama was out and Father was in.

"I'll be gone for a while, Honey," Mama would announce, wearing a shockingly revealing gown and blood red lipstick. She'd kiss him on his cheeks and walk out. Her giant tummy revealing itself below her crimson dress. Her brunette curls hanging like a bundle of serpents let loose.

Hearing that, my heart would coalesce into a lead ball and plunge inside my stomach. There, it would bounce and bounce, relentlessly, until my stomach would be sore with pain, and my mind giddy with paranoid thoughts.

Where Mama went, I wondered. She was not employed, had no friends to catch up with. Very few relatives maintained relationships with her. And she always went out when Father was at home. Was this some kind of unspoken arrangement between her and Father? My mind turning numb, I could think no further.

No sooner did Mama go that Father would summon me under one pretext or another.

"Why is the room dirty?" He'd demand, as if I was the one responsible for cleanup.

"I didn't get time," I said, fumbling, picking up a few pieces of dresses from the floor, undergarments mostly that Mama must have tried and trashed before selecting the most disagreeable one.

"What the fuck you do all day?"

I was silenced. My hand and feet trembled like an epileptic.

"I feel like living in a shit hole," he said, followed by one extended sip from his bottle.

Anger made him look even more malevolent. His lips, red and thick would begin to tremble. I wondered if he was angry or was he pretending? His deep eyes glowed like two balls of fire.

"Stand right here, in front of me," he commanded.

I moved towards him, in full knowledge of the devastating consequence that was to follow.

Father put a slap squarely on my face. Tears flooded my eyes. Then, they dripped.

His rage was of course a momentary affair, for soon, he would pull me closer to him and pretend to console, his greedy palm all over me. First caressing my back, then gradually his hands would reach my growing breasts. He would touch and squeeze them, pretending not to. Until I would feel his steely penis under me. Was he feeling them, my breasts? What did he get by touching me that way? I wondered and wondered.

Those incidents, however shocking, saw a new me. It was another kind of birth. I gradually developed the ability to take my mind away from my physical body. So much so that after a while I did not even notice what Father said or did. Sitting there, in front of him, I was not quite there. I would switch off from my body and remain somewhere outside the periphery of his vision.

And nobody knew. Because nobody could trace my mind.

It was around that time I started noticing a different kind of presence near me. A being, who was only visible to me.

"Whom are you talking to Sona?" Mama would question, noticing me speaking in the kitchen.

"No one."

"Oh, you are. I have been seeing you for a long time," she'd say, convinced that I was talking to someone.

"No one I said," I'd reply enraged.

"You know what we call people who talk to themselves?" she asked.

I looked at her plump face, her swollen under eyes. I shook my head.

"Mad!"

I kept on blinking, thinking what to reply.

"Are you mad Sona?" she asked, gently but her tone was sarcastic.

"No."

"Then stop talking to yourself."

I nodded my head.

Mama sipped at her cup. Her expression changed at once. She made a face as if she had swallowed the bitterest medicine.

"Now, get me some more coffee. This is cold!"

I took the cup and walked into the kitchen, wondering if she was right. That only mad people talked to themselves.

That winter Mama delivered a baby girl, with brunette curls and pink lips. And cheeks that reminded me of ripe cherry. We named her Cherry.

Cherry colored our days, but only for a while. For, Mama grew increasingly irritable and tired, exhausted from nursing. And I burrowed deeper into the quagmire of responsibility. Looking after the house and studying during my free time. Father was out of the picture for some weeks, and I did not miss him.

His absence was a respite that I embraced. I feared to be with him. Feared to see that ugly demon slowly rise in him and then overpower him, taking me in the girdle of his muscular arms; and then scratch my soul with his animal paws... until I was sore with pain... until I bled.

Now, as I look back in time to recapture those bristly memories and write this story, I am appalled not by how much I remember, even after all this time. But that how strongly I feel the agonies of that twelve-year old defenseless girl, who was at the mercy of a wrong fate. Could she be called brave, for enduring in silence? Or was she a coward, for not having the courage to revolt against Mason, against each of his cruel acts and unsavory intentions?

Events that one glides though in life are by default or by design? Who decides? Who designs? Did Mason Palmer design everything so that Sona Palmer would play the prey? Or was there some greater designer who fashioned Sona's days and nights in such a way that she'd end up being a prey?

I still have no answer, exactly the way I was clueless then.

Chapter 2

After all the heartaches and miseries, cruel abuses and unkind beatings, it was hard to believe that not only did I survive but thrive; learnt to live with them as one would learn to walk through fire; learnt to dodge them at times, when things turned unbearable. And yes, more than anything else, learned to switch off at will.

At night, when the house would be quiet, only Mama's snores rattled the walls, I'd remain wide eyed.

"What's keeping you awake?" A voice said.

"Everything! This life," I replied sadly, not knowing whom I was talking to.

"Ah…it happens," the voice replied.

"Does it happen to everybody?"

"To the best ones."

"But I am not the best," I protested feebly.

"Who said?"

"Mama, Father… everybody."

"You got to be kidding."

"I am serious."

"They are not important. What's important for you is to rise above everything," the voice opined.

"How do I do that?" I said, wondering how could one rise above such obnoxiousness.

"Know that you are one in a million. A very special person."

"But everybody says I am a wretched child" I said at once.

There was no reply.

I discovered myself looking at a wall in the darkness. Mama's snores kept me company. Father was out that night, and relief was all that I had felt.

The next few days and weeks passed in relative ease. Father was out of sight and Mama sucked up in her own world. I spent half of my days at school, and the remaining half doing chores. Evenings settled into dusk while we ambled up and down the empty streets. Nights came and went in a delightful spell of peace.

Then one day, when Mama was out and I decided to visit a movie theatre with my siblings. I noticed a tall man in an overcoat and a hat who came forward and abruptly sat next to me, although most of the seats were vacant. I grew uncomfortable and was considering a change of seat when right at that moment I felt his strong hand on my thigh, inching upwards, inwards. The effect was so shocking that I grabbed Lola, and ran out of the theatre. Larry followed me.

Once outside, I met the lady sitting in the ticket counter. I told her about the incident. Immediately she called the cops and the man was taken into custody. Everything happened so fast that I did not have the time to think.

But the cops were good. After a while they drove us home; informed Mama about the incident and told us to be at the court for witness statement.

Father accompanied me to the court, wearing his best navy suit and dark trousers. He looked handsome. The case went on and on, three hours to say it by the clock. But for me, it lasted a life time. Questions after questions were being shot; question that were at once contemptuous and unkind. I did not know where to look at while I answered. And it hurt, not physically but somewhere beyond, deep inside. The hurt was raw, and questions were peppered with spices, that burned my flesh and my being alike. I grew conscious of gazes and stares all over my body.

"What exactly happened inside the theatre?" the public prosecutor demanded, time and again. His voice was rough, his tone demeaning.

I narrated the story, once, twice, thrice. After a while, I lost count. I kept repeating that harrowing experience repeatedly, looking at my brown shoes. Tears dripped from my eyes, and nobody saw. When I raised my head a little and looked at Father, I saw him looking at the convict with piercing eyes. It was as if he was threatening him with his gaze. But every time our eyes met; he quickly pulled his gaze down as if caught in an act of crime. His eyes were red, watery. Something in his appearance told me that he was feeling sorry for me.

In the end, the guy was detained with a minor conviction and I was left. It was a relief to be out of the court, and left alone, removed from critical gazes and judging minds. Silently, I got into Father's Dodge.

All through the journey I thought about the convict and his crime, the small punishment that he had brought on himself. Thoughts gradually drifted to the man who now sat next to me, driving the car in grave silence. My Father! He had assaulted me with many such crimes, abused me as if I was a toy designed for the purpose, and not a daughter meant to be loved. And yet I had endured them without a protest. Was there any court where I could drag him and seek justice? Was there any court where parents could be judged? I wondered as I gazed outside my window.

"You wanna grab a bite? You must be hungry," Father said. His voice was surprisingly gentle, his looks kind.

I looked at him, and kept looking at him. Tears splashed down my eyes, drop by drop.

"It's okay Sona. Don't think too much. Just forget it as a bad dream," he said maneuvering the wheels with one hand, and rubbing my tears off with the other.

The touch!

That was the kindest statement he had ever made. That was his most benign touch. Something inside me softened, I read sympathy in his hard blue eyes. I reconsidered my opinion about him. He might not be as evil as I had thought.

"Let's have some ice-cream," he proposed.

We ate the ice-cream but in silence. Father kept looking at my face, as I nibbled from my rainbow cup, conscious of his eyes on me. But it no longer disturbed me, because his looks were not the same. They had changed too.

The setting was new to me, unfamiliar in a way; the father-daughter relationship. Was he acting? Would he once again turn into a monster when he'd open the bottle? I knocked myself more than once, as I licked and relished the cold blob.

After we returned home, not a word was spoken,

about the case, about me, about anything. Parents didn't make love that night, I noticed. Father did not touch me, either for an embrace or for abuse. And I slept, dead to the world.

When I woke up the following morning, I felt like I had entered into a different life. Father was gone, and Mama was making her coffee. Cherry was cooing to herself, crawling on her fours, following Mama like a pet.

"What is my tiny-winy singing?" Mama said in a childish accent. She smiled.

Cherry looked up, in response as if. She clapped.

"Look, Sona is up," she said looking my side. "Good morning," she greeted. "You want something?"

I blinked. Must be a dream, I thought. And yet the dream continued.

"Hurry up Sona. We are getting late for school," Larry shouted from the washroom.

"It's okay if you want to skip school today," Mama said.

That day I did not go to school, and mostly remained in bed. Sleeping, dozing, remaining awake, and then, after a while falling asleep again. Everything around me was the same, and yet something had changed. It took me a while to realize the change. The room grew calm, peaceful despite its obvious noises, despite Cherry's cooing and cries, despite Larry and Lola's conversations and wrangles. The room resembled home. And we started resembling a family.

Father was gone for a while now. During my evening strolls, at times I'd wonder where he was. What could he be doing? Which city, which state could he be? Was he in some danger? I remembered his pensive look, the sadness in his eyes, the day we sat in that ice-cream parlor.

"Oh Sona, where the hell were you?" Mama screamed, the moment I returned from school. She looked like she had been freshly rescued from a hurricane.

"What happened?"

"I got a call from Grand Pa," she sniffled, "Grand Ma is in hospital. We must go. Pack your bags," she said and rubbed her under eyes with her palm.

"Go? Where?" I said, alarmed.

"To Grand Pa's house," she barked.

"But we just shifted here a month ago," I said referring to our new place of stay.

"Stop talking and start packing," Mama yelled, followed by a long bout of cry that lasted as long as I packed.

Her makeup melted drop by drop that she rubbed with a paper towel and trashed every half a minute. Although she was crying, I felt sad to see her thus, but the scene had a comical effect on me.

Mama and tears, that too for a person she particularly did not like. I doubted if she and Grand Ma ever spoke to each other all through my growing years. If memory did not betray me, they were not on talking terms. Grand Ma didn't like Mama's outrageous life style, and Mama didn't like anybody who dared to speak against her life style. The result was a chasm that never bridged. The sudden surge of uncontrollable tears was intriguing. I wondered if Mama was genuinely sad for her sick mother, or she was feigning Grand Ma's illness as an escape from that motel on Michelson drive. But then, escape from what, I wondered.

"Grand Pa's house is in Sacramento," I said.

"I know that. And you need to hurry up. We don't have much time," Mama replied heatedly.

In less than an hour, we went off to Appaloosa Way, Sacramento. Grand Pa's house was supposed to be our next home, the next waiting room in the journey of my life. Was it my 49th or 50th? Whatever! It no longer mattered.

Peace evaporated from our lives as quickly as it had appeared a few weeks ago. In its wake was a new craziness that Mama was wholeheartedly sold to. She went to the hospital every single day and I was left to care for the family. The only silver lining at Grand Pa's house was that food was always available, and without much effort. And Grand Pa was a darling. He recited us poetry from a hard bound book, while all of us listened enthralled. His voice was deep, full of emotion.

"Lemme see if I can put you to school," he announced one night to Larry and me.

"School?" I hiccupped.

"Yes, school. Children should go to school and not sit at home," he emphasized.

And so, the next day he took me along with him and enrolled me to Bradshaw Christian School. I wondered how long I would attend that school, before the next one.

School was nothing great and neither was learning, because, by then I fell into the disastrous habit of escaping from anything that resembled education. But friendship with Elena Smirnov was good, something I looked forward to each day, every day. Elena's ancestors were Russian immigrants who lived in Grand Pa's neighborhood for nearly a decade.

A new sun rose in my sky. It bathed me with a new

kind of love. Everything about Elena was magical. Now I'd spend more time with Elena than I ever did with any single person in my life time. Elena became my savior, my guide. The warmth of her friendship melted my heart, each time she held my hands. I felt loved.

"Want to join me for piano lessons?" Elena proposed one afternoon sitting in a park. That was her spot; her locus in the world, she always said. I looked into her green eyes when she said it. I wondered where mine was.

"I don't have a piano," I said.

"That's no problem. You share mine," she offered.

Thus, our piano classes started without much ado. Lessons brought us further close. Between the octaves and quartets, we discovered a new bond. Often, I'd borrow clothes and shoes from her, and stay back at her place under the pretext of sleepovers. We spent nights sitting on roof tops under a canopy of stars. Life seemed too beautiful to be real... too good to be mine.

"You are my first love," Elena said one night, as we lay on our backs looking up into the night sky.

"And you are mine," I replied.

"Promise me that we will be like this. Forever." she said extending her hand towards me.

"Promise," I said as I intertwined my fingers with hers.

Elena took our entangled palms close to her face, and then, she kissed. I kept looking at her, wondering what she would make of me if I broke her promise. Would she understand my situation and still love me? Perhaps not. I did not have the heart to ask.

Nearly three months later, one-night Grand Ma's heart suddenly stopped. She expired, and so did my good time.

An evening not too long after Grand Ma's funeral, I returned home from school to discover Father sitting on Grand Pa's couch, smoking a cigarette, chilling. A tornado of activities was going on in the house. Mama was jumping up and down, packing things that were not already packed.

"Pack your stuffs fast, Sona, we got to move," she said in a hurry.

"Move? But where?" I said.

That same question! Quite naturally I got back the same reply.

"We need to hurry up, there is not much time. Pack up your things. Or we go without your stuffs," Mama screamed from another room.

And it dawned on me that we were leaving Sacramento that very moment.

"I need 10 minutes, Mama, please," I begged. Tears were already in my eyes, on my face.

"Stop behaving like a kid. Go and pack your clothes," she barked.

"Please … please. I want to say good bye to Elena," I began to cry.

"Okay. You have ten minutes. Max."

I rushed out of the house, got into a store, bought two Hallmark Date Books and then went to meet Elena.

"This one is for you," I said in a shaky voice. Emotions overwhelmed me.

"You are going?" Elena said incredulously.

I nodded, unable to speak. Tears ruined my face, my expression.

"Where?"

"I don't know," I hugged her and cried, heard her faint sobs against my ear. "I don't know if I am going to come back ever, but I want you to keep this book. And I shall keep this with me," I said in between sobs.

When we tore ourselves apart, Elena's face was red. Tears had ruined the cute expression of her face that I once fell in love with.

"Good bye," she said rubbing my cheeks.

"Good bye."

Elena stood at her door, in an aquamarine shirt dress, waving with both her hands. There was a glint of smile on her lips but her eyes looked sad.

As our car moved ahead, she turned smaller and smaller, until she was no longer visible. I wondered how many more partings and shiftings I was destined to survive before I would finally settle my roots in.

Some years later, Grand Pa told me that Elena was studying music at Yale. She aspired to become a pianist.

"She has turned into a fine young woman, very pretty, very talented," Grand Pa said over phone. I could almost see him smile, as he said those lovely words.

Instantly my mind rolled back to our piano lessons, the small yet blissful moments I had spent with her. Her dainty fingers that I had once held and kissed; cherished. The sparkle in her eyes. Her passion! I was a child then, and yet I knew that she'd go places, far ahead than the ordinary kind that I was. And that one day she would do me proud.

Chapter 3

From Grand Pa's house, we bounced back to a small, rented house on Grevillea Avenue, Hawthorne.

It had two bedrooms with bare minimum furniture, a messy drainage system, many defective faucets and dirty floors. Nonetheless, it was home. A single thought churned inside me ripples of contentment. I would now have an entire room for myself and my siblings. How wonderful! But there was no time to bask in the glory of having a real home.

"Sona, stop dreaming and set up the kitchen," Mama yelled.

I rushed and helped mother set up the meagerly equipped kitchen. Helped? Well, actually not. Because, no sooner did I enter the small kitchen, she evaporated from the scene and got inside her bedroom. Her bedroom! And Father's too. I breathed out a little sigh of relief at the thought.

Of course, the illusion of happiness was transitory, like a whiff of fragrance. For, two days later a couple of burly cops materialized at our door with an arrest warrant and took Father away.

"Don't worry, will be back in a day," he said to Mama, pecking her cheek with a kiss.

Mama nodded, looking glum. There were no parting words from her.

Days transformed and rolled, first into weeks, then into months. Father did not return. He was first detained, and then sentenced to a prison in Milwaukee. Mama never told me what crime he had committed but I suspected that it was something grave. She stopped talking for a while. Cloistering herself in her bedroom she smoked one cigarette after another. Often, I'd notice her looking blankly at the window, her mind lost in some thought that I neither could understand nor pretend to know.

"You want something?" I'd say, peeping through the door.

"Coffee," she said to the wall, in a tone that was new to me. I felt sad for her. Now she and her room resembled each other; messy, stinking, almost upturned.

That night, I feared losing Mama. Her sadness sunk inside me. No longer did she care about how she looked. Or what dress she was wearing? She bathed less and often smelled fowl. Her breasts would leak, ruining the front part of her shabby dress. And yet, she wouldn't be bothered, either to change the dress or hold Cherry to her breasts. It was I who held her at Mama's nipples when her cries grew loud and unbearable.

And our condition fell - from bad to worse.

Then one day, nearly a month later, a bright new star appeared in our dark sky, in the form of Mr. Helpful. His name was Martin Goldsmith and he brought with him a bucket full of opportunities… to start all over again.

I returned from a local swimming club, hungry and thirsty, and there he was, sitting on the couch, smoking, sipping at his cup. Coffee!

"Hello little one," he greeted me in an over friendly voice. He was trying to be nice, and it annoyed me right from the beginning. There was a hamper full of goodies on the table, I observed. "That one is for you," he pointed. He smiled with yellow teeth.

"Thanks," I said and got inside my bedroom. Hunger dwindled in an instant.

"Who is he?" I questioned Mama that night, after Martin left. The room smelled of his cologne. Mama's bedroom! Her bed looked as if an elephant had trampled on it. I looked at her tummy, almost anticipating an outcome.

"He is a relation, a friend. Nice guy," Mama said cheerily.

"Relation? What kind?" I asked, almost expecting to listen, *oh your new father.*

"Grand Ma's step mother's side, 2nd cousin's son," Mama mapped an impossible relation that would require a super brain to decipher.

"I didn't know Grand Ma had a step mother?" I said irritated at her serene expression, as if second cousin's son of a dead mother's step mother's side of the family was a nice little proposition to be hugged and jumped into bed with.

"That's not important," she was saying. Mama took a long drag from her cigarette. There were scars and bites all over her neck. She looked clean and surprisingly well groomed, I noticed.

"Then what is important?" I questioned, annoyed.

Mama was silent. I wondered if she was searching for an answer or averting my question.

"How could you be so cruel? Father is in prison, and you bring this Martin into the house… How could you forget him so fast?" I did not know why, but I felt sympathetic for Father now.

"That's none of your business who I bring into the house and who I throw out. Your father is in prison for no good reason, so let's not get there. You hear me?" she was screaming louder than she needed to.

So, Mama knew why cops had arrested Father. And all those days she pretended as if she did not know a thing.

"Martin is a hero! He has just returned from the Korean War. Mason is a cockroach… a sleazy little cockroach," she spat.

"Hero! Returned from the Korean War! Medal him with a child!"

Having said that I banged the bedroom door and walked out. I sat in my room for a long time. When hunger pangs began to overwhelm me, and my mouth watered uncontrollably, I ate the burgers and muffins from that hamper. The burger tasted heavenly. Mr. Hero Helpful chose well, I was forced to conclude, but I doubted his choice of a woman.

And the war hero was a man of commitment. For, the next couple of months, he visited Mama every now and then; each time with different set of hampers to feed us from. Burgers and fries, pancakes and omelets, muffins and chocolate chip cookies. At times he took us for shopping too, pampering us with ice creams and lollypops, new clothes and trendy shoes. And of course, he catered to Mama's private whims and demands behind the perpetually closed bedroom door.

Mama glowed like a bride. And the deeper he penetrated inside her body and her life, the more disgusting I felt for him, for her, and for everything that was happening around us.

Nearly a month later, one day I returned from school to be greeted by Mr. Hero Helpful, lying cozily on the couch, bare torso, in an ink blue boxer short. Martin was disagreeably hairy, I noticed.

"Come on guys, we are going to Mexico!" Martin announced with a show of happiness on his sun brunt face.

"Mexico?" I asked.

"Yes Mexico. Go quick. Pack your stuffs," Mama yelled from her bedroom. She was dressing Cherry, I sensed.

I washed and cleaned, got myself into the new dress that Mr. Helpful had bought for me during our last shopping trip. It took me nearly an hour. All the while my mind buzzed with that one word, Mexico.

"Why Mexico?" I asked myself repeatedly.

Mama walked out of her bedroom door wearing her maroon gown that she reserved for special occasions. There was a string of pearl hugging her neck. I wondered where that flashy neck piece suddenly came from. Was it a gift from Mr. Hero Helpful?

Larry and Lola enjoyed the ride. Cherry was too small to understand the ridiculousness of a 26 hour drive, where Mama and her Mr. Hero couldn't stop giggling and chatting, at times throwing each other sly glances and inaudible whispers. I felt my stomach churning at the devastating thought. Would Mr. Hero Helpful soon become our Mr. Father, number two? Although he had been kind to us so far, I feared the outcome anyway. Something in his attitude was telling me that he would not remain like that for long. And that, a somersault was somewhere round the corner, just beyond the periphery of my sight.

A sharp break and I was jostled back to the real world. It was the border town of Tijuana, I realized from the glow boards and name plates of different shops. And I discovered myself looking at the city as if I had arrived there in a dream.

"Mexico… Mexico," I heard Lola scream. She looked happy.

A conversation from the past rose to my memory.

"Nobody visits Mexico for any good reason," Elena had once said. She said that a cousin from her mother's side visited Mexico, every time she desired to change her husband.

"Change husband?" I had asked, incredulous. Was there a place where I could change my mother, I remembered to have contemplated, although did not have the heart to ask her.

"People go to Mexico either for a quick marriage or for quick divorce," she added.

I recalled with towering sadness. My stomach tightened at the thought.

"Did Mama and Mr. Helpful come here to marry?"

I began to hate her, and him.

"Will be back in a while," Mama said, as she got

down from the car, slightly lifting her gown. "Look after the children, don't go here and there."

I looked up, unable to believe what I was seeing. Thought left my mind.

"Stay in the car till we return," Martin announced. His voice had a new edge, I noticed.

I did not reply.

Minutes passed, and then hours. One... two... three... four. Temperature inside the car rose to a hundred degree, and so did my restlessness. I felt hungry, thirsty. I needed to pee. Cherry wailed loudly. I embraced her and began to pacify with a lullaby, when I heard,

"*Hola!*"

That was from a beefy man with dark curly hair and bronze skin. He was smiling with a missing tooth.

"*You from America? Need help?*" he said, trying to strike up a conversation.

I pulled up the glass. The heat inside was stifling. Perspiration drenched my back. Sweat dripped from Larry's freckled temples. I began to panic.

"Where are they?" Larry said. "I don't think they are going to come back." His face was flushed.

"They will," I announced but without conviction. Something was turning inside my stomach.

"Am telling you, they are gone," he said rubbing his face with his palm.

"Stop talking shit. How will they go? The car is with us," I said in a fit of rage.

Random thoughts began to burst in my mind. Like

bubbles of air. What if Mama did not return? Okay we have the car with us, but who would drive? Where could we go, if we have to live alone? Grand Pa's house or ours? Worse still, what if Martin killed our mother and returned alone? Would he treat us kindly? Would he still buy us hampers? I could feel anxiety rising and falling inside my trachea like a ball of mercury.

"Pull down those damn windows," Larry screamed. "Am out of my breath!"

It was getting dark outside. Street lights and shop windows began to glow.

"I am scared," Lola whispered.

"Pull down the window, you will feel better," Larry opined. Although he put up a brave face, but he too was equally scared. I could feel it in his voice, in the horror filled look of his red face. He shook his feet constantly, a clear indication that he was nervous. Cherry was asleep in my arms.

I felt as if I was locked inside a time capsule, with no exit. Locked for how long, I wondered.

Nearly a century later I saw her, saw them. Mama and Martin, moving towards the car, tipsy in their amble. Mama held a photograph in her hand. She looked lost; and so pathetically drunk that I feared she would puke right away. And she did, much before she even reached the car. Once, and then again. Mama reeked of alcohol.

When finally, they settled inside the car, I noticed the picture. It was their wedding photograph. None opened their mouths all through the return journey, not even a word of apology for locking four children inside a car for 6 long and torturous hours. They behaved as if it was normal, to lock children in a car in an unknown country. Martin drove, whistling a tune, an odd tune.

Something told me that the drive would lead us into a new life. I wondered what its color would be. What the days would be like? And the nights? If I took that day as a sample of our forthcoming days – with Martin and Mama as husband and wife, life wouldn't be sunny at all.

The miles and miles of intractable darkness beyond my window hinted to me the darkness of my forthcoming days. A peculiar sensation overwhelmed me; a mixture of fear and resignation. My hands and feet turned numb. Hunger left me, although I had not eaten anything substantial that day. Thirst did not bother much. After some time, I fell asleep.

When I opened my eyes next, we had reached home.

A new life welcomed me the following morning. A life with new sets of rules. New person to attend to. New whims to take care of.

Martin Goldsmith was from the army background; and that made living with him a lot worse than I had anticipated. He made a routine for us to follow. Routine that classified me as a slave, and he played the master. I was supposed to make coffee, breakfast and dinner, fetch water, scrub cookware and crockeries, clean washrooms. In a single statement... do everything. He said that Mama had gone through a lot of stress, handling all the children single handedly for so long, so she needed to rest now. Was he so stupidly in love? I wondered, as I listened to him.

"Are we clear?" he barked at the end of his long lecture. That was the first time I heard him speak loudly. Martin never got back to his original tone.

"Yes," I whispered, fearful of his angry look and crimson eyes.

"Are we clear?" he repeated, looking into my eyes.

"Yes," I repeated but gently.

"Are we clear?" he said again. This time almost shouting his lungs out.

Cherry started crying in the next room.

"What happened, Baby," Mama ran out of her bedroom in a black slip that revealed more and concealed less. "You look upset."

"Yes, we are clear," I shouted back looking at him, ignoring Mama.

"Good!" Martin said. "Now move. And yes, school attendance is a must. No compromise on education."

Mama sat next to him and kissed him on his mouth.

I looked outside the window ignoring their passion play. The kiss quickly transformed into a never-ending smooch. I was shocked at the spectacle.

"Am teaching these children a little discipline," Martin said, unhooking from her mouth. His voice changed in an instant, I observed.

"Oh, you naughty naughty boy…wait till I have my coffee."

No sooner did she finish her morning coffee that they both bounced back into their bedroom at once and started making noisy love. Mama screamed and screamed. I locked myself inside my room pretending not to notice or hear anything.

"Why is Mama shouting?" Lola asked after a while,

when the house literally reverberated with all kinds of noises.

"I don't know. You ask her when she is out," I replied.

"Oh that. She is having sex," Larry added confidently.

"Who told you?" I asked, appalled.

"What?" Larry said.

"That sex thing," I fumbled for a speech.

"I just know," he replied, shrugging his shoulders.

"But how?" I asked.

"It's a guy thing," he said with a wink. "All men know."

"What's sex? I want it... I want it," Lola said at once jumping on her toes.

"Shut up," I silenced her.

But Mama and Martin could not be silenced. They went on and on.

Mother married another man; we made a new beginning. And yet, each day that followed was not too different from the earlier ones. Every morning I woke up with a new fear; fear of Martin's strict discipline and unpredictable wrath. Every night I went to bed exhausted and morose, from the day's happenings. Unlike Father, Martin returned from work every night. Where he worked, I had no clue, but he mostly returned home at the same time. And that put me, put all of us in a constant state of panic. He was a lot worse than Father, I gathered. Mr. Helpful transformed himself to Mr. Hell, almost overnight.

Then one day I discovered a book on pregnancy lying

aimlessly on our dinner table. I lifted it, shuffled through it pages and my head exploded. It was as if a bomb had blasted inside my skull. My face turned red, my hands and feet trembled with rage.

"What is this?" I asked Mama brandishing the book.

"Yes, I am pregnant," she replied calmly.

"How could you do this?" I could feel tremor in my lips.

"What do you mean by how could you do this? The way everybody does," she replied.

"You don't even care for your existing children, and you want more? I can't believe this," I turned my back, already beginning to move.

"That's none of your business," I heard her say.

"Of course, it is my business. Because you are going to put it on my head," I shouted and banged the door.

Martin was happy with the news. His over-enthusiastic and noisy labor would soon bear fruit. That evening he took a break from his habitual barking and treated us with beef burgers.

The fruit that Mama was carrying inside was a twin, as we came to know after a few months. Mama began to grow in size while I shrunk. She would sleep all through the days while I was left in charge of the house. Martin grew anxious and crankier with each passing day. His voice and temper touched the sky.

Christmas that year unfurled the gift, a boy and a girl. Martin named them Charles and Cindy.

Then one night, Martin made his first attack on me. It was a calculated move. Mama was in the hospital and all the children were asleep. Nobody would see him doing a thing. His offense would be safe.

I was sleeping in my bed when I suddenly opened my eyes to discover him standing in the dark, looking at me. I turned stiff with fear. Gradually he bent down and started fondling my breasts. His hand was hard, ruthless. I tried to wriggle out but found it difficult. Martin had pinned me down with his other hand. Then suddenly an idea struck me. I began to scream, loudly, so loudly that I was certain it would wake Larry from his sleep. Martin ran away from our bedroom and locked himself in his room.

From the following night, I locked my room and slept.

And yet, after that night, everything between Martin and me changed. However ugly it had been so far, still there was hope; a hope that maybe one day things would be fine. Perhaps one day he would love me, as a daughter and I'd see him as a father. But that possibility now seemed remote, improbable. Our relationship fell apart. I lost all respect for him.

However, Martin kept on trying, subtly, sometimes blatantly, much to my surprise. He would touch me here and there, under different pretexts. He'd constantly look out for opportunities to lay his paws on my skin. One night he twisted our door knob to get inside. When he discovered it was locked from inside, he quickly set up a new rule.

"No child should lock any door," he declared. "It's for your safety."

Out flew all the locks of the house, including the ones from the washroom doors.

Then one day he got inside the washroom while I was taking shower.

"Oh… it's you!" he said plainly, without a visible shred of embarrassment, as I stood naked in front of him.

Water dripped from my nude body. I avoided looking into his eyes. But I was certain he was scanning my body. Swiftly he retreated from the bathroom, closing the door with an unnecessary thud. The incident must have occurred for a few seconds; but the damage lingered for years hence.

Mama returned from the hospital and I breathed out a sigh of relief. I thanked God for that slight piece of luck. For, I was certain that Martin would not do anything with mother around. Perhaps I had judged him too charitably than he deserved, because his cunning moves and quick assaults continued despite Mama's presence.

"Won't you make coffee for me Sona?" Martin would say in a mock politeness. His smile would unnerve me to no ends.

"I'd rather kill you with piss," I was tempted to say but didn't.

Cizzy O'Connor, my school friend had said that human urine has poison, enough to kill a person if fed in good quantity. And thus, I kept on trying, taking baby urine from the potty seat and mixing in his black coffee. Nothing happened. Not even a hair fell out of his body. After many such futile attempts, I stopped trying. But Martin never stopped.

Cizzy and I became friends. What bound us more than the classroom that we now shared was our common agony of dealing with abusive stepfathers.

"Your father does it too?" I asked aghast. I couldn't believe my ears.

"Don't call him father. He is son of a bitch. Fucking bastard," Cizzy spat.

I thought about my own father, how abusive he'd be to me.

"Come, let's go for a walk," she said, holding my hands.

We walked, miles after miles after miles, in silence. I remembered my days with Elena, how happy we used to be, things we'd share with each other. Cizzy gradually went on filling the vacuum that Elena's absence had created. We started falling in love.

Days passed quickly but not happily. With Martin around it was impossible to be happy.

The following November, Mama delivered another set of twins. Two baby girls. Martin named them Anna and Nina. I did not go with Martin to see them. Mama returned from the hospital two days later.

Our house now busted with noises from eight children. Cries, wails, shouts, fights, arguments, laughter and sometimes talks filled up the entire living space. That, and on top of everything, Mama's house rattling snores all through the night. She was a sound sleeper. And Martin was a fucking son of a bitch! I turned increasingly sleepless and panic ridden. Days were sucked up in bone breaking work and nights saw me tremble with fear.

And then, one night it happened. The unthinkable! The monster inside Martin came out and caught me in its demonic clutches. The world around me collapsed like house of cards.

Martin attempted to rape me. Of course, he could not succeed, for, after a bit of struggling I wriggled out of his powerful clutch and ran out of the house in my night clothes. I took shelter in the backyard of a Mexican neighbor, hid behind a bush all night, shivering, feeling miserable. But there was a case anyway. Martin was arrested for child rape and molestation.

The court case was emotionally more devastating than the attack itself than all the assaults and attacks that Martin had invested in me put together. I was made to speak, to narrate each detail an unbelievable number of times, so many times that in the end I lost count. I cried with unshed tears; screamed my lungs out but no sound escaped from my throat.

"Did he touch your breasts?" the prosecutor demanded.

"He did."

"Did he fondle them. Squeeze them."

I nodded.

"Did he touch your buttocks?"

"Yes."

"Did he touch you in between your legs?"

"Yes." My ears became hot. My voice turned wobbly. I shuddered at the thought, when Martin had tried to thrust his dirty hand inside me.

"Did he penetrate?"

I nodded, unable to speak.

"I didn't hear you Miss," he said.

The queries went on and on. Deeper and deeper an axe chopped my heart. I was sore with pain, with humiliation, with sadness of the entire world.

In the end Martin was declared innocent and freed from the rape charges because he did not *penetrate*, as I gathered from the proceedings.

I lost all interest in the case. In Martin. In living with him and Mama. In living. In life.

And yet, I lived. Survived the assaults, survived the case. Survived the vicious proceedings that were more heart wrenching than those cruel acts had been. Survived Martin's angry looks and indecent probing.

Survived!

Chapter 4

His name was Galvin McCarthy; and I was in love. At 16 and not quite a child, I flew like butterfly with happiness on my wings.

I was out with Nora and her friends, to celebrate her seventeenth birthday, when I saw him first.

"That guy is quite a looker," Nora observed.

I turned around, and there he was. Sitting alone at another table, not too far from ours, drinking beer, looking intently at a flower in the vase; a variety of orchid not common in California. The attentiveness of his eyes impressed me, also the color, ocean blue; the meditative demeanor of his face. Although he was sitting, I could say that he was a tall guy.

"Ya, but no need to ogle," I said, already annoyed that Nora was looking meaningfully at his side.

"Jealous?" Nora said.

"My foot," I spat.

"Excuse me," interrupted a baritone voice.

I looked up to discover that the guy was standing

next to me with an orchid in his hand. My heart jumped into my mouth.

"Yes?"

"This one is for you," he said extending his hand. A warm smile graced his thin lips.

"Thank you," I took the flower from his hand and kept it on the table. I smiled.

"The flower will look more beautiful, if you tuck it in your pony," he added gently.

And he was flirting.

I blushed, yet seconds later did what he said.

"Can I get you a drink?" he offered, elated.

Minutes later I was sitting opposite to him, and Nora and her friends were glaring at us.

"I am Galvin," he paused, and then said, "Galvin McCarthy," extending his hand for a formal shake.

"Sona Palmer," I said taking his hand. His grip was powerful, and yet pleasure was all that I had felt. Galvin had a narrow, elongated face with wavy brown hair.

"You are beautiful," he was saying.

I smiled, acknowledging his compliment.

"You love flowers on women?" I said, unable to think of anything to say.

"I am a pilot, flew to Hawaii one million times, am used to seeing women adorned with flowers. It's common there. But..." he paused suddenly uncertain to say more. Galvin bit his lips a couple of times, I noticed.

"But?" I probed.

"May I say something?" he said, looking deeply into my eyes.

I almost thought that he would say I love you or some such thing. My heart raced like a mad pony, as I kept looking at his deep-set eyes.

"Of course."

"You have put the flower on the wrong side," he said making a small gesture with his index finger.

"Is there a correct side?" I asked intrigued.

"Not exactly, but each side tells a different meaning."

"What does mine tell?" I was curious now.

"It means you are married. All married women put flowers behind their left ear. And single women put it on their right," Galvin elaborated. I was amazed at his knowledge of women and flowers.

"What's Hawaii like?" I asked to change the topic.

"Beautiful," he replied. "Lovely beaches, warm weather, friendly people... You must be there to feel the place," his voice trailed off. I suspected that he instantly got transported to Hawaii.

"Are you inviting me to Hawaii?" I said, with a naughty smile on my lips.

"Only if you want," he said peering into my eyes meaningfully.

I looked at him, impressed by his pace; more impressed by his style and genteel demeanor.

"I don't mean to rush into you..." he corrected himself immediately, sensing my sudden discomfiture.

I breathed out, two long and gentle exhalations.

"For now, we could go for a drive," he offered.

"Drive? Where?"

"Malibu…"

Off we went to Malibu in his black Subaru. As we drove, he told me more about himself. His parents, his two elder brothers and their wives; his not so small but happy family. Their pilgrim!

"Pilgrim? What's that?"

"Well, my parents have an eighteen-foot schooner. We named it Pilgrim. We sometimes lease it to movie makers for shooting and all," he elaborated, visibly proud with the announcement.

"That's a nice name, Pilgrim," I observed.

"Oh yea. Mummy's idea," he said. "Am going there to do some fixing job."

"And what will I do while you fix your pilgrim?"

"Talk to Mummy. She is kind of nice," he said.

And he was right. His mother, Evelyn McCarthy was nice, warm, and a lot more loving, quite unlike my mother. She was tall, with broad shoulders, with almost manly features, but gentle and polite in her demeanor. She had a striking resemblance with Galvin.

"He looks so much like you," I observed.

"Who Galvin?" Evelyn paused. "Yes, many say that. And you look so pretty," she added in a pleasing tone.

Evelyn said that she came along with her family to America in the wake of Easter Rebellion. She, a young woman of 15 then, met Galvin's father, Daniel McCarthy in the ship. Daniel was twenty. He had lost his father in the uprising and was leaving Ireland for good. They fell in love even before the ship landed in America.

I blended with the family effortlessly. And it wasn't too difficult. Galvin's family was warm and friendly. They shared food, laughed all the time, cracked jokes with one another, something that was devastatingly missing in my family. It soothed me, the family setting. I felt home from the moment I stepped in.

"You love my son?" Evelyn asked with a hint of smile.

"I don't know," I denied, although I was crazily falling in love with him.

"He loves you?" she added quickly.

"Don't know," I denied once again.

"Oh dear, you need not know. It runs in the family. These men are like that. They fall in love fast," Evelyn said. "And you are blushing, like a bride," she observed.

At that moment all I wanted was to be a bride. Galvin's bride. I wanted to be a part of that beautiful family. I wanted to be one of them.

An hour later Galvin took me to the water in a small boat.

"For rowing," he said.

I sat inside the boat looking at him. My mind buzzed with Evelyn's comment, *they fall in love fast.* He kept on rowing, drifting me away from the shore. Our boat rocked gently below my bottom, and I relished the feeling. Life appeared to be one big dream, blue and translucent, just like the color of his eyes.

"Will you marry me?" he suddenly said.

I was so carried away by surprise that all I could say was, "Now?"

Galvin laughed. His laughter was infectious, for soon I was laughing too. Galvin had perfectly shaped teeth, I observed.

"Well, we cannot possibly marry here, in the water. After we land, of course," he elaborated.

I fell silent, contemplating how Mama would react seeing me married at seventeen.

"Hey, you need not be so stressed. Am not going to push you into the water, if you say no," he joked. His sense of humor impressed me, but what intrigued me was his quick observation.

"For your knowledge, I can swim. Just in case you are thinking to push me," I replied offhandedly.

"Oh… you are too sweet to be pushed into the water."

"I am too young to get married," I said.

"How old is my wild orchid?" Galvin added admiringly.

"17. And you?"

"24, a perfect marriageable age."

"Not mine," I said, somewhat annoyed, for being so young.

"That can be fixed," he said, suddenly taking the boat towards the shore.

"How?"

"Now that's a little surprise for you."

On reaching the shore, Galvin rushed towards his car. I followed him. As we drove Galvin briefed me the plan. He said Nevada was the only place where wedding was quick and hassle free.

"Where in Nevada?" I asked, surprised at the quickness of his decision and the precision of his planning. It appears he had been to that place and married a few times.

"Las Vegas," he said beaming, poking my cheeks with his index finger.

And I thought of my trip to Mexico, when Mama married Martin; the awkwardness of sitting inside a closed car with siblings. Surely Martin was not aware of Las Vegas, as a quick and hassle-free destination for marriage. The thought brought into my mind, the image of Mama, the retribution that would follow after I return and disclose my marriage.

"After marriage we could have a little drive to the Canyon," Galvin was saying.

I was snapped back to the pleasant reality, that Galvin was driving the car and we were going to Las Vegas to marry, and then a little honeymoon in the Grand Canyon. What bliss!

I imagined him as a loving husband; a doting father in days to come. Responsible, matured, and a family man, like his father. *Home is the main thing for Irish men, after football,* Evelyn had said.

"You love football?" I asked Galvin.

"How do you know?" he said mildly surprised.

"From your legs," I faked.

"That can't be true," he pointed. "Mummy told you," he said after a while.

Mention of the word mummy brought an instant softness to his face, I noticed.

"What else do you love?"

"Well... many things. Football for sure, home, Mummy... you," he replied looking my side.

I blushed.

"How is Grand Canyon?" I said, wondering whether Galvin intended to have our first sex there. The wedding night sex! Or perhaps he'd do it in the car. Robin once told me that sex inside a car is a lot more exciting than sex inside a room with shut doors.

"It's beautiful! Quite a sight. Am sure you will thank me," he said.

"Thank you," I said.

Galvin ran his finger across my jaw tenderly and then on my lips. My heart melted at the touch. I breathed love.

"Want to learn driving?" he asked after a while.

"Now?" I exclaimed.

"Why not? Driving is liberating," he lectured and brought the car to a halt.

Then he brought his face closer to mine and kissed. His kiss was soft and wet but passionate. My heart fluttered like a butterfly. I felt wetness in between my legs.

After the kiss, Galvin taught me how to drive, the small theoretical lessons, the do's and don'ts, and then the long practical session. At the end of the lesson, when I was able to maneuver the car nicely, he sat back and relaxed.

He was right, driving was indeed liberating. As I pedaled the car, accelerating it more and more, warm wind brushed my skin and blew my hair. I felt a strange sense of freedom.

That evening, as I drove Galvin's car for the first time, little could I guess the millions of miles I would drive later in my life, from one destination to the next, from one milestone to another, from one crisis to the next.

We reached Las Vegas and entered a wedding chapel. The place was small, but beautiful, and what appeared to be a happening place. Before my third blink I was Mrs. McCarthy.

The next destination was Grand Canyon, where we drove and drove, made merry, basked in the glory of being *just married*. I noticed many couples there, just like us, enjoying their honeymoon. We exchanged cursory glances and warm smiles. We waved at each other.

Almost the entire return journey I drove. Galvin ran a temperature that was unusually high. I panicked all along, about his soaring temperature, my driving a car underaged and without a formal license, our marriage. The terrible outcome!

"You thought of anything, what we are going to say to your family?" I placed gently.

No response. He was fast asleep. His face was red and swollen.

By the time we reached his home, it was dark, and he was unconscious. I stayed back with them, but could not reveal more.

Next morning when he regained his consciousness and slightly better, he divulged the secret to his mother.

"You feel better?" Evelyn said, feeling his forehead with the back of her fleshy palm, when Galvin opened his eyes.

"I have to tell you something," Galvin said.

My heart missed a beat. I was in the room standing behind Evelyn. I looked outside the window, pretending not to listen to him.

"What?"

"We got married, Sona and I," he confessed embarrassingly.

Evelyn's face was blown apart in surprise.

"What will your father say? Is she going to live with us, here?" she said.

"Only if you don't object," Galvin said, much to my surprise and mild rage. I held my breath.

"What have you done Galvin?" Evelyn said, looking worried.

On and on the conversation went, as I shuttled my eyeballs from Galvin to Evelyn and back. It was clear that Evelyn was annoyed, and I felt hopeless.

A couple of times she looked at me with scrutinizing eyes. Her mannerism suddenly changed; I couldn't help but notice.

"Marriage isn't a game you pick up and quit at whim, I hope you realize," Evelyn said.

I did not reply, only kept looking at my feet. But I could feel her eyes on me.

"If I, were you, I wouldn't have done this," she said looking sharply at my face.

Marriage wasn't my idea, I wanted to say. It was Galvin's plan, and I was in no position to protest, given the time and situation we were in. But I kept quiet, feeling embarrassed, shameful.

"Do your parents know?" Evelyn asked me.

Sheepishly I shook my head. And she was shocked.

"Go and tell them at once," she ordered.

I ached to tell her that my parents weren't like them. They were too absorbed within themselves, in their wild and endless lovemaking to be bothered about their children, but I controlled my desire. I walked towards the telephone instead and called Mama.

"Hello," I said uncertainly. I felt Evelyn's pupils glaring at me with silent rage.

"Where the hell are you, Sona?" Mama screamed from the other side.

"Hey, listen, there is something I wanna tell you," I started without a preamble, just the way Galvin did a while ago.

Mother became silent, I could hear her noisy, uneven breathing.

"There is this guy, Galvin… well… we got married," I said and paused.

"What?" came back a sharp reply.

I could almost see her red face. Martin said something in the back ground. A slang, intending to hurt me. I heard a child's cry. Perhaps Anna's. For a second, I felt relieved to be away from all of that.

"When are you coming home?" Mama said after a while, recovering from the shock.

"Am not coming…" I retorted but in a low voice.

"And your school?" she got anxious.

"Am not returning."

"But Sona, how could you leave school just like that? It's important that you finish ..." she fumbled for the right word.

"Oh really? Since when you started caring about my education?" I said and hung up.

That entire day I anticipated some kind of retribution from Daniel, Galvin's father. My throat remained perpetually parched. I couldn't stomach food. Galvin slept all through the day, and Evelyn blabbered to herself. She looked displeased. I sensed she was tensed too, as to what her husband would say; how he would react to the news. Many times, she entered Galvin's room to check his temperature, feed him with soup, give him a sponge bath, helped him change into a fresh set of clothes.

Evening came. And so did Daniel. I was beside myself with anxiety. I was with Galvin in his room and heard Evelyn speaking to him in whispers. I held my breath.

"We will have to take care of everything the best way we can," he said in an even-tempered tone.

I thumped on the bed with relief. Galvin woke up from the tremor and smiled.

I sensed a new beginning, round the corner, about to break open.

Chapter 5

Dawn came and went, and before I could realize what was happening, I was thrust into noon. I got pregnant with our first child. Naiveté and inexperience came with its own price. Nevertheless, I was happy, happy to be a newlywed bride, to be a part of a normal family, and now to become a mother soon.

Galvin resumed his job and was out most of the time. He flew and he flew. But he loved to return home. To me. To his mother. To the family. Exhausted and exhilarated all the same time. Flying was his passion and family, his love.

Galvin's absence from the house made me feel lonely, and often out of place. To beat the boredom, I fished out a job in the telephone exchange as an operator. The work turned out to be more stressful than I had imagined. And it burned me out. Before too long I quit the job.

Months flew by, I was happy, despite my joblessness, protruding belly and rising discomfort.

It was around this time, one day, Galvin returned home with an invitation.

"Party at Bob's place. Cannot say no," he announced. "It would be good if you come."

"Party in this condition," I said pointing to my abnormally giant belly.

"So what? It will be good for the baby," he opined. "It's a pool party by the way. You could dip your feet too."

Galvin smiled naughtily.

But the party turned out to be a rather boring affair. Men had their beer, one bottle after another, absorbed in their own discussions of which neither was I a part, nor was I keen to be. And their wives and girlfriends couldn't have enough of their European vacations and Canadian adventures. They spoke of Milanese fashion and Parisian perfumes, caviar and champagne. I was a misfit and I realized it immediately. Nobody bothered to ask my name. I felt hopelessly ugly in my loose-fitting gown and drooping breasts, in my unadorned neck and non-classy bearing.

I withdrew from them and found a little corner for myself to enjoy the party from a distance. It was interesting to see a group of stylish people, absorbed in their own world, smoking cigarettes and sipping wines. Talking nonchalantly, smiling a lot, showing themselves off, and at times flirting with other people's spouses. I wondered if ever I could be one like them, rich and high handed, suave and sophisticated. I thought of Mama's comment, *finish your school*. Were all these women schooled? I doubted. They looked rich, urbane, but not strikingly erudite.

While I was contemplating about class and education, style and sophistication I noticed that Galvin was nowhere in the vicinity. I looked around; one room after another, when suddenly my eyes got struck at a door, which I sensed was a bathroom door. There were noises inside. I tiptoed and opened the door slightly with a careful push.

The door opened and the ground beneath my feet vanished at in an instant.

Galvin was in the washroom with Bob's wife, Carol. They were making love in the bathtub, half nude and totally unembarrassed. Galvin's bare body was speckled with lipstick marks. I closed the door and ran out of the house.

I sat outside for a long time and cried. Galvin did not come immediately. He took his own time. And when he did, there was no trace of remorse on his face; he looked flushed, almost exhausted.

He came near me and tried to kiss me.

"Come on baby, kiss me," he said in a drunken voice. His hands were already on my breasts, fondling them.

His smell and sound disgusted me. The touch felt insulting. Galvin was reeking of alcohol.

"You are hurting me," I said giving him a rough shove.

"Okay, okay," he said taking his hands in the air.

Again, he moved forward and began to kiss me awkwardly.

"You better go back to her," I said and shoved him again.

"You need not take it so personally. Things like this happen in parties," he consoled, shamelessly.

"You mean to say, you come to these parties to fuck other men's wives?" I snapped, unable to control my rising temper.

"Of sorts. You will get used to all of these," Galvin said getting inside the car and putting on the ignition.

"I don't think I ever will."

"Time will say that. You are just a child," he replied curtly.

I did not take the argument further. For, his attitude told me that it was all too common for him. There was no point in arguing. I looked away, hiding my rising tears. And yet, it fell. A great many of them; so many that I ended up crying the entire journey. Galvin drove in silence untouched by my howls. He had nerves of steel, I sensed that day.

But something snapped within me, in between us. From that moment onwards I couldn't see Galvin in that same light again. He was still my husband, and I was still his wife, but the thread that had once pulled me towards him, had come apart. Our relationship ruptured. We now resembled two planets moving around our individual orbits, not bothering to be coexisting with one another.

I felt betrayed and shattered. I realized what it meant to be married and unhappy at the same time. What it meant to be living with a husband who had multiple faces, of questionable character; was something at home and something totally different outside. He was something in front of his mother, and something else in front of his wife. And so disparate were those faces that at times it was difficult to reconcile which one was the real Galvin and which one, fake.

Strange as it might sound, I thought of my mother, after all this time. Saw her in an entirely different light. Was it the same reason that she went on sleeping with one man after another; went through a string of relationships with hopeless men whom she neither loved, nor were they the kind of men who looked worthy of her love? Could it be possible that marriage was just a farce for her, a big joke that she endured, year after year? Could it be possible that she was never truly happy with even one of them; and that in her desperate search for that spark of happiness she ended up messing up her life to an irreconcilable extent?

All those years when I was with her, I saw her as a mother and always judged her, for the kind of life she lived, the kind of person she was; her horrible choices and disgusting passions. Her strange dispassion towards her children. But now that I was a married woman, and soon to become a mother, I could understand her a lot more than I ever did. And I felt compassionate towards her.

Since I was pregnant, and Galvin appeared to be considerate of that fact, I kept the thought of divorce at bay. I did not want to bring a child into the world, fatherless. I did not want my child to live with a stepfather. Hence, I sealed my mouth and endured my marriage. Endured Galvin McCarthy and his blatant infidelities; endured his blistering remarks and beast like sexuality.

Chapter 6

With the ballast of pregnancy came experience of another kind; rare and unspeakable. I would feel strangely drawn within myself. For hours together, I'd sit at one place and observe the withdrawing pattern of my thoughts, the numb blankness of my mind. The sensation initially felt weird, but as time went by, I felt more in tune with myself. My focus shifted from the world to inside, deeper and deeper within myself. I started having periods of Déjà vu.

Then one night Galvin returned from work and found me in a peculiar discomfort. I was restless and was jumping around the room like a crazy cat. He immediately took me to the hospital and called my mother. The entire family arrived within a short while. Evelyn, Daniel, Mama, and much to my surprise and subsequent disgust, my stepfather, Martin.

Galvin ran up and down the hall the entire time, while I suffered the excruciating pain of a troubled labor. My body and feet swelled up like inflated balloons. I fell in and out of consciousness one hundred times.

After what seemed to be an interminable time, finally

the baby came out. Alone and independent, outside my bizarrely inflated body. The date was 1ˢᵗ April, 1958, and the child was a boy. We named him Harrison.

But all was not quite good, as I sensed from the doctor's mysterious look and worried glances. *Toxemia, pre-eclampsia...* I heard different name being pronounced by different voices, in different accents. But when I asked them if everything was all right, they smiled bleakly and nodded their heads.

"You are going to be fine," they reassured me.

"We need to keep her under observation for at least 24 hours," the doctor said somberly to Galvin, I overheard pretending to be asleep.

I feared dying, all too soon, leaving my son a day old, leaving behind Galvin and his family, and everything that was my life so far. Was Galvin too thinking the same, I wondered. Was he afraid of losing me?

Yet I survived. The problem abated magically couple of days later. I swore to myself, never to get pregnant again. But it was not an easy feat, as I gathered after I returned home with Harrison.

After the initial few months, Galvin would try to get intimate with me more often than he needed to. His appetite for sex seemed to be insatiable. And I'd avoid him feigning one reason after another. He'd fall asleep, irate and dissatisfied. Gradually I started reading at nights, pretending to be engrossed in something with such urgency that sex could wait for a night or two. That too didn't last long, for I could sense Galvin's dissatisfaction steadily rising. He began to show temper.

Then suddenly a solution popped up in front of my eyes, in the form of a newspaper advertisement.

"Camera girls wanted!"

It was an advertisement for a job in some fair in the Pike City, Long Beach. The idea was striking, and I drove to give an interview without much thought. I got the job and opted for night shift. That was the easiest way to keep away from Galvin and his uncontrollable desire. Also, to make some money on my own.

With the job in hand, my life split. Daylight saw me within the enclosure of a secured home. And night saw another version of me, when I dressed up and went for my job as a camera girl.

I took pictures of happy looking people, beaming at the camera, and froze their moments on pieces of paper.

"You look lovely," they would say admiringly.

Those praises bred in me a new contentment. I knew it was a flick of a flame, the illusion of happiness – a momentary affair soon to be extinguished. And yet those compliments and their smiles bred within me a novel kind of happiness.

Fair was my escape of sorts, where I blended with the crowd. Nobody questioned who I was. Nobody posed me with indecent proposals. Nobody cared where I came from, or where I'd return to after my shift was over. Whether I was married or single and available. Everybody seemed to be happy in their own self, enjoying the fair.

At times looking at those gorgeously dressed women I thought about my own life. Was everything worth it? I wondered, feeling spasms of hopelessness rush inside me despite my apparently happy disposition. I smiled a lot to hide my rising melancholy. Age was the only consolation. The thought, that I had barely crossed my teens, and that I had miles to go. My life was ahead of me and I was standing at the beginning. I reminded myself a hundred times a day.

"You were right. My car broke down on the way home, last night," a lady in pink dress and white ballerina shoes came forward and told me. The chamomile fragrance of her perfume engulfed me.

"Is it?" I said, looking up. There was something strange in her face that I could read as clearly as I had read that newspaper advertisement. "You will have a baby soon," something spoke from within. I suddenly grew conscious of my voice. "A boy."

"How do you know?" she said in an eager tone.

"I just know," I replied, casually.

"Oh my God! You must be a face reader…," she said exhilarated.

Face reader. The word struck a chord. Was I? Could I really see things that others couldn't? I knocked myself silently.

"Yea I am pregnant. I didn't even tell my husband. It's just the beginning. You know how it is?" she added blushing.

"I know."

The lady in pink went away leaving me to my solitude. But now thoughts kept whirring in my mind. Face reader! The word repeated itself in an endless loop. And before I could blink next, I discovered a long queue before me. People stood with expectant faces, waiting to be read.

I began to tell them, one by one, all that I could read from their heavily made-up face. Small yet significant details, which I found interesting, worth telling. They felt happy, exhilarated to know the unknown, delighted in knowing the unseen. They thanked me profusely, at times showered me with gifts. I felt flattered.

That was the beginning of a journey, I now realize, decades later, although I had no clue that day. Not even the day next, or the months that followed. It took me many more years to realize that I was blessed with a power, that was rare but impactful.

My job as a camera girl did not last long. And neither did the face reading part of it. All too soon, and way too uneventfully, my journey met with an unexpected halt.

Chapter 7

The next chapter began, as effortlessly and as ridiculously. I was searching for a place to drink, and entered a pub. I settled at a corner, when all at once an important looking man approached me and started talking. He introduced himself as David, the owner of the pub.

"Sona," I said and shook his hand. "Nice place," I said in mock flattery, although apart from the music I did not find anything nice about it. That pleased him.

David looked visibly elated at my compliment.

"The drink is on me," he said taking a seat across the table.

"Thanks," I said, relieved, for the money I had earned from my camera job was coming to an end. And I was still jobless.

"Would you like to join me, here, in this bar?" he offered after a pause.

David Karlsson was of Swedish descent, hailing an athletic body with a nearly perfect sartorial elegance. His gray suit was business-like and crisp, even when there weren't too many guests around to admire his stunning look and red curls.

I thought for a while looking absentmindedly at my beer bottle. The perk looked lucrative. Plus, it would be a night job, I presumed.

"Why not," I said.

David smiled. There was something contagious about his smile that I couldn't disregard. His brown eyes sparkled like two large dots of marbles.

And I began to wait tables in his pub. The job was good, and money flowed in. Apart from waiting the tables I often read faces of guests. That made them happy and ensured a steady trickle. David was happy.

I decided not to share this change of job with Galvin, and hence kept him in the dark. He had no idea where I was going, what I was doing in the name of camera job.

Very soon I became quite popular in the pub. Customers began to admire me. Job offers started flowing in.

"You get in touch with me, if you need a change. He is paying you peanuts. I will pay you more," one beefy man by the name Tim offered, brandishing his card.

"How much?" I said, grabbing the card swiftly from his hand.

"Double. Triple, if you insist," he added.

I accepted his offer and bagged the job.

That was of course one of the many jobs that followed. Each time my salary doubled. The promise of money and the lure of freedom were too great to ignore. I kept changing jobs the way I changed clothes, until I could make more money than I thought I could make with my pruned education and limited talent.

My fourth job was in a bar called Beer Mug. People there were decent and gentler than I expected. And salary was great. I enjoyed a job enhancement too. It was in this place that I met Fred Meyers, a man in his thirties, with an oval face and golden hair.

On and off he would take me out for breakfast. Fred said that he had travelled a lot and would entertain me with stories of distant places; places I did not even know existed. He spoke in a voice that could be spotted from a chaos of one hundred men.

Fred fulfilled his promise of storytelling. And he was great at that. He knew the art of blending facts with fiction.

And the more I blended with the world, the more superficial my relationship with Galvin appeared. Love that had once bound us evaporated. What remained behind was Harrison; the single thread that tied us. I suspected and accused Galvin of infidelity. Because more often than he was aware, I'd discover lipstick marks on his shirt and trousers, stains of foundation and mascara in his handkerchief.

Often, I contemplated quitting my marriage with Galvin and living on my own but could not muster the courage to confront him. He was sweet to the baby, and kind and considerate to me. He had no knowledge of Fred or my life outside his home. In a desperate attempt to be independent, and to evade the string of problems that I anticipated would arise in the name of divorce, one day I walked out of Galvin's house, holding Harrison's hand. Nobody knew what was on my mind.

I went to live with Fred for a short time, in his

apartment. Physical proximity brought us closer, both emotionally and sexually. His expert handlings of my body amused and exhilarated me. I felt complete in the girdle of his strong legs. If not love, but sex was certainly addictive, I sensed with earthling finality.

Fred never talked about my marriage with Galvin, or my life before him. He was happy with the here and now. He was happy just to make love with me, with no deliberate thought of the future.

Association with Fred opened a new world before me; the world of drugs and drug induced hallucinations. It was Fred who lured me to sniff powder for the first time. And there was no looking back. Slowly but steadily, I was sucked up into the quagmire of hashish and mandrax.

After a while, based on Fred's recommendation I started living in another apartment with two other Croatian women. Like me they too worked in the same bar. They took care of Harrison when I was out with Fred. And when both were out, I brought in Fred for a marathon session of love making. The arrangement suited me. For some time, life and I floated effortlessly.

One day while I was out with Harrison on a leisurely walk, Galvin appeared, like a clap of thunder from the clear sky. He looked haggard. I realized my absence had created havoc on him.

"At last, I found you," he started, walking next to me.

"Looks like," I said casually.

"Why did you leave me?" he asked. His voice wobbled, I noticed. His eyes were red and watery. He appeared sleep deprived, perhaps drunk.

I had no answer. We walked in silence.

"Am waiting…" Galvin said.

I was mum. It was difficult to explain all that was in my mind. I exhaled, noisily.

"You must be tired, let's sit," he said pointing a bench.

Soon we were sitting next to each other with Harrison asleep in his perambulator.

"Look Galvin…" I started, but then stopped abruptly. What was there to say anyway? And even if I said everything to him, would he understand? I wondered. I kept looking at him with pensive eyes, blinking, unable to make up my mind as to how to start.

Perhaps he sensed my dilemma from the strange expression on my face, for he said, "I know Sona that I have erred. I have broken your heart. And I am sorry. But please don't punish me forever. Come back."

He was referring to that pool party. I could see that he regretted his deed, but would he forgive me and accept me still if I said that I too had slept with a man after I left him.

"That's not the only time when you slept with another woman. I am sure there were many," I said remembering all the lipstick marks that I'd often discover from his shirt.

"Of course not!" he protested immediately, defensively.

"Let's not create a scene here."

"We can give each other a chance…" he said changing his voice at once. And then after a pause added, "Please?"

"Okay I will come, but give me some time," I said and got up.

"How much?" he added immediately.

"Can't say now. But I will come. You go home," I said already beginning to walk away.

"I love you Sona," I heard him from behind.

But I did not.

Galvin never came back for another effort at reconciliation What came to me was a bundle of paper from his attorney, stating that he wanted custody of my child. The world around me collapsed. I neither had the privilege nor the resource to hire an attorney. And hence lost the battle before it even begun. Galvin was given the weekend custody of Harrison, and I had no choice but to oblige.

"I'll be off to LA," Fred announced one evening.

"LA? Why?" I shot back, surprised at the sudden declaration.

"Have some job to fix. Then will be travelling," his voice trailed off.

Something in his attitude told me that he would be gone for a long time, perhaps forever. I did not question him further. Silently, I went to bed that night, and for the first time, fell asleep without making love. Fred loitered in the dark like a ghost.

Next morning, when I opened my eyes, Fred was gone. And I returned to my job, to keep me distracted, if nothing else.

Galvin started keeping Harrison through the week, citing my job and drinking as an excuse.

"You are an alcoholic," he'd bark, if I tried to argue with him.

"I am a mother too."

"Mother... oh fuck you! Had you had a minimum

sense, you wouldn't have taken up this shitty job of a bar girl," Galvin would reply.

I had no answer, no defense, no voice.

It was then the idea of leaving the city sparked inside my head. I began immediately, looking for opportunities to flee from Galvin and his city.

Then one night, the opportunity placed itself on my plate. One of the customers, Lucas, was travelling to San Francisco, and he offered me help. I accepted immediately. Within a couple of hours, I was in the car with Lucas on the driver's seat and Harrison buckled up in the back seat.

On an impulse I had left everything – Galvin and his family, my job, and the apartment I was living in. But as I proceeded towards my new destination, restlessness seized a better part of me.

Then suddenly I remembered Uncle Earl, my father's brother who lived in San Jose. Instead of getting down at San Francisco, I insisted Lucas to drive me to San Jose. He obliged.

"Hey, listen, if you need any help, lemme know," he said before turning his car and vanishing in the darkness.

Uncle Earl was married to Dorothy Livingstone, a bulky mother of five children. His contribution to the family was his big pay packet that ran the household well. He and Dorothy allowed me to stay with them. Surprisingly he remembered me, remembered Mama and the rest of my siblings. But stubbornly refused to talk about Mason. I suspected he knew certain details that he was unwilling to divulge it in front of Dorothy. I wasn't too keen either, to know about Father. He had long faded from my memory, and I preferred it that way. I had moved too far ahead in my life and looking back seemed absurd.

I shared bedroom with Earl's eldest step daughter, Irina. She was fourteen then, sweet and good natured with a spectacular sense of style and a penchant for the French language. Irina baby-sat Harrison, while I went out for hunting jobs.

Within a short time, I got the job of a waitress in a bar, called Parched. On the second day of my job, I met a Mexican singer, Fellippe Rodriguez. Fellippe had the most amazing voice I ever heard.

Fellippe said that he was from Guadalupe, Mexico and would go back home soon.

"Would you like to join me?" he offered.

"Who me?" I asked surprised.

"Yes."

"But what will I do? In Guadalupe?"

"Well, we have a farm there, you could work," Fellippe was ready with a plan.

So off I went, with Fellippe and Harrison, saying my good byes to uncle Earl and Aunt Dorothy.

Guadalupe was more serene than I had anticipated. The smallness of the town was comforting. Everybody knew everybody and I began to like it. The place was full of warmth and kindness. And so was Fellippe's mother, Nasita.

Nasita Rodriguez was an extremely garrulous woman who could not remain still even for a moment. She was hyperactive by any standard with a warm expression and equally warm bearing.

I fell in love with her, and she fell in love with Harrison. I began to work in their carrot farm during the day and at a beer bar during the night. Nasita looked after the child along with two other toddlers. A four year old boy, Amato and a two year old girl, Zurine.

"Whose children, are they?" I asked Nasita, a week after I arrived.

"Fellippe's," she replied. "Didn't he tell you?"

"What?"

"That he is married," Nasita said.

I shook my head.

"Where is his wife?" I asked averting her eyes.

"She ran away with a Cuban businessman," Nasita replied somewhat morosely.

"Ohh!"

I felt a twinge in my heart. Fellippe could have told me about her, when I spoke to him about my life. But he didn't, and what seemed like deliberately.

That night I made up my mind to quit Guadalupe. I confided to Nasita about it.

"This carrot plucking is too difficult," I said.

Nasita smiled. She looked divine despite her wrinkled face and sunken cheeks.

"It's laborious," she added innocently. "Not meant for city girls."

"Am thinking of returning to San Jose," I lied, so as not to let Fellippe know where I was going.

"Whatever makes you happy darling," Nasita said with teary eyes. "I'll miss Harrison. He is an adorable kid."

"I'll miss you too."

Next morning, silently, I packed my bags and boarded a bus. I decided to return to my mother's place, who was still in Hawthorne.

For a while I considered returning to Galvin, because after all, Harrison was Galvin's son. He could not possibly deny him. But what if he took Harrison away, and then denied me an entry. I would lose my child, I argued to myself, sitting silent and glum in the bus.

Strange thoughts swarmed in my mind. I reflected on all the inconsequential journeys I had taken so far. Was I betting my life on doomed horses? Was I following the same path that my parents had trodden before, repeating the same set of mistakes that they had made?

It was ironical that once I had condemned my parents for being so reckless in their decisions, so heedless of their children's wants and needs. In their incurable desire of jumping from one dwelling to the next, they had always disregarded our desire to feel secure, to feel home. And yet, now I was doing exactly that same thing, repeating those same errors that I had once charged them with; making that same mistake of trusting men too blindly, who perhaps didn't deserve it at all.

I looked at Harrison, now peacefully asleep in my lap. Would he understand me one day, and not judge me for the choices that I made? I wondered.

I doubted.

Chapter 8

Reunion with Mama was an emotional affair and not at all noisy, as I had anticipated. I had expected a lot of screaming and accusing, first, for running away from home with Galvin, and then running away from Galvin and returning home with a child. But Mama did not react at all. Apparently, she did not even notice that I had returned with a child tagged and no husband to support.

Mama was living alone in the house with all her children. My stepfather, Martin was not living with them anymore, but he never stopped creating troubles for the family. Mama told me long and sad stories about the vicious abuses that Martin had thrown at her, his returning home late night, pathetically drunk, and then creating terrible scenes to wake up the entire neighborhood.

"I always knew he is a bastard. You are the one, who didn't believe," I said disgusted, seeing Mama's sad state and pitiful demeanor. She looked ancient, with her speckled face and wrinkled skin.

"Ohh Sona... he was such a gentleman once," Mama started when I cut her midway.

"Gentleman, my foot," I said enraged. "He is an asshole."

"He changed... He just changed one day and never became that person again," she said as tears dripped down her cheeks.

"He didn't change. He pretended to be good to you for a while," I said observing the bruises around her neck. Mama looked emaciated and lean, having lost a generous portion of fat and flesh. The scars brought into my mind all the noisy love makings that Martin and Mama used to have, keeping us free to peer at the spectacle.

Mama fell silent. She lacked an argument.

"You remember the rape case? You didn't believe he could do such a thing. Nobody believed. But it was him. While you slept in your room, he'd come to me and thrust his hand. Bastard! Sick son of a bitch," I spat. That old fury was beginning to show in me, right on my face. I felt my ears turning hot.

"I am sorry Sona, for all that had happened," she said with visible regret. Her eyes grew teary, I noticed.

"There is no point in saying sorry now," I said. "What happened had happened."

Having said that, I looked away, somewhere out of the window. Mama's state was so heart wrenching that I found it difficult to look at her. It was difficult to spot in her the wild and aggressive mother I had grown up with.

"Mason is getting released next week," Mama said after a while.

I was at a loss to understand, what she wanted me to do with the information. I looked at her with curious eyes.

"And?" I asked.

"Will you go to receive him?" she asked me, uncertain.

Receive him. The way Mama said those two words, it sounded like Mason was coming from some battle, victorious. A war hero! And I would go there with garlands and laurels to welcome him.

"Receive him… from where?"

"Prison."

Much to my reluctance, the following week Cherry and I went to receive Mason. Mama insisted that I take Cherry along with me.

"But why?" I said, curious at her odd demand.

"He loved her," Mama said averting my eyes.

"Who loved whom?" surprised, I asked.

"Mason loved Cherry," she replied. "She is his daughter," Mama said as an afterthought, as if I had questioned Cherry's paternity.

"Oh yea… Mason loved Cherry as a daughter, and loved me as a fucking whore," I was tempted to say but didn't. It was pointless to argue, discuss or even talk about Mason.

"Yea… Mason loved Cherry, I almost forgot," I said with a mock smile and walked out of her sight.

A week later I stood outside the prison door for a long time, Cherry by my side. Men, beaten by the burden of age and neglect, walked out. I scanned each and every face, trying to locate Mason. He was nowhere.

One by one, everybody disappeared, everybody except one old man. His head was snow white, and his skin wrinkled like a hundred year old. I moved towards him, slowly, taking cautious steps. And there he was, standing in the corner, looking into my eyes. His tired eyes suddenly sparkled with recognition. He smiled a weak smile.

I tried to smile but couldn't. Something in my face suddenly stiffened, so hard that I found it difficult to smile.

We got into the car and started driving.

Father looked aged; although I sensed that he could not possibly be that old. His hands shook at times, I observed, while he ignited his cigarette and smoked leisurely. Fag relaxed his face.

"That's Cherry," I started, having nothing else to talk about. I was tempted to say your daughter, but then controlled the desire.

"Hi," Cherry said. There was fear in her voice, I noticed. Cherry looked uncertain, smileless. In a strange way, she now resembled Father, the one that I remembered. *Mason loved Cherry*, rang into my ears. Could it so happen, that Cherry was only his daughter, and I had another biological father? I would never know, and it was pointless to ask anything from Mama.

"Ah, Cherry!" Father said, turning his head slightly. "You have grown into quite a lady!" he observed

Cherry did not speak. She nodded her head once and then looked outside the window.

I noticed deep scars on Father's neck and arms. What are those scars? Did they beat him in the prison? For what? Indiscipline, or some other crime that he had committed behind the bars? I thought in silence, as I drove.

"How is your mother?" he asked after some time.

"She is good," I replied, "taking you there."

Father kept looking at me. His eyes grew teary, I noticed. I remembered the disagreeable court case that I had battled in his presence. The accusations, the insults, the unspeakable injury it had incited within me. My heart sank at the thought.

"The case that you ..." he started.

"I forgot about it," I lied keeping my face expressionless. "Let past be!"

My statement comforted him; I could sense. He looked relieved.

I wanted to ask him, why he was imprisoned. Under what charges, but then thought better of it.

Father's meeting with Mama was a hushed-up affair. I was locked out of the room, where the ex-couple exchanged their lives. I loitered in the hall the entire time, taking care of the children who gave the house the feeling of a noisy hostel packed with disobedient inmates.

Nearly a century later, the door opened.

"Would you drive him to the depot?" Mama asked, calmly. Her eyes were red and swollen.

I looked at her, and then at Father. He was expressionless.

"Where? Which depot?" I asked.

"Grey Hound Bus Depot," he elaborated.

Once again we drove, Father and I. Cherry remained behind. The drive was spent mostly in silence although I had a million questions to ask him. I noticed he didn't ask me anything, about my life, about Galvin and Harrison. I sensed that he must have had gathered all those details from

Mama. He remained curiously dispassionate. All through the journey, he kept his eyes closed, perhaps pretending to be asleep.

Was he my real father? I wondered. What made a father, father? I thought of Galvin, the fervent desire in him to meet Harrison. I thought of Fellippe and his two children. Were those men normal, to love their children so ardently, or was Mason abnormal, having done what he did? What he saw in me then that provoked in him an urge to assault? Or were those abuses alcohol induced?

By the time we reached Grey Hound Bus Depot, it was quite dark and foggy. Father got down from the car, closed the door with a bang and limped away, immediately forgetting my presence.

Life is a strange affair! I reflected, sitting lonely in the car.

I followed him with my eyes for a while, until he was no longer visible.

A few weeks later I got a call from him. He said that he wanted to see me. The address was some hotel in a shady part of LA.

I drove and reached the hotel. It was dingier than I had expected. The building was rickety, and looked like it could crumple down any moment. The lift was like a match box, barely fitting two. People walked in and out like zombies. I pretended not to notice them, or even intimidated by them, when all the while my heart ran uphill. The corridor was littered with condoms and a hundred other disagreeable stuffs.

Father opened the door. The room was a slice more than a cage. The wall paper was hot pink and scarred. It was peeling away in ugly scraps. The entire set up was depressing and dark. The room reeked of alcohol.

He sat on the bed and extended his hand towards me. I jumped on my feet at once. His hand was full of stitches and fresh scars. It looked as if he had a hard brawl with someone moments ago. Without being told I could see that he was in pain.

Something inside me stirred. Perhaps it was those ghastly wounds. Perhaps it was the fact that I called him Father. I did not know. I took his hand and washed his bleeding wounds with the whiskey I noticed in his room. Then, one by one I cut out the stitches on his hand, taking care not to hurt him in the process. He squirmed in pain. At times shrieked out, clasping my hand. His hard nails dug into my skin. But I felt no pain.

Father did not speak a word all through the process. But I sensed his eyes on me, saying loads through blinks. Just when I was about to close the door, Father said, "I had killed him."

His voice was impactful, unfaltering. I looked at his face, held my eyes for a moment longer than I needed to. Without being told I understood who was the *him* in his comment.

Once calmed from his physical pain Father lay in his bed, visibly relieved. Or perhaps it was relief from the inner burden, I'd not know.

"Thanks," I said offhandedly and closed the door.

Chapter 9

My return to Mama's house saw me through a year. I joined a nearby pub as a bar girl to sustain the family.

Then suddenly one evening we got a call from a hospital giving us information about Martin. Mama and I rushed at once.

It was a terrible experience; one of the most pitiable sights I had ever seen. Mama nearly fainted looking at his prostate body attached to half a dozen of scary looking equipment.

"Multiple organ failure," the doctor told us morosely, shaking his head.

I looked at Martin's nearly unconscious body. His stitched eyes, his swollen face and bruised body. His battered rectum. Blood and pus oozed out relentlessly from some of his wounds. All his fingers were broken and bandaged. His feet were smashed to powder.

"Oh!" I gasped.

Martin moaned in his sleep, an animal like sound that chilled my spine. Sound of excruciating pain!

"He is in pain," the doctor lamented, looking kindly at him. "We can't do much."

"Is there anything we could do?" Mama intervened with grief-stricken face and wobbly voice.

"Pray for him."

Martin had been a war hero. And yet not a thread of bravery could be scraped out of his wretched body.

Looking at him I wondered what could have happened that had brought him down to that unspeakably pathetic state. The doctor, Gerald William, a lanky young fellow said that Martin was brought in from the streets, literally. He was beaten badly by someone. Who? He had no clue. And neither could Martin say a word. He had lost his speech.

"How did you get our number?" I asked after his speech.

"From his wallet," Gerald replied, handing me Martin's empty wallet.

"Perfect," I said.

And I thought of all the assaults and insults he had once showered me with; all the dirty probing he had invested to bed me. The cruel lies he'd say about me when in public, the unkind accusations that left me nowhere. All the minutes, hours and days when he made my life miserable, made me shed tears of blood. Martin was a stepfather, but he behaved like a gruesome beast, determined to crush me for whatever reason.

Yet, despite everything, I survived. It was he who now lay on the verge of death, breathing out more misery than air.

A part of me was happy to see every fiber of his body writhe in pain, to hear him cry out even when he was barely conscious. He deserved every bit. He had earned it, I reminded myself. But when I looked at his smashed face and blunt nose, my heart melted. Not love but I could forgive him, reminding myself that he was perhaps a product of some extreme circumstances. I knew I could never truly forget what he had done; forgiveness was the least I could give him. And that was that. I forgave him.

After returning from hospital that night, I prayed for his eternal release. After years, I prayed for a soul. After years, I prayed. The sensation soothed me, calmed down my agitated senses. I felt peace.

Two days later Martin Goldsmith died, in extreme agony, the authorities informed us. His funeral was attended by no one other than Mama and me. A life ended unceremoniously. No tears were shed for him, no kind words were spoken in his remembrance. Nobody wanted to speak of him, to remember him. No pleasant memory lingered in my mind that connected me to Martin, however vaguely. Mama seemed to be happy that he was gone. I was happy too, seeing Mama happy.

For some time, life settled down into a kind of smoothness that was never there in Mama's house. They were no assaults and attacks, no beating and punching. The house was filled with noises of children. Mama too smiled, when Harrison giggled. I loved coming back home after my job. House meant home for the first time in our lives.

Galvin would meet Harrison over the weekends and take him back to his house. My hands were tied legally. Although I resented those visits but could do nothing to prevent it. Something in his attitude told me that a plan was brewing in his mind, and one day it would explode.

Perhaps he would snatch Harrison from me and never return. But then, a child needed a father too. I rationalized. Hence, I kept my calm.

Gradually Galvin won Harrison's admirations. Evelyn pampered him with gifts that he'd return home with, car loaded with packs of toys, clothes and chocolates. I feared the subtle bribing.

"I love Granny more," Harrison would say loudly, in my presence.

"More than whom?" I'd question, feeling my accelerated heartbeat. Did Galvin teach him that? I wondered.

"You...," he'd reply.

And I could almost see ripples of a force drifting Harrison away.

On his fifth birthday, Galvin took him to New York, saying that it was his birthday present.

I was at the rock bottom of my grief. I was convinced that by the time Harrison would return from the trip, he would no longer be mine.

it happened exactly the way I had feared. Not too long after his return from New York, Harrison moved out of my place and began to stay with Galvin's family. Initially it would be three to four days at a time, gradually moving to one entire week. Then quickly it turned into a month, until one day Harrison completely evaporated from my life.

I lost my first child. The sadness was overwhelming, unspeakable. Galvin claimed that I worked in a bar and hence held questionable character. That I was an alcoholic. He wanted Harrison to be raised in a normal household, which an alcoholic mother like me could not guarantee.

I remembered the enormous amount of pain I had to endure, the vicious Toxemia I had to battle with, to bring Harrison into the world. The endless miles I had travelled with him, hungry and thirsty, but ensuring that his mouth was always fed. Now, Galvin's family mattered, and I was nobody. He trashed me like a paper napkin. I felt just the same, used and trashed, futile.

Chapter 10

With Harrison moving away and Mama taking care of her children, I had dived headlong into my job.

Mama managed the household and I brought in money. It was a new kind of experience for me. After work I'd return home, hungry and exhausted, and Mama would bring me a bowl of beef stew and warm bread from the kitchen. The gesture touched me. She had finally become my mother, as if. I had lost a son but got back my mother. I felt bubbles of happiness rise inside me despite a bottomless emptiness.

The vacant existence, of course, at times was made up with one-night stands with men boasting a good physique and irresistible sex appeal. I enjoyed those brief interludes that lasted as long as the nights. Most of them I never met again. Some returned with renewed vigor and special interest in me. I liked their admirations; the flirtatious way they talked to me, with lingering gazes and seductive gestures. I could not say that I disliked those flings; however transient the relationships were.

One day the bar door opened and strode in, Stephen Aitken.

"What can I get you for a drink?" I asked professionally, ogling at his beautiful face for one straight minute.

He looked up, taking in my blunt expression.

"One double black, large, on the rocks," he replied. His voice was deep, enough to create an impact.

"You got it," I said and moved away.

His eyes followed me, everywhere I went. I smiled behind my pursed lips; felt butterflies in my stomach.

Stephen said that he was the head of dispensary, from the United States Navy. Single and thirty-one. And that egg noodles with garlic and bacon were his favorite food, and double black, his all-time favorite drink. He said all that and much more, matter-of-factly, I noticed, as if he was reading some news bulletin. Stephen's eyes were a strange shade of blue, marked by rings. He smiled less. His face wore an expression as though he was perpetually attending to some grave procedure.

There was something about his demeanor that attracted me towards him. I craved to see him, every night, all night. The days he wouldn't come, I'd keep looking at the door, anticipating. I'd check the clock every now and then.

"You didn't come last night," I said placing his drink on the table.

"You noticed?" he said arching his brows.

I smiled a smile that pleased most men.

"You didn't reply," I added softly.

"I didn't know you were looking out for me."

"Had you known, you would have come?"

Stephen thought for a while. His face turned instantly old, I noticed.

"That depends on..." he said.

"Depends on what?"

"What you are looking for," he said. The unpretentiousness of his attitude pleased me. The candid way he spoke. The conversations!

Stephen was not chatty; conversation did not overwhelm him. But when he spoke, about something – about anything, whether it was the American Navy or JF Kennedy and the American politics, or the Academy Awards or the Nobel laureate, John Steinbeck, or the recently released film, The Guns of Navarone – he revealed knowledge, and confidence.

I knew it right from the beginning that we were different, almost two worlds, yet I felt strangely attracted towards him. I fancied a relationship with him, I imagined sex.

"Would you share a drink with me today, after your job?" he asked one night. Stephen looked exceptionally glum that evening.

"Sure," I said, elated.

That night I joined him for a drink in a pub not too far away from where I worked. I bartered sleep and Mama's stew with double black and a company.

"You like being alone?" I started, darting in the dark, after my first sip.

"What makes you say so?" he questioned in grave voice, looking puzzled.

"Never seen you with a friend," I added.

"Aha... that. Yes, I enjoy my own company," he reflected. "When you make friendship with yourself, you don't need another one," he added as an afterthought.

"True," I said, wondering if he was recovering from a failed relationship.

"Why am I feeling that your heart has been broken recently," I said in a flirtatious tone.

Stephen raised his brows and looked quizzically at me.

"Are you a face reader?" he asked.

"Many say so," I confessed with a faint sense of pride.

"What? Face reader?"

I nodded, wondering if I did a right thing by telling it to Stephen.

He took in the information, looking into my eyes. Then he nodded his head meaningfully.

"What do you see in a face?"

"In any face or in your face?" I asked with a sly smile.

"Okay, let's take my face. In my face?"

"You are a part of a twin. But he, I mean your twin brother died three weeks after you were born. Your father had suffered several strokes and is no more. You have a sister, about a dozen years younger than you. Very recently you had a heart break," I heard myself say.

Stephen's eyes grew wider in what I took to be disbelief.

"But don't worry, you will live long," I added smiling.

"That's incredible... Sona," he said flabbergasted. "How did you do that?"

"I don't know. It just happened," I said shrugging my shoulders.

"But how?"

"Something that ought to happen happens. The how's, and why's don't matter," I replied confidently.

"That's intense," he said, clearly impressed.

"Maybe it is. Or maybe not. Who cares?" I added jovially.

That was when he told me about Bridget Kennedy, the astonishing lady who had splintered Stephen Aitken's heart.

Bridget was Stephen's colleague, a surgeon in the Navy, a lady with olive complexion and melancholy eyes. That's how Stephen still remembered her and wished to remember for the rest of his life. She and Stephen had been together for a while and were dreaming of tying the knot when suddenly Bridget fell in love with another man and broke her three-year old relationship with Stephen.

"You are not destined to grow old with her," I said absentmindedly, after his short Bridget story.

"That was cruel."

"Who me?"

"Of course not. Ken... I mean Kennedy. Bridget Kennedy."

I noticed Stephen struggled to pronounce her name. I wondered if Galvin was also having that same problem, taking my name in public. What was Galvin telling Harrison? I thought.

"Now what are you dreaming about?" Stephen observed.

"Nothing," I lied bringing back my attention and eyes on him.

"There must be something," he speculated.

"I have a son, Harrison," I blurted out.

"And?"

"He is with his father. We are... separated. I mean divorced."

"I don't see a problem there," he said.

"He thinks, I mean Galvin, my ex-husband thinks that I am not a good mother," I said looking at his empty glass.

"What motherfucker says so?"

"Galvin said. His family said. His lawyer said," I replied, embittered, remembering the long and distasteful battle I had fought repeatedly, only to lose it in the end.

Perhaps there were tears in my eyes, for Stephen said, "Hey let's not waste tears for fuckers who don't deserve them."

Having said that he rubbed my cheeks with his fingers.

And a journey began... with Stephen Aitken this time.

That meeting was followed by several others, and in quick successions. Small talks leading to gentle conversations. And before we knew it, we ended up in the bed, finding comfort and solace in each other's arms.

Stephen's love making was like him, mellowed down, less noisy, unpretentious. Intense! I was head over heels in his love. Perhaps his straightforwardness was the reasons. He never said a word more than necessary. He never over did an act.

We began living together, emulating a couple. I cooked for him, his favorite food. That he ate thankfully, always concluding it with a kiss on my cheek, as a mark of gratitude. One night, after love making, while we were still in the bed, he declared that he got a transfer order from his department.

"Where?"

"Hawaii," he said, and looked my side.

That same place! I thought of Galvin; his proposal, our marriage. *Are you inviting me to Hawaii;* echoed in the dark. I exhaled, noiselessly.

"When are you relocating?" I asked controlling the wobble in my voice.

"Let's see, haven't decided anything," he said. That's when he noticed the tears dripping from my eyes.

"Hey, you okay?" he said at once, alarmed.

"Am fine," I said and turned to the other side.

"Let's get married," he proposed, in a flat voice.

I turned around, and looked into his eyes, trying to gauge what had exactly played catapult in his proposal. My tears? His love? Or our impending separation?

"Are you sure you want to get married?"

"Of course, I am. Don't you?" Stephen smartly volleyed me the question.

Something was warning me to pause, to breathe and then decide. Perhaps he was not the right guy. Perhaps time was not conducive. Maybe the reasons were not enough to get into matrimony all over again. We needed to give more time to each other. There were a hundred other reasons to reconsider before marrying a man. Yet, when I opened my mouth to answer, I said, "Yes."

Stephen smiled; one of those rare smiles that flummoxed my mind.

Not too long after that, we married. Stephen and me. And not too long after our marriage I realized that getting into a wed lock with Stephen had been a mistake that I had jumped into with the recklessness of a 16 year old. To begin with, he had loads and loads of idiosyncrasies to deal with, which was not an easy feat, as I increasingly gathered. He was ridiculously finicky about cleanliness. He wanted everything in the house to be spick and span, and in the correct order. Perhaps his training in the Navy had taught him that. And I was just the reverse. Untidy, at times clumsy, and to a great extent disorderly, as Stephen had, quite rudely, pointed out.

A week after our marriage Stephen went to Hawaii to resume his job.

"Lemme arrange a house and stuff, then you join," he said before boarding the military air transport.

I nodded; I too had many things to fix before I could leave California.

Stephen left, and I discovered that I was pregnant, an information that nearly freaked me out, remembering the horrible experience I had endured during my last delivery.

I wrote to Stephen every now and then, informing him all the details that was my life now. He responded, at times more sweetly than I had expected.

I receive maximum number of letters in the entire base, he once wrote. *Am turning into quite an enviable stuff.*

I smiled, caressing my tummy with my other hand, remembering him, remembering our intense love making.

Months passed, without trouble of any kind. With

Martin dead, and Mason lost in his own world, and Stephen in Hawaii, life seemed to settle down into something smooth and predictable. Mama and I enjoyed that brief period of peace. I began to love her, and so did she.

Looking at her, at times I wondered had Mama been only a mother and did not chase those useless men to make herself a lover, would she have been better? Perhaps.

"Am coming next month to bring you to Hawaii," Stephen wrote after a while.

That night I remained awake for a long time, anticipating my reunion with him; the joy of being together. Sitting beside that unadulterated joy there was also a fear, a feeble paranoia to be clean and tidy and in order, all the damn time. For, I still remembered those brief days of staying with him, when he literally ran after me to clean the mess, I'd often create in the house. Those brisk arguments, and his flaring anger.

Stephen came to California, as he had promised. But destiny had another plan. The military doctor voiced his concern pertaining to my travel.

"Long air travel would be too much for her," he said indicating my seven months swollen belly.

Stephen looked worried at the announcement. I sighed.

"She might deliver there, right in the plane... midway," the doctor added gravely as an afterthought.

"You go back to the job, I'll join after the baby is born," I consoled Stephen.

He obliged but with a heavy heart. Couple of months later my baby was born; a girl child with deep blue eyes, like Stephen. I named her Isabella.

Stephen flew back a few days later to take us to Hawaii.

It was during the process of some medical tests that we were supposed to go through for clearance from the Military department that a volcano of problems erupted. To begin with, we discovered that Isabella was born with a heart condition, and that she needed special care and extremely special diet. I was on the verge of a nervous breakdown at the news. Nevertheless, we moved to Hawaii and took Bella to the Army Hospital for treatment.

"There is a hole in her heart," the doctor informed us, after a host of tests and check-ups.

"What's the treatment?" I asked, nearly on the verge of tears.

"For now, she has to be in the hospital…" his voice trailed off.

Something in his attitude told me that it was the tip of an iceberg; and that I was perhaps destined to take up a lot more struggles than the doctor was willing to reveal.

Unfortunately, it happened exactly the way I had anticipated, perhaps feared. The Hospital kept Isabella in their children unit, and like a ping pong I shuttled between barracks and the hospital. Many a night I cried myself to sleep. The pillow soaked my tears but couldn't abate my sorrow.

Gradually Stephen's attitude changed too. His temper rose at whim and often without a reason. He would shout himself hoarse at the messy house that I had no time to clean. He'd fuss over everything under the sun.

"Why are the pots and pans not cleaned?" he'd bark from the kitchen.

"I didn't have time," I'd reply from the bedroom.

"I can't believe, you are such a dirty person," he would retort.

"Dishwashing liquid makes my hand scratchy," I'd shout back.

"What about the mess you have created with clothes in the bedroom. You don't need dishwashing liquid to clean that," he'd say.

"I was in the hospital," I'd reply disgusted at his fault-finding attitude.

Stephen came into the room and saw me sitting in a loose shirt and without an undergarment.

"All you know is to show your fucking cunt!" he screamed and then banged the door.

On and on it went, for hours together, until a heated argument would flare between us and rot our moods and turn our relationship sour.

One day Stephen returned home from work and wanted to go to some beach party he had been invited to.

"How can you go partying, when Bella is not well…," I demanded in a not so pleasant voice.

"Bella is not well… Bella is not well… all you do is parrot like an idiot. What the fuck can I do, if Bella is not well?' he screamed back, red in his face.

I sensed his desperation. "You want to go… you go," I said and locked myself into the room.

Stephen noisily went out and did not return for the next three days.

Of course, his absence mattered, especially when

all the money was with him, and there was not a dollar in the house to buy a grain. I was hungry, I was desperate. I searched his closets and cabinets for money and to my surprise discovered an envelope.

The envelope was sealed. I tore open the letter and read it. It was addressed to someone by the name of Andy. The signature at the bottom was Stephen's. The letter said that Stephen was not happy in this marriage, it made him feel shackled, almost a loser. He wanted his freedom. Being single was far better than having a sick child and a hungry wife, who wanted sex all the time.

Sometimes I wonder if Isabella is really mine. Or did Sona dump it on my head, taking advantage of our marriage. How could my child be so sick, right from the birth?

Tears came to me so suddenly that I didn't realize I was crying. How could Stephen say such cheap things about me, his wife? How could he even think such? Something inside me broke, and broke down to splinters, which was impossible to unscramble. I had always known him as measured, but his coldness was due to lack of happiness, that I couldn't realize.

I tore the letter into pieces; and realized that I had to get a job. Perhaps that was what he also wanted but couldn't say.

I started reading newspapers for jobs and soon landed up in an 'opening soon' sports pub by the name Speed. The owner, Jian Durand was a well-known footballer of Honolulu. Jian was a second generation American with a French father and a Chinese mother. Jian held Oriental looks but a temperament that was strikingly French.

The interview was only a formality, as I discovered after a short question answer round.

"Would you like to join me for the opening bash?" Jian said in a flirty tone, looking admiringly at me.

"Only if I have the job," I bargained cleverly, taking advantage of that look.

Jian smiled. I bagged the job, and life seemed better.

Bella was out of the hospital but needed regular shots. I paid for her treatment and ran the house with my income.

Stephen's coming and going became increasingly unpredictable. He'd come late at night and would lock himself in his room. I'd sleep with the child by my side. Sex flew out of the window and loved seeped into the earth.

My job as a hostess in Speed made me quite popular among the rich and famous of Hawaii. And the more successful I grew at my job; the more distant Stephen became. In short, our relationship fell apart.

"Stay on for a drink," Jian would plead me, after my shift.

"Sure." I had nobody to return to anyway.

It was thus our relationship began; Jian and me. One thing leading to another, we ended up kissing and feeling each other like teenaged lovers, until it was full-blown sex; first with nothing other than our burning desires, gradually moving towards powder.

We made love, sometimes in the pub itself, after all the guests had gone. Sometimes we'd lie on the couch in his chamber and discover with renewed vigor the pleasures of wild sex. Jian was quite a feat. And I enjoyed my time with him.

Yet, it was like jumping from the pan to fire, from Stephen - one married and dissatisfied man, who was my husband, to Jian - another married and dissatisfied man, whom I worked with.

Stephen got annoyingly critical about each of my gestures at home, especially when I'd dress for the evening and sit for my makeup.

"Who are you putting that red lipstick for?" he'd critique obliquely.

"It's a part of my job, to get dressed nicely," I'd reply, looking at the mirror.

The mirror was reflecting a new me. Could Stephen see those blushes that now rouged my cheeks? What was he making of it? I covered my neck with a lilac scarf, fearful of revealing those scars and bites from his piercing eyes.

"I see…"

And then after a short while, he'd started again.

"There you are painting your lips and going for some fucking night job, and here I am babysitting after a hard day," he said looking at the wall.

"When it's your own child, it's not called babysitting," I retorted at his senseless comment, also at the senselessness of his comment.

Stephen fell silent, while I strode out of the door without a word. The lure of money and fame from my job were ardent enough to take me out of the house, but relationship with Jian was even more strident. I wanted to be with Jian, and for that I could go to any damn extent, however absurd.

For the next few months, life was like that, Stephen and I, absorbed in our respective worlds, separate and disparate. We crossed each other's path, only twice. Once, when he handed me Bella's responsibility in the morning, when I returned from work. A second time, when, I handed him Bella's responsibility in the evening, when he returned from work. We shared no other domain. Sex became a rare feat. We neither had emotional attachment nor the desire to derive carnal fulfillment from one another. I drew mine from Jian. I was certain he too had an alternate source, which he hid from me.

Then one Saturday evening, he returned from work and said he had to attend some party, and he could not take care of Bella.

"I am sure you can take a day off," he argued heatedly.

"Of course, I can, but I must arrange for an alternative. It's a Saturday night," I protested, half dressed and fully made up.

"You can fall sick," he replied. "Or you could get injured suddenly."

"But I am not sick," I said, wondering where the idea of injury came from.

Stephen moved forward briskly and put a slap squarely on my face. The effect was so sudden and shocking, that I toppled from its effect.

"Okay… then tell them you fell down from the stairs and got injured."

Having said that he lifted me from the floor and pushed down the small flight of stairs that separated the kitchen from the hall. I slided down and bumped my head into the refrigerator.

I was thunderstruck at his audacity.

Stephen packed a few of his clothes and left. He

did not turn to see if there was a cut or a fracture, serious enough to be attended to. He didn't return home for a while. Instead, he reported to his office that he had moved out of his office accommodation. And that his wife, was a lunatic. As per rule, if he moved out of his residence, the accommodation was no longer valid for his family. I was forced to search for an alternative residence.

I resorted to Jian. He seemed more than happy to help me.

"Don't worry Sona, I know a place where you can stay. Come let's go," he offered. "I am sure you will like the place."

I nodded, still recovering from the shock of Stephen's unnecessary violence.

I wondered if there was someone in Stephen's life, if Bridget Kennedy had come back. If Stephen wanted to get rid of me and marry Bridget? If he came to know about my increasing intimacy with Jian? Disturbing thoughts stirred in my mind. So much so that I barely noticed the road that Jian and I drove through. Bella was at the back, suckling her thumb, oblivious to the storm that was rising in my life.

The house was in Kalihi valley and had lovely wild orchids surrounding it. There was a Hawaiian family settled in a small house next to it, where the father was the gardener and the mother became Bella's baby sitter and cook.

Life felt good, with Stephen away, and a baby sitter to take care of Bella, and a job that paid me well. My child was comfortable, and I was happy. Jian was a good employer, and my love story with him was growing in leaps and bounds. The only problem with him was that he was already married, and at times prevented us from showing our affections in public. We had to restrict our feelings for indoor amusements. When in public, we acted as a warm employer and a devoted employee, good friends at best.

Initially it did feel odd to share two different relationships with the same man, but gradually we fell into the habit.

The good time however did not last long. Stephen started spying on me. My growing success and happiness became increasingly muddled by his ugly and ill-mannered presence. He'd often come in the pub and observe me with stern eyes and meaningful glares. And when I would not respond, he'd pass stray comments. It was this one time, being possessed by alcohol and insecurity; he thrashed me on the floor and kicked me hard in the stomach. That was when Jian barred his entry into the pub.

Then one day, I got a wire message from Hawthorne. The date was 5th of July, 1964. Jian brought down the message. He said that one of my sisters had been killed.

"Which one?" I asked, shocked.

"One of the twins," he said in a glum tone.

I thumped on the couch. The world around me spun like a typhoon until it ended in a complete blackout.

"Nina," I said, sadly, looking out of the window. Tears rolled down my cheeks. "It's Nina."

"No name is written," Jian said extending me the sheet.

"I know its Nina. I can feel it… her absence."

Jian's eyes grew wide for a moment, and then his face relaxed. He patted me on my shoulder.

"She was run over by a speeding vehicle," he said and stopped.

That was the saddest thing I ever heard.

Yet it was an information I already knew.

A dream from the past flashed in my mind. A car accident: a girl with golden curls and peach colored dress ran across a street when there was the noise of a sharp brake followed by a piercing shriek. I woke up at the sound and realized that I had a temperature and was bleeding miserably from in between my legs. The temperature ran for a week; and the bleeding continued for nearly two months.

I did not remember what happened next, for a long time I remained like that, silent and sad. I thought about my dream, repeatedly. Did Nina die that way? I wondered. That was when my eyes fell on my lap and I noticed bold patch of red coloring my groin.

Grief was a very heavy thing, for, within moments, I felt burdened. I felt old, menstruating and yet quite not a woman.

"I must go and meet Mama," I said.

"You should," he added, emphatically.

It was Jian who arranged for the air tickets; and dropped us at the airport. Stephen was nowhere around. Not that I was unhappy about it, rather it was the reverse. His absence made everything easy, it ensured peace of my mind.

I travelled to Hawthorne the following day.

Mama was devastated. She had aged about twenty years more since our last meeting. I sensed it was the death that had taken a toll on her health and mental peace.

"How am I going to survive this, Sona?" she said

helplessly, wiping tears from her shrunken face. Mama appeared lost. And I felt irreconcilably sad.

"It's okay to grieve, but don't let that bird of grief build nest in your hair," zI quoted Jian.

She looked up, perplexed at my philosophy.

Mama narrated me the incident in between her sobs. It was a version of my long-forgotten dream. The car had smashed her head into pulp, she said and howled. Tears overwhelmed me.

"What was she wearing?" I asked slowly, feeling a terrible tremor rising inside me.

"A peach-colored dress... but now its red."

I sighed.

The funeral was a sad affair, and I felt glum. I looked at Bella for a long time, wondering if I had to lose her one day, what would be my state of mind. Would I survive the shock? Perhaps not. And yet, I had survived Harrison's parting. Wasn't that parting from him akin to death of a kind, not knowing, where he was now, what he was doing at that point of time?

Mama too absorbed the shock of Nina's death. She survived. Perhaps that was life all about. Learning to deal with losses and live on, learning to move ahead at whatever cost.

I reflected on my life so far, all the random and absurd things I had done, the two men I had married in frenzy and separated, the children I made, the job that I was doing to earn my bread. The countless men I had slept with, without any serious intention of living with them, or spending my life with. The friend who now made me smile: Jian Durand.

Chapter 11

Jian visited me in Hawthorne while I was with Mama, sorting things out, still not completely recovered from the shattering grief.

"I got a meeting in San Francisco, so thought of catching up with you," he said first, upon meeting.

I nodded, smiling. I was happy to see him.

"How is Speed doing?" I asked.

"It's going in speed," he replied in his usual way.

I observed him looking at me with strange eyes. Jian always confused me when he looked like that.

"You have put on weight," he observed after a while.

"Yes, because of the outside food we are having, pretty often," I replied, truthfully.

"Hmm," he said and stopped. He absorbed the information mindfully, and yet, he did not ask me how I. was I noted with mounting sadness.

I could sense that something had cropped up between us or perhaps the relationship got truncated somewhere. I grew anxious to know. Was it my sudden absence? Or was it something else? I was desperate to return to Hawaii.

"So, when are you joining?" he asked.

"Soon," I said without revealing too much. Already I was chalking out a return plan but did not reveal it to him.

"Tell me the date, I can book tickets for you," he offered.

"Will let you know," I lied.

Jian returned to Hawaii. I returned two weeks later without informing him. I wanted to surprise him. But in the end, it was I who was shaken and stirred by surprise.

I entered Speed from the back entry that directly led to the anteroom. I opened the door soundlessly and discovered Jian playing a dirty little game with Hanna, another female staff of the pub. Jian and Hanna both were nude and looked comfortable with each other's nudity. Hanna had beautiful tits.

"Sorry I barged in at the wrong time," I said and closed the door with an extravagant thud.

Jian came out running, with a towel wrapped around his waist.

"Sona… listen to me. We'll talk about this," he said embarrassingly.

"Oh yea…" I said without turning and left. "Put on your undies first."

I did not even feel like looking at his face. Talking with him was out of the question.

And yet, as promised Jian arrived that night, sobered and over-dressed by any standard. He brought a bottle of expensive wine for me.

"Your welcome gift," he said extending the bottle, smiling his most beautiful, all pleasing smile.

"Thanks," I replied coldly.

Jian fidgeted for a while before he finally opened his mouth.

"You know...," he began and then suddenly paused. "I can explain that... what you saw."

"I know."

"Look Sona, you were gone for a long time, And I was kind of missing you... and one day... this Hanna comes to me... really bad, really really bad... pathetic..." he said.

"I understand," I said avoiding his eyes.

Jian fell silent.

"You know what, you have two options. Either you throw that bitch out, or I walk out. Of course, I have plenty of options to choose from, and you need not worry about that," I eased out his problem.

"Hanna is returning to Germany anyway... I will arrange for her travels. You stay... please," he said.

Although Jian said *please*, but he sounded least pleasing and certainly not regretful. I knew my relationship with Jian was officially over and I had to look for a new job.

I started right away. Getting a job was not difficult; not at all difficult. For soon, I fished out another pub to work in, and with a backhouse to live in. The proposition was lucrative and I moved out of Jian's house.

I changed my job and settled into a new one, and Stephen came back to me. Perhaps he was keeping an eye on me, for no sooner did I move into the new house that I discovered Stephen standing outside it, one evening, waiting for me. He was looking sober, and in control. Back to the Stephen Aitken, whom I had met and fell in love with.

"What the hell are you doing here?" I screamed, the moment my eyes fell on his lean frame.

"Waiting for you."

Stephen had changed, and it did not take me long to realize.

"For me? Why?"

"I heard about Nina's death... am sorry. My condolences," he said in a deep voice.

So, he did his homework, I thought but didn't say, only nodded my head. Immediately that dream came to my mind. Was I with Stephen then, when I had that awful dream? I couldn't recollect.

"Whatever has to happen, happens," I replied.

"Can we talk a bit?" he proposed.

"About what?"

"About you, me... us. About Bella," he said looking at me expectantly. Stephen had reduced a lot, I observed. Was he ill, or was it the lack of happiness?

About Bella. I liked that the most. Something inside me stirred at the mention of her name.

"Okay... let's catch up at my place after my shift is over," I said, sensing a peculiar desperation in his voice and attitude.

"Sounds great! Will come."

That evening working turned out to be a messy affair. Rather, I was too messed up from the inside to focus on work. I mixed drinks incorrectly, thrice, took incorrect orders twice, and delivered wrong drinks to the wrong table so many times that in the end the manager had to ask what the matter with me was.

"Am not feeling well," I lied, looking at the floor.

"Why don't you take off," he suggested warmly.

"I think I should. Look I am really sorry for..."

"That's okay Sona, happens sometimes. You rest tonight."

Relieved from my job, I returned home early, showered, dressed up with a flower in my hair and waited for a long time for Stephen. I wondered whether he regretted what he had done in the past and was contemplating reconciliation; whether he was looking forward to start everything all over again.

"Looking beautiful with that flower," Stephen pointed at once.

I smiled, trying to remember the last time he said that. I could not. Was Stephen an event of my life so deeper into the past? Or did the depth of time that I spent without him had erased out his memories so neatly that I had already begun to forget the details? I kept on wondering and wondering.

"You have become silent," Stephen observed.

"No, it's just that..." I began to fumble for words.

"I understand..." he added sensibly.

Something was beginning to crumble inside me. Was it my ego? Or the wall of anger that stood between us?

"I am sorry Sona..." he said and paused.

"That's okay," I replied

"No, don't stop me. I need to," he said taking in my hands. "Things I have done to you..." his voice trailed off.

I looked at his teary eyes. Should I tell him all that I had done, behind his back, I wondered silently. Would he be as apologetic, knowing that I had slept with Jian even when he and I were together? I doubted. Wisdom was in remaining quiet and observing the world as one saw a cinema.

"Let's not go back. Let us start afresh," I said.

Stephen looked pleased. He embraced me warmly and did not let me go for a long time. The familiar smell of his flesh mixed with cologne engulfed me. I was overwhelmed with a sense of longing, of nostalgia. I sniffed the fresh scent of a new beginning.

Old flames burst into new fires. Stephen and I ended up making passionate love that night, and the few nights that followed.

He hugged and cuddled Bella too, more often and with much affection than he did earlier. The sight bred in me peace, the father-daughter reunion. However good Jian had been to me, but I always noticed a sense of estrangement between him and Bella. Often, I wondered if I was doing the right thing for her. If I wasn't repeating Mama's mistakes? But now, seeing Stephen playing with Bella, I knew that I had made the right choice.

Stephen moved into my apartment and we began to live like husband and wife; one happy family that we had once been, that I always wanted to be a part of.

Soon I discovered that I was pregnant, yet again. I was beside myself at the discovery. Remembering my experience of Harrison's delivery and Bella's ailment since birth, I began to have second thoughts.

"I will be with you," Stephen affirmed. "Will take care of everything, Sona."

I reconsidered his proposition.

"Call Anna for help. It will be too much for you to handle everything alone," I opined.

For the first time, Stephen obliged, and without a protest. Anna flew down and took charge of Bella. She was 10 then, quite a child herself, but her efficiency in handling Bella amazed me. Looking at her I often thought of my previous versions, how I'd babysit my siblings while Mama relaxed.

As days progressed, my kidneys began to bother me, so much that one evening I lost my consciousness and fell on the floor. When I regained my senses, I was in the hospital.

"There is a blockage in her kidneys," the doctor said to Stephen. "We have to keep her under observation".

Stephen looked serious, perhaps sad. I could tell that he panicked inwardly but tried his best to hide his feelings. Was he afraid of losing me? I wondered. Was death standing near? The thought bred in me a strange sensation. Fear mixed with anxiety and puzzlement – an odd combination. I could feel spirits twirling around me, all night, half the day. And the remaining half I slept or was unconscious.

The doctor advised that I should stay in the hospital until the baby was born, which was approximately six weeks away, he calculated. I obliged. Soon I was transferred to ICU and tethered to all kinds of instruments, put on restricted low calorie and salt less diet.

It was a difficult time! Very difficult for me to deal with all the physical infirmities that I was so shockingly suffering from. I thought about all the abuses that I had been doing to my body; the narcotic pills that I had swallowed one after another, the countless bottles of vodka I had swigged down, the cigarettes I had turned ashes into. I remembered those wild sex sessions I had with multiple partners, the abortions that emptied my womb time and again, the sleepless nights, and the stress and strain of being part of a dysfunctional family.

The price was perhaps, too heavy to bear. My heart sank; I began to contemplate the extreme. What if my child is born deformed? Worse still, what if it is a still born? What if I die right now, without even delivering the baby? I felt guilty and sad, and numb with grief.

"Your child is going to be ok," I heard somebody whisper.

Turning around I discovered a frail looking Japanese lady looking at me and smiling.

"Your child is going to be fine," she repeated.

"How do you know?" I asked.

"I just know."

"You are an astrologer?" I said, curious. I noticed the deadly looking machine attached to her body. Was she hallucinating? I wondered.

She nodded her head. Her face was pretty, and yet it was not difficult to see that sickness had claimed a lot of her beauty. What was she suffering from?

"One day you will travel the world and predict people's future," she said. Her breathing was deep, noisy. I could see that speaking was effortful for her.

"Really?" I said excitedly.

There was no reply. The Japanese lady spoke no further. She drifted into sleep, or perhaps lost her consciousness from which she never recovered. She died two nights later and was removed from the ICU without a stir.

I thought about her prediction. Was she speculating? Or could she really see the future? I did not know. Time was only to prove.

A few weeks later, I delivered a baby boy. We named him Bill. I recovered from the kidney blockage too and returned home, healthy.

Stephen was happy to be a father again. I thanked Anna for the support she had been to me.

Not too long after that Anna returned to Hawthorne. We resumed normalcy; a warm and cozy home, two children, a responsible husband and a wife. I returned to work almost at once, given that my house was at the back side of the bar. I hired a baby sitter to take care of my children. Life appeared beautiful. Or was the happiness only an illusion, I wondered at times.

Months passed as if they were days. Another year appeared: 1966.

Couple of times I met Jian, but the meetings were casual, more of a chance encounter than a deliberate converge. Each time Jian was with a different woman by his side; tall and slender, sexy looking with big boobs and light eyes. Jian pretended not to notice me, all the while throwing sly glances my side. I too disregarded his presence, reminding myself of my reunion with Stephen. Jian Durand was a station that I had crossed in the journey of my life, never to return.

It was around that time, one late evening while taking

a stroll in the neighborhood, I was hit from behind by a beefy man. He thrashed me on the ground and tried to take away my purse. The tussle grew, he beat me miserably. I countered him with the little strength I could muster. Soon people in the street called the cops. The man ran away before the cops arrived. I lay on the ground with blood in my mouth and ugly bruises on my face and arms. My stomach was sore with pain.

Somehow, I managed to return home, limping like a maimed human being. I told Stephen everything that had happened; and that cops would be knocking our door to record my statement. He dressed up my wounds. That night the cops did not come. And we slept on the couch like that, embracing each other as if we have returned home.

Love was an emollient, I realized despite pains and bruises.

Chapter 12

The pain abated in a week's time, but the memory lingered, a long

time after that incident. I feared going out alone when it was dark and the roads, deserted.

Meanwhile, Stephen was transferred to Illinois. I was reluctant to move to Illinois. Stephen of course wanted otherwise.

"Children need you, need me... and at the same time," he emphasized.

"I know that honey, but I have this job..." I tried to argue, somewhat reluctant to part with my job so abruptly.

"Fuck your job! You will get better ones there."

And the argument continued, day after day, night after night, until we decided that Stephen would go right away and I, along with the kids would join him a month later.

Initially he grumbled, but then budged. Not too long after that Stephen left.

The police case with the robber was under process. I

was ordered not to leave the town until settlement. For hours together I sat with the police and detectives, discussing the case. At times, I regretted my decision of taking the case to the police. Could have left the guy just like that. If nothing, it would have spared me the horror of sitting in a police station, hungry and thirsty, with a pair of wailing children to take care of and a job to attend to.

Then one day a lady came up to my apartment with two mixed children; a five-year-old girl with brown hair and grey eyes, and a boy of three with yellow hair and black eyes. The boy held spectacular resemblance with the lady.

"Yes," I said looking at her lovely grey eyes, wondering who she could be.

"I need a favor from you," she began without a preamble.

"Have we met before?" I said, taking in her picture-perfect figure and stunningly gorgeous looks.

"You don't know me, but I know you," she added confidently, as if she was a school friend, who remembered me while I forgot.

"I am Melissa," she said extending her dainty hand for a formal shake.

"How come you know me?" I asked doubly surprised now.

"I am his wife," she said in a mellowed down voice and paused, "whom you beat in the streets."

You beat in the streets, I noted but didn't react. I also noted that Melissa was observing my lips quite minutely to the exclusion of every other detail of my face. It was as if only my lips were visible to her. Did I put my lipstick too gaudily? Or was she obsessed with that body part? I wondered.

"Oh!" I said and stopped, wondering what to say next.

And the drama began!

"Look at them," she said in a wobbly tone pointing the two children standing on her either side. "You could make them fatherless," she added sobbing in a voice that was loud by any standard.

"Come inside and talk," I said opening the door wide for Melissa and her children.

Melissa walked inside and sat on the couch exactly opposite to me. She gazed at my children for a brief while.

"My husband could get ten years of imprisonment..." she continued, sniffling.

"He should have thought that before attacking me that night. I could have lost my life. My children could have been motherless," I added heatedly.

"I understand ... what you are saying. But my husband is a good man. He never behaves like that. I don't know why he did what he did. Maybe he was drunk..." her voice trailed off.

I looked at the bewildered children, and then to Melissa.

"Help me please.... Save him."

"Give me a day to think," I said.

"Please consider these two children, before you decide anything," she pleaded again. Having said that she moved towards the door.

"Where do you live?" I asked.

Melissa did not reply.

"Where have you come from?" I asked again.

She continued walking without paying any heed to my query. I noticed that her daughter tugged her hand and pointed back, towards me.

As if awaken from a sleep she turned abruptly and said, "You were saying something?"

I shook my head, denying.

"She asked you, where do we live?" the girl said loudly.

Melissa's eyes quickly drifted from my face to her daughter.

"Kalihi," she said loudly and smiled.

That was when I realized that Melissa was hard of hearing, and all this while she had been lip reading. Melissa must have read the puzzled look on my face, the befuddled expression, for she quickly added, "Sorry about that. I am hard of hearing," she said pointing her ear.

"You are doing fine," I replied and smiled.

"Help me please," she said again.

Then she was gone.

I stood at my door for a long time observing her car glide away. I thought about Melisa that night. The challenge she might be facing – running a family, raising two children with her impairment. Probably she could not hear her children's wails, or her husband's alcohol induced shouts. Did that make her life easy, smoothing out the rough edges? Or was it difficult to live with an impairment? I was left confused and thinking.

Using my sources, I inquired after the guy, Melissa's husband, Richard Pereira. And she was right. Richard was a nice guy, many said. He owned and ran a Dairy Queen joint in Kamehameha Shopping Center, which, for some reason wasn't doing well.

I called Melissa a few days later and told her to postpone the trial, so that when I'd come in the court, I could pretend that I had practically no memory of the incident. And Richard could be saved.

For some reason, I felt sympathetic for Melissa. I admired in her the courage to come up and confront me. I admired her commitment towards Richard.

I wondered if I did the right thing. Because I was certain that the police would be after my life after I'd say that in the court. And yet, a part of me felt sorry for the children. Whatever reasons Richard had had for the attack, the children were innocent. Melissa was innocent. And I had no right to punish them. In the process of teaching Richard, a lesson, I would ruin a family, I reasoned.

Two months later I appeared in the court and said that I could not remember the face of the man who had attacked me. And that I was too drunk to take a note of the incident.

The police and attorney turned red with fury. They kept looking at me with scrutinizing eyes, as if I was a criminal who needed to be punished and not Richard.

"Will come and meet you," the cop said menacingly.

I nodded my head, unable to speak. Silently I walked out of the court room and returned home. That night the cops returned, as if to charge me.

"Do you have any idea Miss how hard I worked on your case?" he barked.

"I do."

"And you went ahead to ruin it. I don't understand why? What possessed you?" he asked fuming.

How could I make him understand the endless agony of fatherless children? How could I explain to him the helplessness of a woman whose husband was in jail? What kind of days and nights would befall on her, on the family?

"I was confused… may be that was another man," I lied looking at the floor.

"Fantastic!" he said and marched out with thudding steps.

Nearly twenty minutes later, Richard came in, with a bag of chocolates and two tubs of ice cream.

"For your children," he said offering me the bag. "Thank you for your help. That was nice of you."

"I did it for your children," I replied, straight.

He didn't reply but walked out, his head held low.

Richard was embarrassed to meet me; I could tell it with that one look of his face. I was tempted to ask why he did what he did, but then thought better of it. Weren't we all like him in a way? How often and how many of us act, keeping in mind the full consequences of our actions? Not many, I guess. Perhaps that night he was drugged and had lost his balance of mind. Or perhaps he was under the influence of alcohol. I would never know.

A moment later, Richard returned. He fumbled for a speech.

"You want to say something?" I asked.

Richard nodded.

"Please take care of yourself," he said and paused.

Something in his face told me that was not all. Richard did not return to say, *please take care of yourself.*

"And?" I probed.

"There is this guy… who wants to injure you… that night… I was paid… I didn't want to… but then… this debt… he paid me… to … but… police siren… I got… scared… I ran," Richard said, haphazardly.

I was beside myself at the revelation. Who would want to kill me? I wondered and wondered.

"You can tell me the name… I won't tell anybody," I said putting up my bravest face.

"Somebody you know," he said, still skeptical to reveal the name.

"All the more reason to tell," I said meeting him in his eyes.

"Jian," he said and vanished from my sight.

I was thunderstruck.

All those incidents were beginning to crush me, first the unexpected assault for which I neither could trace a reason nor a conclusion. Then the case. Then Melissa and her children, and then my unanticipated and unpretentious backing out from everything sighting a reason that nobody bought. Nobody except Melissa of course.

And finally, the revelation. Jian!

Not too long after that I got a call from Mama. She said she was not well, and that she would need me there, for a while, to help her run the household. I needed a break too. And more than anything I wanted to be away from Hawaii. Hence, I packed my bags, booked my tickets and travelled to Hawthorne. It would be a vacation, I decided while boarding the flight with my children.

Little did I know at that point of time, that the trip I was considering a vacation would never end. And that I was leaving Hawaii forever, and for good.

Chapter 13

The truth revealed itself the moment I stepped inside Mama's house. Nina's death and her sickness seemed to have aged her a decade more. Mama looked weak, incapable of running a house with six children. Apart from Larry and me, everybody was still living with her.

Larry was somewhere in Arizona, Mama said, working for a printing company. He rarely called and never came to see her.

"You are my only support Sona," she said trembling.

I nodded smileless.

I settled down in one of the rooms with my kids and started looking for a temporary job using my connections. Getting a job wasn't difficult, given my popularity in Hawaii, for sooner than expected I was called for an interview in a bar called Hawaiian Breeze. I got the job and started right away.

The job paid me well, enough to take care of Mama, my children and all my siblings. I sensed a deep relaxation in Mama, seeing me taking charge of her family.

Then one day uncle Earl arrived, in a navy suit and English hat. He appeared younger than I remembered.

"Hello Sona!" he said with his charismatic smile.

"Uncle Earl!" I almost hiccupped. "What a surprise to see you."

"Well, life is full of surprises," he said, moved forward and kissed Mama on her cheeks. "How are you, my sweetness?" he greeted her.

Mama blushed.

True. Life was indeed full of surprises; so many of them that I started feeling dizzy. My head was about to burst open and the ground beneath my feet crack up. I feared, if I dared to stand there a while longer, I could very well be sucked inside.

"Feeling a lot better, after she turned up," Mama replied smiling, pointing my side.

For a second, I had an impulse to run away from that place that very moment and never see her face again, but then thought better of it. Controlled my thought, restrained my impulse.

Uncle Earl and Mama chatted for a long time, and quite animatedly. Mama did not look sick at all. It was the reverse, she looked healthy and happy. They touched each other often, and what I suspected endearingly. There was a different kind of bonding, between them now, that pinched me in the eyes. Under the pretext of work, I excused myself, but kept an eye on them.

"What was that?" I asked Mama that night, after he left.

"What was what?" Mama feigned innocence.

"Oh, come on... you know what I am talking about," I spat in a fit of rage.

Mama fell silent.

"You two are in love?"

"It's not that simple," she said.

"Of course, it is..."

I did not know why but I was beginning to feel a bizarre tremor raising inside me, overtaking me.

"I am a woman Sona, a lonely woman who needs love," Mama said in a tone that was loud but measured. A new development in mother, if I knew her correctly.

"Oh yea..."

"It's easy for you to judge, but, if possible, try to understand me. See the world through my eyes."

Having said that Mama walked out of the room. For a long time, I sat in the patio, reflecting on what she said, observing the gradual descent of darkness.

Perhaps she was right. It was easy to judge her. For, it was true that she was a woman with a desire to love and be loved. I too had slept with countless men in the vacant desire to be loved. Worse still, I had a string of one-night stands with men with whom I had no other connection other than those fickle moments of shared carnality. And yet, I was now judging Mama for the exact vices for which I could be held guilty. Who knows perhaps one day Bella would judge me too and condemn me for what I was doing now?

Having said that I reconsidered my opinion about Mama, and her growing intimacy with Uncle Earl.

"I am sorry," I said, first thing next morning.

"Sorry for what?" Mama looked surprised.

"For having said what I said last night."

"Its okay. I understand your anger. You are not wrong," she said trying to put up a happy face.

"No, I was, last night. And you are right when you said that - you are a woman too," I moved forward and hugged her.

"I love you Sona," she said endearingly.

"Love you too," I said feeling a strange sensation washing my shores, overpowering me,

"Thank you for understanding. Means a lot to me," she said kissing me on my forehead. I felt like a child all over again. "You know something, you are my biggest blessing."

Not too long after that morning, Uncle Earl and Mama married in the church. It felt strange to see a mother's wedding. I recollected another wedding like that when Mama and Martin had married in Mexico. I was a child then, waiting in the car all along when that dramatic union had taken place, and yet I had felt myself on the verge of a change. It had happened exactly as I had thought, feared. Martin's arrival changed our lives forever.

I wondered if my life was on the brink of another change.

Uncle Earl said that his wife Dorothy died a few years ago from ovarian cancer. Mama and he met at the funeral. That was when then they began to meet. Romance sprung in the autumn of their lives. I thought of Aunt Dorothy the entire time, how kind and considerate she had been when I came to stay with them briefly.

Mama and uncle Earl looked happy, when they were together. They enjoyed each other's company. At times, I felt like an unwanted intrusion in their love story. Often at nights, new kind of sounds would reach my ears. Sounds of matured love making, I guessed, amused. Mama smiled incessantly all through the day. Having found love and a good husband, she appeared contented. Mama finally discovered love again. I felt happy for her.

With Mama's new found love and matrimony there were times when I began to feel lonely. Job kept me busy, but I was beginning to crave for emotional fulfillment that was now totally missing from my life.

I contemplated visiting Stephen. Anticipating a warm welcome, I called him one evening. Stephen appeared cold.

"Hello," he said in a slurry tone.

"It's me, Sona," I said and paused, expecting him to something.

Stephen fell silent. I heard the sound of his inconsistent breathing, loud and unpleasant. What he was doing, I wondered.

"How are you?" I asked after a while.

"You remember me now? After all this time?" he retorted. There was an edge in his voice. A deliberate roughness perhaps crafted and invested to insult me.

It was my turn to become silent. I wondered what I should say, for he wasn't far from the truth. I really didn't care to call him all those months.

"Was kind of busy..." I fumbled.

"You and your kind of busy ness," Stephen said

enraged. "I know what you were busy with. Fucking men…," he spat.

My ears turned instantly red, as if somebody had slapped me right across my face. I was about to open my mouth, when he said,

"You know what, marrying you had been a mistake."

Darling what's the matter, you sound upset, I heard from the background. It was a female voice, slightly husky and grossly slurry. Perhaps he had a company that night.

"Who is that?" I asked gulping humiliation.

"That's none of your business."

"Of course, it is my business. You are still my fucking husband," I spat.

"I was…" he said and paused.

"What the hell do you mean?"

"Exactly that," he replied.

"Stephen, listen to me…" I began to fumble. "Listen to me please…"

"Oh, shut up you bitch. You think I don't know what you do behind my back. You bloody whore… you fuck men and then trash them. The way you trashed me…"

I banged the phone and cried my heart out. Tears flooded my eyes, rushed down my face, and drenched me in its unforgiving brine.

Within a month's time I received a divorce notice from Stephen. I knew it was over between us. Whatever I'd say or do after that would only add to the loss. Stephen would not change his mind. I signed the papers, certainly not happy but not grieving either.

Stephen Aitken was an episode of my past, I told myself. I had travelled with him, mothered his children, and now it was time to move on. Five years of marriage ended in a divorce for which I neither got a settlement, nor did I get to see Stephen's face. I signed a bundle of papers before a stranger in black coat and grey moustache, as he kept looking at me, blinking and smiling nonchalantly, as though I was a spectacle.

If anything, marriage is a big farce, I realized with monumental regret.

Chapter 14

A new chapter began. Although Stephen and I lived separately for the last couple of years, but now, being officially divorced meant new set of struggles and obstacles to battle with and overcome. I was defenseless and felt vulnerable most of the time. Sleep slipped out of my eyes, and restlessness once again found residence in me.

Mama's attitude changed too, and for worse. She became surprisingly disinterested in me and my problems after her marriage with Uncle Earl.

Uncle Earl's five children shifted from his residence and started living with us. Our house now rattled with the noise of twelve children: my mother's five, uncle's five and my two. If our house had once resembled a hostel, now it reminded me of an asylum; noisy, unruly and annoyingly chaotic. The halls turned into bedrooms, washrooms turned into dumping grounds, kitchen metamorphosed into store rooms. There were even nights, when the two bath tubs were used as beds. Clothes were everywhere; books, toys and shoes dotted the entire living space. As for the kitchen. the sinks overflowed with used dishes emitting foul smell. The dinner table was loaded with a wild hotchpotch of fruits, cut and un-cut vegetables, cooked food, untouched soup, half-drunk coffee mugs, wine glasses and what not

Often, I noticed Mama treating Bella and Bill unkindly, shouting at them even when there was no reason to. In a month's time, she bounced back to her original self; apathetic, distant and self-obsessed. The kind of mother I had grown up with.

I sensed she wanted me to move out of her house and create space for Uncle Earl and his children. It was obvious I no longer constituted her family. The delicate bond that we had been creating during my stay ruptured, leaving both of us spinning dizzily in our own respective orbits.

Around that time, we got news of Mason's death. He had died of some unknown malady in a shabby hotel room in Milwaukee. He was seen with a prostitute the previous night, Uncle Earl informed. His voice was flat as he spoke, devoid of emotions. I noticed. He did not have any great reverence for Mason. Mama did not speak a word after she heard the news. She did not arrange for a funeral either.

I thought of our last journey together, when I drove him to the bus depot. And then our meeting in that hotel room where I attended to his wounds. I remembered the look on his face, the sad mixture of pain and resignation; and the final moment when I had closed the door, while he lay in his bed, alone and vulnerable. He could have said a lot to me that evening, after we were done with the procedure, but remained eerily silent. I wondered why. And then his confession, *I had killed him*. Was it an act of vengeance or an escape from guilt? Why did he kill a man with whom he had no personal enmity? Was it to punish the man of his folly or was it to wash off the scars from his own hands, having committed the same crime? I wanted to know. And now, with his passing away, I would never know.

Although he had never been around, to care for me or protect me when I needed it , officially I was fatherless now. With my divorce with Stephen, my children were fatherless too, in another sort of way. The thought sunk inside me like a rock.

Soon I moved out of Mama's home to a rented apartment. Bella and Bill became my new world, and I loved it that way.

Unexpectedly one day I received a letter. It was from Stephen; the postal address was Vietnam. Emotions overwhelmed me. Nostalgia drifted past me like a gush of fragrant wind. He said that he was about to complete his twenty years of naval service, when he got a transfer order to be posted to Vietnam for a year. Many of the American doctors had died in the war and hence his service was needed. That was his first experience in a war zone, he wrote. While on duty, he saw hungry and naked children eating garbage from bins. Many were incurably deformed. Looking at them, often he thought of Bella and Bill. He missed them. He said that he regretted the decision of parting. In a way he had made his own children fatherless. The experiences he was now going through was the fruit of his own sin.

With the letter, there was money too; nearly five hundred dollars. I felt thankful to him, not for the money but for the emotional banter that brought into my mind our good days.

I read the letter time and again, reminding myself that a letter was all I now had, in the name of a relationship. The man vanished from my life, only his scribble was there to console me, to smooth out the rough edges of my being.

A week later, Mama called me to her place for Easter.

I went there and stayed for a couple of days. The entire time I saw Nina, moving around in the house; playing in the garden, laughing, dancing, singing. Nobody could see her apart from me. I kept looking at her side, and at times smiled at her silly pranks. She was a kid when I had left home and married Galvin. I did not see much of her. But now, seeing her like that, I felt a deeper connection growing between us.

"Who are you smiling at Sona?" Mama pointed.

"No one," I lied, getting suddenly conscious that I was being watched.

"Of course, you are. I have been seeing you for quite a while now," she protested.

"I said no one," I replied, annoyed.

"Don't tell me you started talking to invisible beings," she said, looking menacingly at me.

I saw Nina, first looking at Mama and then at me. She giggled, putting palm on her little mouth. Nina shook her head, as if to tell me, not to reveal mother the things I saw.

"You won't reach anywhere, if you continue doing silly things," Mama warned.

And I thought about the Japanese lady's forecast. One day I'd travel the world and read people, she had predicted. I wondered if it would ever come true.

That night, I had an extra body sensation. I could see myself from somewhere atop. For some time, I felt so light that I feared I would be swept away by the wind and perhaps land in another galaxy, far away from where I was. I saw my children too, deep in their sleep, unaware of my strange state of being.

When I woke up the following morning, that lightness remained for some time. I drifted in and out of sleep as if I was shuttling from one room to another. I became aware of a transformation within myself, a new beginning round the corner.

Chapter 15

Meeting a galaxy of people in the bar in a way lured me to scan faces, predict their temperament and happenings, both past and present. One thing leading to another, I started reading cards as well, and to my surprise, turned out to be good at it.

I began to like the work, a hundred times more than the bar job I had been doing for more than a decade now. Gradually I became popular too. A lot of people flocked around my house to know their future. They paid me handsomely, if they were satisfied by my reading. In a way it felt good to meet new faces every other day, talk to them for hours, read their faces and predict their futures.

Once, an Indian engineer by the name Karan Singh came to visit me. He was the first Indian I ever met. Tall and brown, with sharp features and dark beard, quite a looker he was. Karan said he was from a place called Amritsar.

"What's that thing on your head?" I asked pointing the turban on his head.

To that Karan laughed. He said, he was a Punjabi and a Sikh. He hailed from a religious community where men didn't cut their hairs and covered them with a turban.

"So, you are Punjabi, and not Indian," I asked confused and curious.

"Both," he replied.

"But how could you be both?"

He replied that India was a huge country and Punjab was a state in it. People who originated from Punjab are called Punjabi. India comprised of many states, and that people from each state were different.

"Different? How come?"

"They speak different languages, wear different clothes, eat different food, have different festivals…" he went on and on.

The idea intrigued me. One nation with 29 states and each state different from the neighboring one.

"Your country must be one interesting place," I presumed.

Karan nodded his big head aggressively.

"Yes, it is. Interesting and very very colorful!" he remarked.

Next time Karan visited me he brought an exquisitely carved wooden elephant. I was touched. Ever since I became a woman, no man had ever brought me gifts. Karan was the first one. We became friends soon and began to spend a lot of time together.

Karan nostalgically spoke about his country, his culture, his cuisine, his festivals, as I listened enthralled. I began fantasizing about a visit to India.

"What's your country like?" I kept on asking him, time and again, unable to grasp its cultural diversity.

Karan laughed; a laughter that reflected happiness, I noticed.

"If you want to understand my country, you will have to go and stay there," he added.

"Are you serious?"

"Of course, I am. Tell me when you are ready. I will take you."

That night, for the first time I contemplated visiting India. The idea was fascinating. But to take a tour of India, I had to arrange for my children, which was no easy deal. Mama refused point blank.

"You are going all alone to that faraway country and I will have to take care of your kids?" she bellowed, clearly annoyed.

"Please Mama, try to understand. I may not get an opportunity like this. I wanna see that country. Please," I begged. That was all I could do to convince her.

Yet, she remained unmoved.

"And what if somebody kills you there?" Mama asked.

"Nobody is going to kill me. Plus, I have a friend with me. An Indian, I will be safe. You need not worry about my safety. All you must do is take care of my kids for a couple of months. That's all I ask from you. Please," I said.

"Of course not!" she replied. It was difficult to convince her.

Uncle Earl came to my rescue.

"If she wants to go, let her go," he said looking at Mama.

Mother fixed uncle Earl with an angry stare. I looked away, from both of them. I returned home with a long face, and heavy heart. India seemed a remote dream.

Next day I received a call. It was from Uncle Earl. He said that he would look after my children while I was away. I could plan my trip.

"But Mother?" I asked him, nervously.

"Don't worry about her. I will convince her. You book your tickets and enjoy your vacation," he said cheerfully.

"Thanks," I said. "Means a lot."

"No problem. Be safe," he said and hung up.

I smiled for the next ten minutes straight.

Almost immediately I started preparing for my trip. Karan helped me with all the formalities. Not too long after that we boarded the flight. My first flight to a country that was only a story so far. I was anxious, nervous, I was excited, enthusiastic, I was happy, and at the same time panicky... I did not know which one more.

"This will be an experience of a life time," Karan kept on repeating, all through the flight.

And how true he was... experience of a life time. The sights and scenes, the fragrance and the beauty of India overwhelmed me, so much that the time I was there, I forgot every other aspect of my being. I forgot the family I had left behind in the United States. I forgot Stephen Aitken. I forgot myself.

Karan and I landed in New Delhi. The freedom was exhilarating; a new continent, a new country. New hope. I basked in the thought under an unforgivingly hot Indian sun.

"You, okay?" Karan kept on asking with annoying monotony. He looked concerned, even worried at times.

"Have never been more okay," I said, looking at him, smiling with my entire skin that was wet with perspiration.

"Now listen, there are things I want to tell you," Karan started, uncertainly.

I looked at him with a knot in between my brows.

"This is India, so no getting cozy, in public. Especially not in front of my family," he warned. "No holding hands, no hugging, no kissing."

Was he terrified to take me before his family? I wondered.

And yet, I followed his instructions with surgical precision. I did not touch him for as long as we were in India. Not even a casual brush of palms, or a peck on the cheek. And it was not that I was terribly missing sex. There were other pleasant distractions.

After a halt in a hotel in Delhi, we went to Agra for a tour.

"The Taj Mahal!" Karan said smiling with pride.

And he had reasons to be proud; I realized the moment I laid my eyes on that unbelievable monument of love. The tomb reminded me of the beauty of longing. I breathed love, I felt beautiful.

From Agra we went to Rishikesh, Manali and Kulu, and then to Dharamshala. The Himalayan Mountain and the crisp air cooled my agitated nerves. Clad in those enormous mountains, shrouded by a perpetual mist, I discovered happiness, a feeling of home miles away from home.

Finally, Karan took me to Amritsar, his home town. He introduced me to his big family, who stayed in a giant house, happily and with a hell of a lot of noise. I was allotted a guest room on the terrace; a small room with a single bed, a table, a chair and a window that opened to a never-ending stretch of colorful rooftops. Karan's three brothers, two unmarried sisters, his parents, and his grandparents, all occupied different portions of the house. Two of the three brothers were married and had children. One of the sisters was to be married soon, as I gathered from their conversations and Karan's interpretation. All of them were curious about me.

His family was cordial without being over friendly. And I liked the distance; the feeling of being a part of a loving family and yet remaining alone. Indians made very good mothers, daughters and sons. Relationship was their forte, something I lacked, and devastatingly so. Looking at Karan's mother, I often thought of Mama. The dispassionate attitude that guided our relationship, her multiple relationships that ended more often in disasters, the abrasions those relationships had caused in my soul. Instinctively I thought of my own children too, now that they were so far away, I thought of them with a different mind. A part of me regretted for leaving them behind with Uncle Earl. And another part was thrilled with the journey, from which I drew more than the superficial experience of a tourist.

One late evening Karan's mother came to meet me. Her English was quite rudimentary, and I fumbled to fish out the right word from my pathetic Hindi vocabulary to express my feelings. Nevertheless, I tried. She sat on the chair and spoke, very slowly and what I took to be candid. I struggled to understand her point.

"You, marriage?" she asked, pointing her index finger towards me.

I nodded.

"Your husband, no come?"

I realized Karan had introduced me as a woman married to another man. He did not reveal our relationship. But again, had he had the courage to reveal that truth, would they have accepted me into their house with so much warmth, with such bountiful spring of love and hospitality? Perhaps not.

"No," I said.

"Children?" she said, asked. She adjusted the white *dupatta* on her head.

I nodded.

"How many?" she said with an added gesture of her beautiful hand.

I lifted three fingers, in reply. She understood. She smiled.

"You husband, and you children together?"

I nodded. I lied. Immediately I felt solid and stubborn pangs of guilt, having lied to the woman who had been cooking and feeding me, playing the role of that perfect mother which, I never had. But my life and family equations were so complicated and so incomprehensible, that it would have been impossible for me to make her understand.

"You no feel alone?" she asked etching a frown on her shiny forehead. Her eyes were big and bright, I noticed, and bore striking resemblance to Karan's.

"All of us are alone, in a way."

She thought for a while, making a strange face. I kept looking at her, wondering how well and how far she would understand my statement. She was a woman, around 65 years of age, surrounded by two in-laws, a husband, four sons, two daughters in law, two daughters and five grandchildren, on top of that, two house maids and one man-servant. Perhaps she had never been alone in her life time. The house so clatteringly bustled with noise all the time that one could never be lonely. Yet, she understood my point, magically as if. Or at least she pretended to.

"Right you are," she nodded her *dupatta* clad head twice, in understanding, in acceptance. "All alone in the end."

"You are very good, very kind," I said with a cherry expression.

"You good too," she returned the compliment. If eyes were wells, hers would have been two oceans of love.

I thought for a moment. Did I truly deserve the compliment? Was I nice in its real sense of the meaning? The lady who was calling me good was surrounded by her family, her children. She had been with them, taking care of them all her married life. Things might not have been easy for her, and yet she had never given up. Never thought of quitting her marriage or her children. She had nourished them with her life and kindness. What had I done in comparison? Married two men, quit them in frenzy, slept with countless others, just for fun. Produced three children and now left them with my second step father to visit a country I had no practical reason or relationship with.

"I am no good, I made mistakes," I said finally, having mustered the courage to speak my mind. Perhaps her lack of English proficiency had eased the process. For, somewhere

I was certain that she'd understand less than what I would confess. And hence her judgment of me would invariably be inaccurate, partial.

"All make mistakes, you not one," she replied, kindly with a small smile.

Tears welled up in my eyes. And before I could realize it or even control it, they leaked. Karan's mother got up from the chair, and then moved towards me. She rubbed my cheeks with the free end of her *dupatta*, then patted my head gently and went away.

It was a human gesture. And yet, the effect it had on me was profound. A woman, with whom I had practically no relationship with, touched me so deeply that I began to squirm with sadness. I plunged into thoughts and memories of my mother, my children, the shallow things I had done and accepted as my life. The unforgivably stupid decisions I had taken so far, and altered multiple times, the course of my life. The pathetic waste of everything!

I remained awake that night. Her touch of kindness was a moment of intense truth. I had rarely felt such strong emotion before, if at all. Had rarely been loved in that way, simple yet profound, and innocent. I never met Karan's mother after that. And yet, she remained somewhere deep inside me in the form of love.

In our desperation to be loved, we do crazy things. And my life was the biggest proof. I went to the most impossible extents to love, to be loved. And yet, more often than I had cared to notice, love came and touched me from the most unexpected sources. From people whom I had no relationship with. From people with whom I had nothing to do.

Every evening that I spent in Amritsar, I visited the

Golden Temple, listening to *Gurbani* and soaking peace with my entire being. The temple promised me a kind of peace that I had never felt before. It felt amazing to be there, as the sun would set, filling the air with a crimson glow that would make everything appear golden. All the struggles I had faced so far, all the hurts and insults, the accusations and abuses that people showered on me got washed away in that gentle spring of peace. I felt light; felt forgiving. Life appeared like one big blessing, and for the first time ever since I was born, I thanked the universe for everything that I had got so far.

Having said that I realized with a strange finality that events and situations in one's life are linked with one another in a never-ending succession of events, however random they'd appear to an onlooker. And that my life, having travelled through the rough valleys and terrains of suffering and abuses was meant to reach at that spot, to stop, to think, to look back and reflect on the fact that life was not too bad after all.

Before I knew it, three months were over. And it was time to return. I left India with a bowl of memories - happy memories, serene memories, memories that would be my companion for a long, long time.

Chapter 16

L anding in New York, we drove straight to Colorado, to collect my kids from Uncle Earl, who was there at a friend's place for a brief holiday. He decided to take my kids along with him.

Collecting Bella and Bill, we drove back to California. Reuniting with children bred in me a new kind of contentment. But then gradually disturbing thoughts began to haunt me, like an evil memory. What would I do to make a living? Where would I stay with my children and with Karan? Would my children like him? What would I tell them who Karan was? Would he rent a separate accommodation for himself? All kinds of thoughts played rugby in my mind.

Then suddenly an idea struck me. I called Nora Griffith. Nora had a big house in San Ramon and was a good friend.

"Sure, you can stay here with your family," Nora said over the phone, smiling. "Need to catch up."

I began to stay at Nora's place with Karan and my children. It was difficult, I realized soon enough. Nora's husband was a California based businessman who was killed in a devastating road accident. The accident of course made Nora richer than ever. Too much of money had made her a slave to her crazy and often incorrigible whims. It had spoilt her children too. Nora's children and my children fought, and they fought like pole cats. They did not like each other and were perpetually complaining about one thing or the other. Soon I moved out of her house and arranged for a separate accommodation for us.

One day, Karan called his home in India, and learned that his father had expired. He was requested to return. He packed his bags and bid us goodbye. I came to the airport to see him off. He hugged me and kissed me with all the passion of the world. He was reluctant to part ways.

"I'll come back soon," he said with sad eyes.

"You take care," I replied.

Karan never came. I knew it even then, when he said *I'll come* standing in the airport. Our paths diverged, never to meet again.

Anyway, with Karan returning to India, I dived headlong into card reading. After my trip to India, I started meditating, having completely sold myself to the delightful concept of meditation. I went far and wide to take up classes on meditation; visited all possible places where there was a promise of peace. The idea appealed me. It invariably brought into my mind the experiences I had encountered in India.

I took my children with me, all along. There was a strange comfort in their presence. And they loved travelling with me, in cars, literally living life on the roads. When the car broke down, we travelled in buses. At time we hitch hiked in other people's cars. We lived on meal-to-meal basis but felt happy and contented. We craved for nothing, we wanted nothing more.

Gradually roads began to comfort me, and journey, soothe me. It brought into my mind the string of homes that I had made, one after the other, and then after a while trashed them like old garments and moved on, when I was barely a child. At that time, I had considered the whole affair a vaguer, an absolute and ridiculous wastage of human effort that my parents had indulged in with bizarre longing, year after year. But now, I was a grown-up woman and a parent myself, yet I considered the idea, adventurous and totally thrilling.

I loved the perpetual shift of my landscape, the ever-changing nature of my days and nights. The different beds that I slept in, and observed the sky change its color. All the numerous bathrooms I had showered in, the various eateries where I ate my meals and sipped my coffee without having any idea where my next cup of coffee would come from. The incertitude of my existence excited me, it bred into my mind a passion and penchant for travelling, for exploring the world beyond the fringes of cognizance and certitude.

Chapter 17

The thought struck me one night, when I was lying in my bed, alone and sleepless, after a long day's drive. Tired down to my bones, and yet sleep would not embrace me. It eluded me beyond the darkness of my closed eyes.

Bella and Bill were sleeping in the bed, adjacent to mine. I kept looking at their reposed faces. The luminous darkness of the motel room was clear enough to observe their features. They looked beautiful and healthy, and yet I felt sad. I couldn't help but feel sad.

Was I doing the right thing? Am I really being a sensible mother? I thought, repeatedly. They were my children. They still had their father alive, somewhere. And I was robbing them of their education, their childhood, depriving them of a real family, a decent father. In the pursuit of finding happiness for myself, I was denying them the most basic joy of all - the joy of having a family.

That was the exact moment when I thought of Stephen. Of course, as a couple, we had parted our ways for a while now, having signed the divorce papers; but Stephen was still the father of my children. That was the truth I had to accept.

I embarked on an immediate course of action. After a few phone calls, investing all the telephone operator's tricks I had learnt, I could finally locate him. Stephen was in Biddeford, Maine, after his retirement. He had settled there and taken up the job of a manager in a local hotel called Swamp Fox.

I reached the town around late evening, got his address from the hotel and then knocked his doors. Stephen was beside himself, when he discovered us standing there, hungry and tired, looking as emaciated as we were.

"Oh my God!" he exclaimed, and not without surprise. He looked stupefied. "How the hell are you here?"

"Won't you call us in?" I added, playfully.

"Oh sure… please," he said and moved aside, making space for us to enter.

We ambled in, taking in the cozy décor of his house.

"Children are hungry," I said after we settled down.

"Don't worry about food. We have plenty," he said opening his spectacularly over loaded refrigerator.

My stomach twisted at the sight of food. I felt ravenous.

After shower, all of us sat down at the table and ate hungrily. Stephen sipped his beer and looked at the children admiringly, I observed in between my avid gulps. A satiated stomach, fatigue and then the booze. An impossible combination! My head felt heavy, eye dropped as if pulled down by gravity. But even with my partially numb faculties, I noticed love in Stephen's blue eyes. Was he missing his children? Why didn't he reach me? He had Mama's telephone number. I thought behind my pursed lips.

I looked at his small but beautifully decorated home; the tasteful furnishing, the stockpile of food in his refrigerator. The fragrance of home. The placid happiness of having a family. A stable life!

When I finally settled my eyes on him, I discovered him ogling at me with longing. Immediately, he looked away. But even in that fraction of a moment I read in him something that I had seldom noticed when we were a couple and shared lives. Perhaps it was the effect of the war. Or his increasing age. Maybe it was both. I did not know. All I realized was a strange vulnerability in him that pleased and confused me equally.

Any other woman would have sunk inside Stephen's home, perhaps taking advantage of the children we shared. And if instincts did not betray me, he was emotionally ready to accept the responsibility all over again. Play the role of a husband and father that he had once played with so much of joy.

But I was I. Getting tied to Stephen would mean the freedom that I was nurturing and chasing with maniacal determination would be lost. I would have to return to the cage and perhaps spent the rest of my life raising children and being a wife. The idea unnerved me, because by then I was beginning to fall in love with the freedom that came with homelessness. The romance of being a nomad! Thoughts of home intimidated me, and having real relationships scared me, enough to make me run away from anybody who would propose to me.

After dinner, the children went to bed. Stephen and I sat for a while.

"You have a nice home," I said eyeing the room we were sitting in.

"A home is home, only if there is family to live in," he said looking at a spot invisible to me.

"I understand," I added uncertainly, wondering where the conversation was going.

Stephen paused. I could see that he was framing something in his mind.

"Can't I have my children... for a while?" he began, somewhat cautiously.

"Of course, you can!"

My answer eased him; I could sense. His face relaxed.

"You could stay...," he started. That was when I cut him.

"I want to be alone for a while. I don't crave for a home," I added candidly.

Stephen nodded. He appeared as if he understood me. Or at least he pretended to. I contemplated telling him about my recent trip to India; all the places I had been; play wife, even if for a while. But that would also mean telling him about Karan, and a lot more than he deserved to know. For, I could never really forget the statement he had made before he banged the telephone down on my face.

Oh, shut up you bitch! You think I don't know what you do behind my back. You bloody whore... you fuck men and then trash them. The way you trashed me...

I trashed the idea at once.

Those words left an unsavory flavor in my mouth. No matter how hard I tried to forget, no matter how much I tried to ignore the scalds those few words had created on my mind, but it lingered, like a birth mark.

"What I suggest, you keep Bella and Bill with you,

here. Enroll them in a school. I think that would be the right thing to do, for their future," I proposed.

It amazed me how, after ceasing to be husband and wife for so long, now, we conversed like matured parents. Perhaps that is the role children play in a parent's life.

"How long will you be like this?" Stephen asked.

I sensed his worry, the repressed love in his voice, his care for the vagabond mother of his children.

"I don't know…," I paused, "Really Stephen, I don't know," I replied.

"You get fun out of these?"

"It's not always for fun. I do things that I like that I get happiness from," I added passionately. "It may be difficult for you to understand. I don't blame you if you don't. Home may comfort me for a while but it does not give me the joy that I look forward to."

"I don't know what to make of you," he said and got up for a refill of his scotch. His voice was laced with frustration, I noticed.

"This is what I am Stephen, you accept it or not. But now that I am a mother too, I understand that my choices are hampering their upbringing, their education, their lives. That's the reason I came to you. Give them a home they deserve, a proper upbringing, education. Love."

"I will… don't worry. You are free to fly. Go wherever you find your kind of joy," Stephen said.

I sensed it was time to quit.

The few days that followed brushed us past in unimaginable craziness. We enrolled Bella and Bill to school, bought clothes and stationeries for them, took a few small picnics at Fortune's Rock, like one happy family. Together we attended dinner parties, like a couple, leaving the children at home. It was during one such private gathering at Ralph Henderson's place that a strange encounter happened.

Ralph was a childhood buddy of Stephen. He was a cop, with broad shoulders and a heavy face. Somewhere when the party was on and people were drinking themselves silly, suddenly I asked Ralph, "How is Rosaline?"

The name, Rosaline, slipped from my tongue unintentionally. I really did not intend to know how Rosaline was. Or for that matter who she was in the first place.

Ralph looked thunderstruck, his breath on hold.

"Honey, his wife's name is Zelda and not Rosaline," Stephen interrupted.

"Oh, I am sorry!" I exclaimed half embarrassed, half puzzled, not knowing what to say next.

Ralph kept looking at me with curious eyes for the rest of the evening.

We returned home, and an hour later, Ralph knocked on our doors, much to our amazement.

"What's up buddy?" Stephen said opening the door.

"I need to talk to Sona," Ralph said.

"She has fallen asleep, I think," Stephen replied, I heard from my room.

"Then please wake her up. I need to talk to her," he added quickly, nervously.

I got up from my bed and joined them in the hall.

"Hey..." I said in sleepy voice.

"You got to tell me from where you got that name?" Ralph pleaded with teary eyes. He looked disturbed.

"I don't know, the name slipped from my tongue," I said defensively.

"But still... please, it's important for me, please..." Ralph pleaded.

"Actually, I can read people's faces," I blurted out.

Stephen rolled his eyes at me, I observed but ignored.

Ralph jumped from his seat and hugged me.

"It's okay Ralph," I said patting him on his back.

That was when Ralph told us the story. He said once he had met with an accident and had to stay in a hospital for a long time. That was when he fell in love with a nurse, called Rosaline. He was alone there and was missing his wife. So, he and Rosaline had a brief affair. But then, their paths diverged once he was discharged from the hospital. Here, Ralph began to weep.

"It's okay buddy, things like this happen all the time," Stephen added emotionally.

"But I can't believe you could tell it. This was so long ago. You are something! You must have some power," Ralph said looking at me. I could see that my awkward revelation had rattled him.

"Most people say that about me," I acknowledged making it sound as modest as possible.

Ralph went back after a while.

That night I remained awake for a long time. Thought of what Ralph had said. Though of the precise moment when that name, Roseline, sprang out of my mouth, unconsciously. The effect it had created. I certainly did not know her; neither did I intend to blurt out the name of a woman with whom I held no connection. And yet, I did. I thought of all the incidents when I could predict a person's past, foretell the future with deadly accuracy. Their trust on my prophecy, their blind faith.

As night wore one, I began to feel more and more certain about myself. The path that I would follow from now; the purpose of my life. I knew that I was not destined to nurture a family or raise children. I was meant to read people; I was meant to travel the world.

I expected a lot of repercussions from Stephen the following morning, as we shared our coffee, but to my surprise he said nothing. Not a word about the previous night. Not a word about my journey, when I declared to him that that was my last day with him, in that house.

"You tell me, when you are ready, will drop you to the bus depot," he said offhandedly. But something in his voice suggested that he was upset, and that he showed no inclination to hide. And yet, he did not stop me, did not ask me my destination. Or what I'd do for a living. He was cold about my departure; unperturbed about my decision.

Bella and Bill did not cry, when they came to see me off. I sat in the bus. From that height they appeared smaller. But I could read their expressions clearly. They didn't look particularly sad. Bella was eight years old then, and Bill six. Although they were little but grown up enough to understand that they would not see their mother for a long time. Had Harrison been there, next to them, he too would have behaved the same? I wondered. What puzzled me was the apathy in their looks. The composed way they had accepted my departure from their lives. It was as if they had known all along that one day, I'd desert them and move on.

And I remembered their births with ghastly details, the pain I had to endure hour after hour to bring them into this world. My personal struggle with death, after each delivery, the endless hours and days I had spent with them, feeding them, nurturing them, making countless visits to hospitals to cure them of ailments, the sleepless nights I had spent to earn money for their keep, the hundreds and thousands of miles I had travelled with them to reach at the exact spot where they now stood.

I might have not been a very intelligent mother, having failed to choose the right action for them, the right decisions that would have given them a safe and secured home; a sound upbringing. I was certainly not an educated mother who would set an inspiring example before them. But I was a mother nonetheless and loved them as dearly as any mother would. Where exactly did I err, to deserve such apathy? Or was it the fault in my stars? That I would never be loved by my family and destined to be alone.

Tears welled up in my eyes, Then, they leaked. Relentlessly, as if someone had left a tap open. I realized with mounting conviction that what we call family and children are a bundle of vacant moments that drift past you, or you drift past, leaving you as empty and as solitary, as a forsaken oyster shell on a deserted beach.

By the time I reached California, my tears dried up, or they just stopped coming, having exhausted the stock. But I carried within me a vacuum that no time could ever heal.

Chapter 18

California once again welcomed me with outstretched arms; this time in the form of Sophia Johnson. She was an anonymous person for whom I had once read cards. I did not even care to ask her name. But Sophia remembered, and with striking accuracy, every detail that I had predicted.

Sophia now ran two upscale restaurants: one in Palm Springs and another one in State Street, Santa Barbara, both with enviable success. And that made her rich, way too richer than my prediction.

"Oh Sona, my life changed after I met you," Sophia said with emotions in her purple eyes that always brought into my mind the image of Elizabeth Taylor.

"I haven't done a thing. It's your destiny," I said humbled.

Sophia offered to play my host, and I accepted her proposition without drama. There weren't many options anyway. The truth was, I was a woman with no future and very little money. Returning to Mama's home would have been difficult, now that she was married to Uncle Earl and was living with him and his family. I felt happy for her. Really happy! Although I remained mum the entire length of conversations, but I sensed happiness in her voice too. Uncle Earl was a good husband and Mama was happy to be with him. In the autumn of their lives, they discovered happiness.

I was put up in Sophia's house and loved the solitary state of being. Sophia was a kind person with a big heart, who'd always be there when I needed her, but never overwhelmed me; whether with her love and care, or with her apparently endless list of unsolvable problems. Staff problems at her restaurants, a parade of difficult to please customers, her offensively drug addicted boyfriends, her three ex-husbands, who extorted money from her under one pretext or another; her current girlfriend Zaina Khoury, who at times spent nights with her and remained nude all day. Or her squishy dog, Puddle, who regularly sneaked out and fucked the next available bitch.

"He appears to be a great fuck," I once pointed, humorously.

Sophia laughed showing her two sets of beautiful teeth. Something about her reminded me of Elena, my first girlfriend. She was one of those little keepsakes that I carried within me. Sophia had sparkling white teeth and was extra particular about dental hygiene.

"Hey, listen love, I have booked a few classes for you," she added professionally.

"I don't know how to thank you," I said.

"Just be yourself. Do what you love. Touch people's lives, the way you did mine. That would be enough….," she said looking at me with a naughty grin of her red pout.

I started right away, reading cards for people in a small chamber at the back of her restaurant. Twice or thrice a week, I gave lessons to people on card reading techniques. That made me doubly famous. I was happy. Money trickled in at a speed and volume I could hardly believe. Soon, I had more money than I ever had in my life. It was a strange sensation. I felt on top of the world.

Sophia brought in clients, and I read them. Time flew faster than I could keep pace with. Clients went home happy, satisfied. Gradually I sank into a state of bliss I had never known existed in me. Money bought me the instant freedom to buy all that I needed, and much more. Success and recognition invited professional love and diverse friends. I realized that my world was slowly opening up. My clients were not exclusively restricted to America. People from Venezuela, Spain, Portugal, Chile, Japan, India and many more would visit me. They listened to my readings enthralled, as if I was God and not a human being, sitting in front of them, holding their hands. I was touched by their unabashed belief; their trust in everything I said. Often, I read affection in their eyes.

I was always intrigued by them, those men and women, who resembled me in one way or the other, yet so very unique. If I predicted their future, they taught me to live in the present. To look and feel accurately the 'here and now' of life. The greater my horizon stretched, the more I was pulled within myself. The more my wings spread, the more rooted I felt.

Around that time, I met Anand Chitnis, a lanky Indian guy with honey skin and brown eyes.

I read his cards and told him all I could see. He looked intrigued; but retained his calm. He asked me a few questions that I answered. Then came an explosion. I asked him a few questions and the answers that came from him, flabbergasted me. I was no longer certain whom I was talking to.

Time and again Anand referred to something called 'soul'. He said that 'soul' is present in every human being, like heart or brain, and that after one's death, the 'soul' moves to another dimension which we human beings cannot perceive. In other words, 'souls' don't perish, when the body perishes. Anand appeared to be a man of the world, while people called me, a psychic healer. And yet, he knew more than I did. He was saintlier than I was, on any given day.

"If ever you decide a trip to India, don't forget me," he said placing a card on the table.

"Where are you going?" I said looking up. His gaze lingered on mine.

"Will be off for a while…" he replied skeptically.

"Off to where?" I persisted.

"Will travel here, in America, then will return to Pune, but will be in touch," he assured. "Give me your address."

Something broke inside me, noiselessly. Surprisingly Anand seemed to notice.

"You look sad. What's wrong?"

"Nothing," I denied.

"Look, I have already made this plan, now I can't back out. But will meet, that's for sure. Trust me!" Anand added gently.

I nodded looking at my feet. Speechlessly sad.

After a while Anand went away, kissing me gently on my cheeks. His touch was comforting but could do little to abate the rising sadness inside me.

That night I felt a shift, somewhere, outside me and yet, not too far from the inside. I wasn't too certain but something was telling me that with Anand, perhaps my good time was leaving me too. And that I was on the brink of something.

Chapter 19

Henry Richardson zoomed into my life like a brake failed car. I was driving aimlessly one breezy afternoon, when Henry's shiny black Stutz Blackhawk drove in from the wrong side and hit Sophia's AMC Gremlin. Two cars smashed with theatrical extravagance; luckily not a life was touched or injured. Henry came out of his miserably damaged car in a navy-blue Armani as a hero from a 1960 film.

"Don't worry about it. I'll get you a new one," he said, referring to the car, Sophia's car that I was driving that day.

"Am not worrying anyway. That's not my car," I said banging the half-broken door.

"You don't look like a car thief," Henry said.

"Precisely that," I replied.

Henry laughed and so did I. That was the exact moment when Henry and I became friends.

I dived in his friendship with such ridiculous alacrity that I disregarded every other fact of him. Facts that were in front of me all along, and yet I decidedly chose to keep my eyes shut. For example, a week after our accident Henry bought Sophia a brand-new Pontiac Firebird and brought himself another Blackhawk. Where did the money come from? The accident was quite a big one and yet no police case existed. Was it a deliberate one? Henry trashed his old car like one would trash a paper cup and insisted that Sophia did the same. Why? Henry declined to answer. He pretended that the accident never happened in the first place, and stubbornly refused to answer any of my queries pertaining to it.

There was something suspicious about him that I could not deny. And I knew right from the start that he was a man capable of holding secrets. Yet, I came dangerously close to him, so much so that he pulled me inside his orbit and I started revolving with him with maniacal steadfastness, leaving aside my tarot readings, my classes, the patrons who regularly visited me, and last but not the least Sophia.

"Lemme warn you Sona, that man... Henry is a bastard. He deals with drugs. Stay away from him," Sophia warned me menacingly.

"He is a friend," I replied.

"Okay... but he has Mafia connections too. Be careful," she said.

"How do you know?" I protested.

"I know Sona, I have connections. Everybody says he is fucking dangerous!"

"He has never told me all these... Mafia connections and all," I said.

"What do you expect? He will take you on a date with his ring leader?" Sophia smirked.

"Not that... but he is a decent guy."

"Decent... my ass! Next time you meet him, ask him, where does his money come from?" Sophia said and walked out of the room.

"Will ask him," I said in a raised voice.

Of course, she did not wait for my answer. For, she was convinced that Henry was a drug peddler and held mafia connections. And I was convinced to prove her wrong.

And Henry did not meet me the entire next month. Where he was all that time, I had no clue.

At times I thought about Sophia's comment. Was he really a drug peddler? Did he hold connections? All those days when he supplied me with drugs that I sniffed and got so deliciously stoned, I never questioned him about the source. From where did he get such high-quality drugs? Next time would surely ask him, I promised myself. But would there be a next time? I doubted.

In moments such as those I looked at the card that Anand gave me. I was tempted to call him and speak, but then thought better of it. He could be busy elsewhere, I justified myself, pushing it inside my closet.

Two days later, exactly six weeks after he vanished, Henry rang my bell. He was wearing a red T shirt and beige pants. His pink face glowed in the light. Henry was in gay mood.

"Good morning sweetheart!" he greeted with an extra pleasing voice.

"Where the hell were you?" I retorted but was mildly pleased to see him.

"We could do the question answer session in my car. I have a surprise for you. Come on... get ready, we are going for a drive," he said quickly.

"But... where?" I fumbled. "Did you get another car?"

"You will know... come on, quick," he said.

And off I went with him; without looking back; disregarding Sophia and her well-meaning warnings; disregarding the little rationality that I still possessed, or at least claimed to possess. Disregarding my life!

If ever there was one mistake, I could point my finger at, that blasted my life apart, so much so that I practically never recovered from the shock, that was it. And it all started with my journey with Henry that fine August morning of 1973.

The sun was warm, smiling on us as we started in a Dodge.

"Since when have you started driving a Dodge?" I observed.

"At times I do," Henry replied casually.

"Where is your hawk?"

"At home."

"Don't tell me you trashed it," I said.

Henry laughed.

"You wanna grab some coffee?" he said. "It's going to be a long drive."

"Where are we going?"

"Mexico," he revealed, smiling, as though Mexico was a destination, I was keen to visit.

The very name of Mexico rang an ugly gong inside me. At once I remembered all the experiences that I associated with the place, starting right from my mother's marriage.

The place somehow had been unlucky for me. Sitting next to Henry I squirmed at the thought.

"Can't we go anywhere else?"

"Why, what's wrong with Mexico?" he asked. Henry sounded defensive.

I sniffed something odd.

"Why Mexico?" Something in his attitude was telling me that he was concealing something.

"Why not?"

"Is there anything you are hiding from me?" I probed.

Henry was silent for a while. He drove as if he had not heard me. I was panicking below my skin.

Henry spoke after a long time. He said that he intended to bring some Marijuana from Mexico. He had made all the arrangements beforehand. That was the reason behind his sudden absence all those days, he highlighted. We would be joined by two other men and that, we might have to halt at a motel for further instructions.

"What arrangements?" I asked.

"Money," he replied.

"Where is the money?"

"In the bonnet."

"How much Marijuana are we picking?"

"500 pounds," he said.

A crisp answer that nearly blew my head apart. A scream let loose from my throat involuntarily.

"500 pounds … are you kidding me?"

"No sweetheart… am not at all kidding you. But you

need not panic. You don't have to do a thing. Just be my side, like a friend. It's easy that way. Border police never suspect when there is a woman," he elaborated.

Henry told me that such large consignments never happened just by one group of people. There would be more men in the chain, waiting at vantage points so that pick up and drop could be made safely, deceiving the border and state police. And it was perfectly safe that way. He had been doing that business forever, and nothing had ever gone wrong.

I let out a sigh remembering all that Sophia had told me, warning me time and again. She had been right all along; and I was so fucking wrong! I did not know what to do. Should I go ahead with Henry, just the way he wanted me to, pretending to be his family? Or should I get down right at that moment and hitch hike my way back? I was at a fix.

"Don't look so worried, Sona, police would sniff right away," he observed.

"Why the fuck you did not tell me all these before I boarded the car?" I screamed.

"You would not have come?" he questioned.

"Of course not! I had no idea that you deal with all these," I blurted.

"Where did the money come from? For your Firebird? I always thought you knew," Henry replied casually.

I was silent. Again, I thought of Sophia and regretted not listening to her.

"Trust me Baby, nothing's gonna happen to you," he added in a composed voice.

I looked into his eyes. It was difficult to say whether he was being honest or was trying to placate me. Whatever it was, I had to take everything at his face value. I had limited options anyway.

Soon we were joined by two men in a different car. Henry passed them some code written on a currency note. They instructed us to follow their car. We did; blindly followed their car as if we were on a tow. And we were! The car moved into the desert that separated Mexico from America. Soon another car joined the troupe. Those two cars had the Marijuana, I suspected from the pungent order that emanated from them. We were made to halt in the desert at night. Next day, we reached a small border town. Henry gave me money to buy a car with a big bonnet.

I went ahead and bought one. I registered the car in my name; another mistake I realized soon. I brought back the new car into a predetermined place where I met Henry and the rest two cars loaded with Marijuana. Quickly, they started loading my car with all the packs. Their cars became empty and my car was filled with 500 lbs. of the drug. I began to panic, but Henry assured me that it always happened like that. They bought multiple cars in one delivery and burnt the old vehicles along with their registration plates. That way the police could not trace them. It was a common practice. And just as Henry said, they took the two cars into woods, showered them with 16 gallons of gasoline and put them on fire. I saw two cars char down to two mounds of ash.

Out of nowhere, magically as if, a huge jeep arrived; and the consignment was quickly shifted from my car to the new Jeep. It was decided that I would drive my car and the other guy would drive the Jeep. I sighed in unspeakable relief seeing the hushed shift. I admired the way they worked. It was as if everybody knew what to do. Nobody spokes to anybody. In fact, other than a few yes and no's, a few grunts and quick signals, they never said a word. I wondered if they knew each other from beforehand. Or if that was the way they operated?

Anyway, after the shift I took my car for a car wash and instructed them to clean it thoroughly, so that there was no smell of any kind. The entire consignment was in the Jeep now, and I felt comforted. If anything happened, I was in a safe vehicle, I reminded myself.

"Is that a good clean?" one of the guys joked.

His name was Eric; a tall, lean man with a frightening look and shaved head.

"Looks like," I replied smiling.

"Give me the keys. Lemme take a test drive," Eric said.

I handed him the key and off he went for a drive. He returned after some time, smiling from ear to ear.

"Yea, its good. Smelling soap," he opined.

Henry and I got into the car and drove out. It was decided that the Jeep with the consignment would come after a while. We drove in silence, until we reached the border.

The border police caught us and asked me to get down. They had guns with them. I obliged. Then they asked me all possible details. Our purpose of visit, my ID, what all the places we visited, the car registration papers, if I had any offensive or narcotic material with me. I denied. Somewhat convinced, they let me go. Soon I was on the road, but before long I observed a strange car following us.

"Henry, did you see that car?" I said observing the rear-view mirror yet another time.

"Which car?" he turned back.

"That one… it was not there earlier. Now it's following us since our last check. I feel everything is not okay," I said in a panicky tone.

"This is the only road from Mexico to Brouli… thousands of vehicles pass, every day," Henry argued.

I looked at him, taking in his composed face, reminding myself that I had not done any crime, and hence was safe. I looked at the mirror again, and to my horror discovered that our car was now being followed by seven other cars. Before I could blink next, they surrounded us from all sides.

"You are under arrest," I heard in a loud speaker.

Hell let loose on my head, before I could breathe. I was bathed in an incessant shower of misfortune, misery and wretchedness of such extreme kind, that the remains lingered within me forever.

Henry and I were taken to a nearby police station; and from there to a prison.

As it turned out, Eric had surreptitiously placed 50 lbs. of Marijuana in the bonnet without my knowledge. While the Jeep had the remaining 450 lbs. which they drove into the desert, intending to take a halt. The drivers thought it was a fantastic victory, having acquired the huge consignment and at the same time, evading the border police. To celebrate, they drank heavily and fell asleep. When my car was caught for the first time at the border, the security people sniffed something odd and quickly sent three choppers into the desert to trace another vehicle. Those two guys woke up by the noise of the border control choppers and were caught red handed.

Henry and I were in deep shit.

Chapter 20

Jail in Mexico was my first real time experience of purgatory. It housed small time criminals, smugglers, drug peddlers, people who attempted murders and people who were caught crossing borders, illegally. A room of 50 by 50 had about 30 convicts with hardly any place to sleep in, decently. Everybody was fighting with everybody else for toilet, or a place to crouch in. Each one of us was rationed only three liters of water. And that included drinking and cleaning.

Walking into the toilet would mean walking through a muck of ankle-deep urine and human excrement that had accumulated for days. The authority would only clean the toilets once a week, and only if the obnoxious stench bothered the staff, which interestingly enough, never seemed to be the case. They appeared to be ridiculously comfortable while my stomach made a little somersault every three seconds.

I was already in the prison for 10 days with no official charge pressed on me, all the while reminding myself that only 50 lbs. of Marijuana had been discovered in my car.

And that I would be released soon. All until an officer called me and broke my delusion with a blow harsher than a hammer weighing 5000 pounds.

"You have been charged for smuggling 500 lbs. of Marijuana," he added menacingly, scanning me from head to toe a few times. His eyes lingered for a long time somewhere in the middle.

"What?" I grasped, ignoring his vulgar gaze.

"The two guys in the Jeep have told us everything," he added.

The world around me started spinning dizzily. I felt as though I'd faint right in front of him and would never come back to life again. I wondered why the officer announced it with such élan. Soon my doubt was answered.

"You will be transferred to another cell," he ordered, and not too kindly.

And that was that. The next thing I knew was that I was transferred to a high-security prison that was meant for hard-core criminals, prostitutes, and dangerous murderers. The bail amount was 5000 dollars. And to my horror, Henry was out with a small bail amount, as he was a co-driver in the car.

"I will do everything to bring you out Sona," he assured before returning to California.

I did not know what to say. I looked at him, speechless, as tears of desperation dripped from my eyes.

"Don't worry, everything is gonna to be fine," he said patting my shoulder casually.

"When will you return?" I asked in a wobbly voice, despite my tears.

"Very soon," he added assuring.

And it would be three months, before I would see him again.

Those lonely and sad months, I had another friend to keep me company. A violent bout of stomach ulcer that made me scream at the top of my lungs, and still there was no respite. No one bothered to ask me how I was, no one bothered to look at me with kindness or even attend to my ailment. No one cared.

Although I was surrounded by scores of women, prisoners and jail staff, I suffered alone. On the third day when I collapsed, out of excruciating pain, they took me to a hospital, but with a heavy chain tied around my waist. I returned from the hospital four days later, feeling better but not totally healed.

Lying in my cell, I'd pray for my release, day and night, every waking moment. Even in sleep I'd call out for help, for some random power to interfere and get me out of that shit hole. I was helpless, sick and irreconcilably sad. I felt as though my life would be cloistered in that cell and I would never be free again. Time and again I thought of Sophia and wished that I had listened to her warnings. I thought of Anand too. Where was he? Would we ever meet? I had no answer. Having nothing else to do, I spend my days and nights thinking.

I thought of Stephen and my children and prayed for their happiness. The last time I was with him, he had offered me to stay back with him, like a good wife. But I had rejected, sighting that I was a free bird and a cage would not suit me. Marriage was no better than a cage, I had thought then. I would die in the absence of freedom. And yet I was in that cell for... I thought a bit... but couldn't calculate the time. How many days, weeks, months flew past I had absolutely no idea. The worst part of prison life, after the lack of freedom, was the loss of your grasp on time. I realized with painful certainty.

After what seemed to me an interminable stretch of time, one evening an officer came to my cell and opened the gate.

"Roll up," he barked.

It took me a while to understand what he said. And when I did, I was beside myself with joy. Henry returned with my bail money. That was the happiest moment of my life. On an impulse I hugged him right in front of the officers.

"Now Miss, there are rules," commanded an officer.

Quickly, we disentangled.

The officer said that I was not supposed to be seen within 25 miles from the Mexican border and if I was, immediately the border police would take me in their custody. I had to find a lawyer who would fight my case. And that I'd have to go for a monthly reporting to a police officer during the entire length of probation, failing which I'd be brought back to the prison immediately. The terms were complex, but I had no option but to follow them. I signed the papers and made my exit from the prison, promising myself that I'd rather die than return to the place and serve my term like those ugly and intimidating criminals I had spent my nights with.

The return journey was spent in silence. Of course, I was thankful to Henry for having kept his word and returning with the bail money, but the entire length of the journey I could not bear to look at his face.

"From where did you manage the funds?" I asked looking into the windshield.

"I sold off my mother's apartment" he said, but I knew he was lying.

"I trusted you so much, I cannot believe, I am a branded criminal now, all because of you," I blurted out.

"You will be fine. We will win the case. I have spoken to lawyers," he tried to assure.

"You better do," I retorted.

That was the last time we were together.

The few times we met afterwards, it was at his lawyer's office, discussing the case. There was no intimacy between us. Henry gathered the bail money and I arranged the lawyer's fees.

Not too long after the case officially began, one day, I read a surprising piece of news in the papers. The article said that a person by the name of Henry Richardson was caught by the Federal police with 75 million dollars' worth of cocaine in his vehicle. He got arrested while trying to sell the consignment to a man, who turned out to be an undercover cop. He was sentenced to ten years which constituted 3 years of imprisonment and the remaining 7 years of probation.

Of course, the news rattled me but I was not shocked. If anything, I was expecting something like that. Because, during my Mexican odyssey, I had sensed his deep connections with the drug mafia. He was far more dangerous than he looked, than Sophia could even contemplate.

"So now you know," Sophia said waving the newspaper.

I nodded, speechless, embarrassed, ashamed... all put together and a thousand times more.

"Listen Honey, am going to be in Colorado for a while," she said.

I looked up.

"You can stay here if you want," she said tentatively.

"Don't bother, I'll shift into a rented apartment," I said hurriedly.

Something in her attitude was telling me that she perhaps desired me to vacate her house. The effect was disheartening, but I understood her problem. Sophia was doing a legitimate business and had a decent reputation in the society. No one in the right frame of mind would want to have relationship with a woman who had a criminal case on her head and had been aired on television for the same disrepute.

Sophia agreed to my proposal without fuss.

"Whatever you think better," she said looking away.

Two days later I moved out of her house and took a rented accommodation. For a while, I enjoyed being alone, after the horrible and rowdy encounter with the prison mates. Solitude comforted me and healed my inner wounds. The ulcer in my stomach also got better.

Soon I began working in a bar to raise funds for my case. After Henry was arrested, I had to make my own arrangements.

Then one evening, few days later, I met the bar owner, Justin Kendell. Justin was a beefy man in his late forties, with piercing eyes, one golden tooth and knuckles that appeared to be made of iron. He had an outrageous sense of humor, enough to impress me in the very first meeting.

But the meetings swiftly turned out to be least interesting. Justin would get annoyingly intimate with me, in his cabin or at times in public. Under the pretext of dropping me home on numerous occasions, he would try to kiss me so hard that my lips would remain sore for days together. His over sexuality was repulsive.

Once, he pushed open my door and thrust his huge body on me. His giant paws ripped open my cotton dress in an instant. He scratched and bit my nipples like a hungry beast. When I resented and tried to shove him, he kicked me in my stomach with his boots, so hard that I fainted from the blow.

When I regained consciousness Justin was nowhere around. There was an ugly scar on my stomach and the pain was unbearable. My face was swollen beyond recognition. I had to swallow a cavalcade of pain killers for the next three days to abate the pain. It took me a week to regain normalcy.

When I resumed job, Justin behaved as though nothing had happened. His casual attitude disgusted me, but I could do little to protest. He was a powerful man and I was a pretty woman in need of money, at any rate, a dangerous combination.

A few days later, one night I returned from the bar to see Justin, waiting for me outside my home. I was beside myself with shock. Cleverly, he had parked his car a little away so that I could not notice him. The moment I got closer, he jumped on me and hit my head with the butt of his gun. I lost consciousness.

When I regained consciousness , I discovered myself lying on my couch, naked with legs parted; and there was a crushing pain in my head. Blood was gushing out of the wound like an open tap and Justin was there, nibbling at my nipples.

"What the fuck," I tried to scream but no voice escaped my throat. Only a deep animal like sound reached my ears, groaning, grunting. That was Justin's. His hard penis was already inside me.

I tried to shove him, but now with the head injury I lacked the strength. Justin was all over me, biting me here and there, thrusting himself with such aggression that I was defenseless. It must have been a few minutes, ten minutes at the most, but to me it appeared interminable.

When Justin was done, he shoved me from the couch and lied on his back. I rolled down on the floor with a thud but felt no pain. Already there was so much pain in my body that I did not notice that the abrupt banging on the hard floor had injured my back.

When I felt slightly steady, to get up on my feet and walk, I reached for my refrigerator and brought out some ice cubes, wrapped them in a kitchen towel and pressed it on my bleeding head. I could feel blood dripping from my head, and now after the rape, from my groin. I tasted blood in my mouth, on my lips.

Staggering, I reached the washroom and when I looked into the mirror, I screamed in horror. My nose was broken and bent towards the left; my entire face was red from all the blood that had dripped from the devastating head injury. There was a huge crack in my skull and I could see the inner materials. I felt dizzy.

Gradually I sat in the bathtub and put on the faucet. Cold water from the shower fell on my bleeding head, and then ran all over my naked body. The feeling was soothing, although not totally healing. For some time, I sat like that, relishing the water all over me. The cascade of water felt like the mother I never had; comforting, all-encompassing, loving. Silent tears dripped from my eyes.

And for the first time in my life, I wanted to die, knowing that it could not be more harrowing than the life I was forced to live with. Instead of thrusting his penis in between my thighs, had Justin thrust a bullet into my head, things would have been better; I contemplated, sitting nude inside the tub.

Gradually I felt shivers overwhelm me and I lay down in a foetal position. With all the blood loss and the shock, I slowly drifted into unconsciousness.

Chapter 21

Iwoke up to a loud mechanical sound and discovered myself lying inside an MRI machine. My head was stitched and nose plastered. The cold appeared brutal, and I shivered like an epileptic, despite being wrapped in a blanket.

A doctor was attending to me. He smiled.

"You are going to be fine," he assured.

"Who brought me here?" I said through my clattering teeth.

"There, that gentleman," he pointed at a corner.

I followed his finger with my eyes. My head felt too heavy to move. Justin was there, white in his face, standing against the window, looking outside. He turned and walked towards me. Justin looked shaken. There were blotches of dried blood on his white shirt. Were they mine? Did he pick me up from the washroom and in the process stained his shirt? Or did he purposely sprinkle blood from my wounds? I wondered. My groin pained as though somebody had hit it with a hammer. Was I still bleeding?

"How are you feeling, darling?" he asked gently placing his hand on my injured skull.

I squirmed, more out of disgust than pain. Justin waited for the doctor to vacate the room.

"Listen Honey, am sorry," he started without a preamble.

"You think it's going to amend everything?" I said stiffly, looking into his cunning eyes. Had he been drinking all night?

"Please…," he begged.

"You break open my skull, you beat me into a pulp, you fuck me like an animal, and now you are saying sorry? What do you want me to do? Clap with joy? That you are sorry?"

"Please don't file a complaint, that's all I want to say. Please," he begged again, this time more sincerely. "For that I would give you anything."

"What did you tell them?" I asked, feeling sick in my stomach. The pain in my groin returned with vengeance. I felt a warm mass sliding down.

Justin informed the hospital that he came to my place last evening and discovered me lying inside my bath tub; naked and bleeding with a fractured skull, unconsciousness. He requested me to tell everyone that the assault had been done by somebody I didn't know.

I thought for a while. I could very well lodge a complaint against him and get him behind the bars. But he was a powerful guy and would come out unscratched in no time. And once out, he would chase, perhaps, kill me. Worse still, he could frame a case against me and put me in jail. But if I took money from him, pay for my case, then go away from Palm Springs forever, that would make sense. First, all my worries about raising money for my case would be solved, and secondly, I could be freed from him forever.

"Okay," I said after a long time.

"Okay?" he hiccupped.

"Yes okay, but I have two conditions."

"Anything…" he blurted out, energetically.

"First, you will pay me money for my case."

"Done!"

"Second, you would never bother me again, where ever I am and wherever you are. Even if we cross paths, you do not know me," I said.

Justin kept looking at my face for a while. I wondered what he was seeing in me, now that I had bandage almost all over my face and neck. But then a quick thought crossed my mind. Perhaps the cover of bandage was my alibi. It made my face unreadable, inscrutable.

"Okay. I promise," Justin said at last.

Justin left after a while. It was then the thought sunk; everything I said to him. The deal! I recollected the injuries Justin had given me the day before; the brutal rape, the violent attack with his gun. It could have taken my life. Justin was a criminal and deserved to be punished. But if I let him go free, against a bundle of cash, it could free me from another bundle of shit that I had led myself into. Did the act make me more forgiving or more self-serving? Perhaps both.

Justin released me from the hospital, dropped me home, gave me a briefcase full of cash and then silently vanished, closing the door from behind.

That was the last time I saw him.

Then one day, not too long after my release from the hospital, out of nowhere, a flyer reached my hand. It was from the Divine Light Mission Ashram, San Francisco. I had absolutely no clue what it was all about, and yet I felt a deep restlessness within me to go. The flyer spoke about meditation. I remembered Anand speaking about meditation. The delicious effect it had on the mind.

"If ever you want peace, the kind of peace that would last and last, you should start meditation," Anand had preached.

"Meditation? What's that?" I had asked, curious.

"Observing one's breath!"

I sold off whatever I had, and a week later, left Palm Springs.

Divine Light Mission Ashram, San Francisco was more enticing than I had anticipated. There were communal houses too, where one could stay and volunteer for the ashram. I signed as a volunteer. They gave me a small room to lodge in.

I started practicing meditation. The kind of life that I had lived so far, it was difficult to claim peace right away, but yes, after a couple of weeks of ardent practice, I began sinking into a state of unruffled calm. Old wounds began to heal, and in its wake was a new kind of happiness that overwhelmed me.

The time I did not meditate, I worked for the Ashram. Industry bred contentment. Gradually I became friends with other women staying in the Ashram. They had no idea about my past, and that helped me blend with them.

"Tarot? What's that?" Tulsi, an Indian woman asked, when I declared that I read Tarot.

"It's like cards. That predicts your future," I briefed.

"Really? You can do that? Can you read for me?" she asked, immediately, impulsively.

I nodded, wondering if I had done a right thing by disclosing Tulsi about my card reading.

"Okay, will do it for you, but you should not tell anyone," I bargained.

Tulsi agreed. Two days later I read cards for her in my room.

I told Tulsi that she had got married at the age of eighteen and then within a couple of months, her husband had died. She was single now, a full-time devotee, but also very lonely. She craved companionship, perhaps sex. Tulsi's eyes went progressively larger as I went on adding details.

"Oh my God!" she exclaimed. "How did you know all these? These are old stories, nobody knows."

I smiled. "That's my job. That's what I do."

"You are good," she said. "What next?"

I looked at her brown face, large eyes with upturned lashes. There was a large mole on her right cheek.

"You are going to meet the love of your life soon," I added smiling.

"Here? In this ashram?" she exclaimed, blushing.

I nodded.

"But I have vowed celibacy," she said looking instantly worried.

"When love touches you, you will forget every other vow," I preached.

"Love?" she said, as though she no longer believed in it.

"Yes, my cute darling!" I said endearingly. "Love is the biggest magic of all!"

"But how will I know its love?" she asked

"You will just know," I added confidently, as though I was well schooled in the business of love.

Tulsi was too happy to speak.

Sitting in front of her, I kept on contemplating in silence my observations on love. When was the last time I had felt loved? Or for that matter, did I? Had I ever been loved?

For me life had been one string of futile and hopelessly non-fecund relationships. Men entered and exited my life like the way people entered and exited a monument, taking refuge in its beauty or grandeur or whatever, only for a while. Nobody intended to linger - to last. Nobody intended to love. Sex! Yes, that I had plenty ever since I became a woman, even before that, if memory did not betray me. I had so much of sex by then, touched and abused by so many men, that if I vowed celibacy right at that moment, I would not miss sex for the rest of my life.

But things were different for Tulsi. Although a devotee, but something about her told me that she desired a male company. She did not reveal her sexual urge or intentions to me. That was beyond her. But she was a grown-up woman, ripe in age, appealing, and what I gathered from the bits and pieces of information she told me after the reading session, she was a virgin. For her, sex was an unquenched thirst, a curiosity, a fantasy.

From that evening, for as long as I was there in the

ashram, I discovered Tulsi, forever lost in another world with dreamy eyes and a gentle smile on her lips. I knew where she was, and what she was contemplating. I began to wish for her happiness, pray sincerely that she should meet the love of her life. And magically as if, my prayers were answered. Not for Tulsi, but for me.

One day Anand appeared in the ashram looking for me.

"I have come to meet you," he said beaming.

Tears of happiness ran down my cheeks seeing him standing in front of me with that familiar graceful smile. His eyes sparkled with tears.

"How did you find me?" I asked after a while, when the joy and surprise of meeting him subsided.

It so happened that after hearing my predictions Tulsi became so happy that she told many people about my card reading. Gradually people started approaching me for a reading, which I did, at times voluntarily, at times taking a small amount of money. Very quickly news spread outside the Ashram that a lady had psychic powers and could predict people's future.

"There is this friend of mine, who told me, there is a woman in this ashram who has powers. She can read people like book. And I knew right away that it's you. I had to come," Anand elaborated.

I was only too speechlessly joyous to respond. I kept looking into his eyes, remembering the time we last met. All the days and months that I had spent without him appeared to melt away.

Gradually I told Anand everything, my encounter with Henry, the Marijuana case and the Justin episode, my broken skull and the terrible rape that I had to endure in cloistered silence against a bundle of cash that in the end had helped me survive. Finally, my escape from everything and reaching San Francisco.

Anand listened, patiently as ever, holding my hands, looking deeply into my leaking eyes. His eyes flowed all the same. He did not say a word to interrupt, to admonish me for my stupidity or even to advice. I read love in his kind eyes.

"Things happen in our lives for a reason Sona. Our job is to seek the reason, transform ourselves and rise above it," Anand observed after I stopped recounting him those harrowing details.

I kept on looking into my lap, wondering what to say.

Perhaps he was right that things happen in our lives for a reason. But everything that had happened to me so far, was it needed at all, I pondered.

Although I was a psychic healer who could read people like a book; or living in an ashram for a while now, meditating, trying to find calm, I felt incapable of peering into my own future, what life had in store for me? Like a leaf I kept on fluttering in the breeze, dancing at its subtle tune, reaching places that were beyond me; temporarily settling myself into the soil, and then again, with the next storm, flew and reached another destination.

It was my 34th year in the world and I had no house that I could call my home, no family, no relation, no money, no security. Practically I had nothing other than my physical body that people still said, was beautiful. It was Anand, and only Anand, who pointed that I had a beautiful soul too. I was still unsure what he meant, nevertheless I felt happy, admired; and more than anything, felt grateful.

"Am returning to Pune," Anand declared during his next visit.

"Pune? What's there?" I asked.

Immediately I thought of my previous visit to India, the places I had seen, the serenity I had felt.

"My home and Osho Ashram," he added. "You wanna come?"

I did not know what possessed me, but I nodded my head, without having any clue either about Osho or Pune.

Perhaps that's how destiny plays. It catches us at the most unexpected of places and forces us to make choices that forever alter the course of our lives.

Anand was only too happy to hear my consent and started preparing. Tulsi was sad, hearing my plans of not only leaving the ashram but the country for a while. But when she heard the destination, she couldn't control her emotions. On an impulse, Tulsi hugged me.

"Sona, you will love Pune,' she said with dripping eyes.

Little could I gauge at that point of time that Pune would be my home for a very long time.

"You know Pune?" I asked her, impulsively.

Tulsi nodded.

"Went there once, as a child. But I remember. It's green everywhere. Beautiful place! Full of Banyan trees," she elaborated, with visible nostalgia.

Couple of weeks later, I left San Francisco... America.

A new life was beckoning me. Once again, I floated high and low at destiny's call, like an autumnal leaf dancing in the breeze. This time, across the Atlantic, traversing several continents, I landed in India, yet again.

Chapter 22

The day was 10th March, 1975 when we landed in Bombay, took a taxi to Dadar station, and then another one that drove us to the beautiful city of Pune.

Koregaon Park, Pune was greener than I had imagined, or even anticipated. The effect was so magical that I burst into tears the moment I stepped in. I felt at home!

And yet getting a house was not easy for a foreigner. Outsiders were looked upon with suspicion. Finding a decent accommodation was no easy feat. Anand came to my rescue to find one.

The next step was to enter the Osho Ashram, which turned out to be surprisingly easy. Anand took me to Lakshmi, Osho's secretary and undoubtedly one of the most powerful persons there, with anytime access to Osho. Lakshmi fixed up a meeting.

I was taken into a room where Osho was already there, sitting. I sat in front of him. For the next few seconds… minutes… I was not sure; my eyes were fixed on him in speechless wonderment. And then, I heard him, for the first time.

"What took you so long? I called you twice."

But there was no sound, no noise of whatever kind. I noticed that his lips weren't moving either. Was he talking telepathically? I wondered.

A scene from the past rose to my memory; not one but two. First one, during my previous visit to India, I had met three completely separate people who at that point of time held associations with Osho, and had spoken to me about him, insisted that I should meet him. Obviously, I had disregarded them, not knowing who Osho was.

Another time, in California, there was a spiritual congregation called the "Consciousness Movement", where I landed up accidentally. There were hundreds of people inside, many more waiting to get inside. My chance of entering the auditorium was dim. Although I could buy an entry ticket, but the security would not allow me inside.

But then, a miracle happened. I saw a woman come out and hand me her ticket. She said she had a family emergency and had to rush. I could use her place. I was only too happy to accept the offer.

There, in that auditorium, I saw Osho's picture for the first time. In the photograph, he was leaning against a wall. There was something about his eyes that struck a chord inside me. I did not know his name at that point of time, I did not know who he was, and yet I had felt his eyes piercing into mine with a kind of deep meaningful intent.

"Who is he?" I asked Sushila, referring to the photograph. Sushila was heading the organizing team.

"Bhagwan Sri Rajneesh," she replied in a gentle voice.

"I feel like he is looking at me," I blurted out nervously.

"Possibly he is," Sushila had said and moved away.

I stood there for a while, transfixed, not knowing what to make of it.

A stir brought me to the present, and I realized that I was remembering all those long-forgotten events, looking into Osho's eyes. And I knew immediately why I was where I was. Why had I suffered so long and in silence? Why my life took one ugly turn after another? Why I never admired the concept of having a family and raising children? In that brief encounter, in that strange, unspeakable moment, I got back answers to all the why's of my life. I must have felt like a sweater, whose thread had been tugged and was unraveling rapidly. I felt loose, opened up.

Tears streamed down my face in a relentless downpour. Of joy, of sadness, of ecstasy...I did not know. I could barely control myself. For some time, I was beyond myself. My past, my present, my future, my emotions, my agonies, my ecstasies, whatever little, every drop that I could call me, was not mine any more. I was totally, absolutely and blissfully dissolved in one giant meditative moment, where time and space receded into a black hole, where time and space did not matter, where nothing mattered.

And the conversations continued, between Osho and me. Although there were other people, sitting around in meditation, but nobody seemed to be bothered by us, nobody seemed to hear us speak.

"I have left my children behind," I blurted out in a moment that was powerful but vulnerable.

"You have shed a lot many children, if you count your previous lifetimes. This is no different," he replied in meditative silence, looking at me with deep eyes.

I told him everything that I had been through, all the harrowing stories ever since I was a child. It was like reviewing my entire life with him.

"You have been working with the wrong hemisphere

of your brain," Osho said. "When you were 7, they switched you from left hand to right."

I was shocked. How he could know that I wondered in silence. For, it was true, I was born lefty but my father forced me to use my right hand. The effect was more than physical. It was traumatic, because my entire orientation got changed, wired in a different way. Often Father would put my left hand in a sling and force me to use my right hand. Mama saw everything, but never protested. Silently, she observed my difficulties, silently she saw me suffer, like a spectator watching a film.

But the striking thing was that I forgot all those events of my past. With Osho mentioning it, all the memories came to me at once, rushed into my mind like a gush of water.

"Now do that same thing again. Put your right hand on a sling, and do everything with your left hand," he advised. "You will set everything right."

I considered his advice. Perhaps it was time to start all over again, right from the beginning. To correct the first mistake of my life, I pondered.

"Have you made up your mind?" he was saying. "For *sanyas*?"

I had no answer. And yet I found a great relief from inside hearing it coming from him. The effect was exhilarating. It was as if he was seeking my permission to initiate me in the spiritual path.

"Yes," I replied impulsively, although I had not come prepared for it, or thought about it until then.

"You have a heart of gold. You are precious," Osho said.

Then he took a piece of paper from Lakshmi, and

scribbled a line and handed it to me. The paper read: *Maa Param Sona*, Supreme Mother Sona.

Slowly but steadily, sex receded from my shores. In its wake was a new kind of ecstasy, a sublime joy that no words could describe. Presence of Osho himself, trances that I experienced while meditating with him, the peace, those long and silent conversations, the sense of belonging … life flowed at the tune of some divine symphony.

Repeatedly I thought about the hemisphere change that Osho had spoken to me on the first day. At seven, I had been oriented from left to right, unconsciously, without taking into consideration the disastrous consequences it would inflict on my subsequent life. Here in Pune, after all these years, again I went through a transformation, from right to left, in full consciousness. For me, it was like travelling time, going back to my childhood and starting the journey all over again. A new kind of birth; a fresh beginning.

Regular visits to the retreat and spending a lot of time there came with its own set of benefits. Gradually I got to know many people; famous in their own right, and yet ardent devotees.

One of them was a German lady by the name of Francoise Ruddy. Francoise along with her second husband, Albert Rudy had produced the film, The Godfather. She was a dedicated disciple and a passionate human being. Soon we became close and spent a lot of time together. She grew curious about me when she discovered that I too had come from America. Another one was an Austrian artist, and a great astrologer, Sebastian Wagner, who could read face and could get into another person within seconds. An Italian musician, Luca Romano, another devotee of Osho, whose music and flute I had heard back in America was there too. He was nominated for Grammy awards once, I remembered.

And yet, despite their worldly success and money, fame and fortune, they behaved humbly. Inside the ashram premises, everybody was equal. No one was a star or a pauper. Nobody was above anybody. We all were seekers sharing a common space. We were one! An undivided whole; a unit.

Maybe it was the common search that brought us together. Maybe not. Perhaps the place was like that, easy to accept and embrace people, easy to love. It could also be we were all attuning ourselves to the mode of compassion. For, quite naturally and very soon we all became friends, and ended up conversing for hours together, like one happy family. We loved each other, showed sensitivity to the other's feelings. They welcomed me with outstretched arms. I couldn't ask for more. Perhaps Sebastian could read me, more deeply than the rest, and yet he never revealed his knowledge to anybody, not even to me. And neither did I reveal anything.

Slowly my past and all the traumas that came with it ebbed away. I began to forgive everybody who had injured me. With that forgiveness came a new kind of love that I felt for my mother, my father, my step father, all my siblings, my husbands, my children, all the men I had had a relationship with, all the people I had hated so far... everybody. The transformation was slow, but certain. And steady in its unraveling.

I rented an apartment. Anand helped me abundantly in getting it. I bought some wooden and bamboo furniture to decorate my house. And then bought a few Indian saris to use them as curtains and upholstery. The apartment was very near to the ashram and hence commute was no problem. Mornings and evenings, I went there for meditation.

"Let Sona live here, in the ashram," Osho said to Lakshmi, one evening after *Darshan*.

Lakshmi was about to open her mouth, when I intervened.

"Oh please, don't put me here," I blurted out, perhaps a bit thoughtlessly.

I could come and meditate, I could volunteer my service too, but I was reluctant to live inside the ashram premises. Of course, I was still unaware of the inner functioning of the ashram, but by then, I had seen enough of myself to realize that ashram setting would not suit me for long. I was happy to live in the apartment which Anand and I had set up with so much of joy.

For some reason Osho agreed, for he did not pester the matter further, much to my satisfaction.

A day later he ordered Lakshmi to get me some work in the ashram.

"Put Sona to work in your office," he said.

This, I accepted readily, and with immense gratitude. For, money was running short, and I had to meet my expenses. I had no other way of income.

Lakshmi promptly assigned me a desk to work at. I was required to be there at night, when people came out of the evening *Darshan*, I had to give them forms to fill in, gather information about them, co-ordinate with them, and plan *Darshan* for the following day. And my day job was to interview people who wanted to have a meeting with Osho and decide if their case was relevant or important enough. I had to interact with people from around the globe.

Given my lack of experience of working in an organized setting, I found the task onerous. It drained me off. I soon discovered that I couldn't handle people, and many of them did not even care to listen to me. They were all over the places, and I was running away from them under one pretext or the other.

It did not take Lakshmi much time to understand my incapability in handling an office, my sheer callousness in handling a crowd. Promptly she fired me. I could not say that I was shocked at her decision, realizing my shortcomings.

So once again card reading came to my rescue. I'd read cards for people and earn a living. It helped me earn fame too, for very quickly people came to my doors.

'Read cards for people or teach them how to read one. Or for friendship, if nothing else.'

Chapter 23

A lbeit alone, but I was living a normal life; had a house, was earning an honest living, making friends with people who owned and raised normal families. That was the longest time in my life when I neither smoked, nor touched alcohol. And drug was out of my galaxy.

As a part of my volunteering activities, I was scheduled for a few days to an ashram in Lonavla, about 50 Kms away from Pune. Lonavla was a small hill station with an unbelievable number of waterfalls and virgin hills. The weather was magical during monsoons, with all the waterfalls coming alive and the mountains turning greener than green.

The head of the ashram, Rishi Khedkar, a pious looking man with a deformed eye ran a home for the blind. In the process, I got to mix with a bundle of children who were more deprived than I ever was. All those years I considered myself ill-fated for having such a devastating childhood but being doomed with a crushing disability right from one's birth, was unthinkable. I could not imagine a life like that. I could not pretend to know what those little children felt like, every single day, every single moment of their waking hours.

Helping them with some of the basic activities reminded me of the time when I had handled my children. It brought to my mind sweet memories of a time when life was crazy and I was off the track, and yet, being together, laughing and crying together meant meaningful, even if our stomachs were half empty most of the time.

Did my children, remember me, I wondered, as I was remembering them now with melancholic affections. I had not been in touch with them for years now. Had never set my eyes on them. I had never tried to contact them in any way. All this for so long. Did that make me a careless mother? Or a mother who loved her freedom more than her children?

The month was August, and rain came pouring down in threatening gusts. For days there was not a speck of sun in the sky. Rain, rain and rain was all that we had. It rained so much and so heavily that the roof of the orphanage began to leak. Water dripped inside, on the beds. What struck me as amazing was how those blind children helped each other. With the deformity, it was not easy for them to locate a dry spot, yet everybody tried to be helpful to everybody else. Each one was taking the other by his or her arm and shifting to a dry spot while his own bed was getting increasingly soddened.

The sight touched me, so much so that tears flowed down from my eyes. I couldn't help but fall in love with them.

Osho had warned me against having a relationship.

"No more relationship," he had said on my second visit.

And yet, standing there, seeing those children a relationship was already made, despite me; a new kind of relationship the taste of which lasted on my mind, long after we parted ways.

The next day I received a letter from Osho. It said, *drop everything, come at once.*

I packed my bags, put all that I had in a large plastic bag, got a taxi and reached Pune.

"You look beautiful, so much graceful," Lakshmi observed upon arrival.

I was overjoyed to see Osho again. We spoke for some time, when he asked about *Mouna*, (remaining in complete silence) that he had earlier asked me to practice for 28 days in Lonvala. I had no answer. The kind of person that I was, it was impossible for me keep quiet for an hour, let alone for 28 days at a stretch.

"I knew you would not," he said after a while, realizing my discomfiture. "Someday there would be golden silence for you," he then said, predicted.

******

The year was 1975. The then Prime Minister of India, Mrs. Indira Gandhi had declared emergency across the country. Police, Foreign offices, Bureaucrats started behaving rudely with the people who didn't have a valid visa.

After months I fished out my passport and was appalled to discover that my visa had expired long ago. I was too busy doing all my voluntary activities, reading cards and socializing that I forgot entirely about my visa status until a Brazilian friend of mine informed me that she was constantly been harassed by the police for her expired visa.

"I think they will put me in a lock up... how could I be so stupid?" she said in a sad voice.

"Don't worry nothing is going to happen to you. Will work out a way," I consoled, in a voice that wasn't my confident best.

Without saying another word, I vanished from her sight. Rushed home at once and discovered to my horror that I was outliving my visa by a number of months. I began to panic.

In India, living with an expired visa that too without informing the officials was a punishable offence. They could imprison me any moment as an alien. It was a tough time. The entire country was under emergency, freedom of press was curbed, and foreigners were looked down upon with suspicion. All kinds of horror stories reached my ears daily; people being picked up randomly by the government officials.

I was loitering in the ashram garden, when the thought struck me. That it wouldn't be long before I'd have to leave behind everything and perhaps go and live in another country.

Attachment, whether to a person, a thing, or even a way of life is dangerous, I realized. The simple thought of leaving the place and not being able to see it again made me sad; a kind of sadness that no amount of meditation could abate. I felt like deserting home, deserting the love of my life.

That was the moment when my eyes fell on a gorgeous

lady coming out of Osho's room. She was tall, wheatish with a well-toned body. She wore a pink gown. The lady appeared to dazzle in the light. For a second our eyes met, and then she smiled.

Perhaps somebody had told her about me, for she moved forward, where I was sitting in the garden and said, "Would you read cards for me? Please?"

I nodded.

We spent some time together, in my apartment. Then, I read cards for her. She was breathtakingly gorgeous with a perfect body. I felt ugly sitting next to her, in my loose *kurta* and fading pajama. She was a successful woman, with more money and fame, as I later came to know. But her eyes were hollow, lacking happiness.

After some time when she was about to leave my house, I realized I had not asked her name.

"Am sorry, I didn't get your name," I said uncertainly, looking as embarrassed as I was feeling.

She turned, and then very slowly smiled.

"People call me Sakina, Sakina Hasan," she said and vanished from my sight.

Later I came to know that Sakina was a popular cinema heroine, giving the industry many hits.

"Where are you planning to go?" Anand asked me gravely; when I informed him about my expired visa. I sensed concern in his voice.

"Nepal," I replied at once. "But I need to have an exit visa. Will do it from Delhi, instead of Pune," I continued.

Anand nodded.

The next day when I was sitting in front of Osho, and

contemplating about my card reading, whether I should continue it in Nepal, or should I peruse something else. Osho said, "You will be a successful card reader in the years to come!" I was only too overjoyed to ask anything further. I bowed to him and came out. That was the last time we met.

Soon I wound up my home in Pune and made way to Delhi to get my exit visa. Like a good friend, Anand accompanied me.

Chapter 24

Like every other reality of my life, the exit visa too did not happen easily. It came with a greater number of challenges that I could anticipate or even overcome at that point of time.

To begin with, handling all the bureau staff at Delhi, at a time when the country itself was going through the crushing trouble of a political emergency was stiff. It proved to be one of the biggest obstacles I bumped into. They were annoyingly particular, as far as paper works were concerned, and I was slowly beginning to lose my ground. And my temper.

"Is there a way I could get my exit visa?" I asked an officer with a no-nonsense face and bushy brows.

He looked up, menacingly. His thick moustache scared me enough to consider the proposition of running away from him that instant

"And you are?" he asked.

"A woman," I blurted. Immediately I regretted my lame answer. Obviously, he knew that he had his own eyes to see. He was asking about my nationality.

"I can see that," he replied annoyed. His voice was edgy.

"Am an American," I replied, in my gentlest voice.

He was not happy. And even if he was, he didn't look. He retained his serious face and irritable tone.

"You have any Indian connection?"

"Connection as in?"

"Husband?"

I thought for a second, and then nodded. Speaking blatant lies made me uncomfortable.

"Where is he?" he asked.

"He is in the hotel," I lied yet again.

Anand had come to Delhi with me stating that I, being an American woman, would find it difficult to get a visa. He could come to my rescue, he insisted, before we started our journey.

"And your marriage license?" the officer asked.

"I can bring it later," I said skeptically, not knowing from where the hell I'd get one.

"Bring with you next time, and will give you an exit visa," he pronounced.

"In case I cannot bring one," I added tentatively.

He looked at me in a way as if with his sight alone, he'd burn me down into a bowl of ash.

"In that case, we will give you 10 days to sort things out, before taking you to the prison. In those 10 days, you must come here every day and report."

I deduced that I was between fire and frying pan. I vanished from his office and returned to the hotel. Anand looked worried after hearing the details. Then, suddenly leaving me alone in the room, he went out for a long walk. I wondered where he could go, and more than that what I would do, if I could not provide the authority, a marriage license.

When Anand returned, he was visibly happy, and at peace.

"What?" I asked, mildly annoyed at his gay disposition.

"Have found a solution," he said, taking a seat.

Anand said that he had spoken to someone, who would provide us with a fake marriage license that would show us, Anand and myself, as married. That would get me an exit visa without any trouble, he informed.

Tears dripped from my eyes, hearing all that he said, realizing every little thing he was doing for me, most of the time going beyond his principles and ethics. For all I knew Anand was an honest man. Corruption was neither in his blood, nor his forte. And yet, in the process of rescuing me from trouble, he was sinking into the dirty quagmire of deception and forgery.

"Are you sure you want to do this?" I asked, feeling tightness in my chest, and pangs of guilt in my stomach.

"Is there another way?" he asked plainly.

There was none.

Sitting in that shabby hotel in Delhi, I embraced him with all the love I could muster from inside. He reciprocated, without being pushy. We sat like that for a long time, letting our feelings sink.

As for me, I would have straightaway signed an

original marriage license with him, right there, right at that moment, had my relationship with men and marriage not been so disagreeably rocky. In my life, men were good as long as they were sexual partners or friends. Husband was a proposition that almost invariably brought me troubles. Anand was a friend, and I was happy that way. I did not venture for more, knowing the disastrous outcome I would perhaps suffer, if I muddled our beautiful relationship with matrimony.

Perhaps Anand understood me more than he was willing to accept, for he too never tried to push our relationship further. He was happy to be by my side, to be a friend when I needed one.

Anand procured a fake marriage certificate within two days.

"Here," he said, beaming, handing me a petty paper that I would carry with me for decades hence.

"Thank you," I said.

Those two words were too insignificant against all that he had done for me.

Anyway, I supplied the bureau with the certificate, and secured my exit visa without further trouble. A day later, I travelled to Nepal, via Bihar. The journey was exhausting; nevertheless, it brought me relief, realizing that for the time being I was out of danger.

Anand came with me up to Bihar but refused to cross the border.

"I thought we were going together," I said, already heartbroken to realize that he had already made up his mind.

"I should be returning to Pune," he said.

"But why?"

"This is your journey Sona, you should take it alone," he said in a grave voice. "My path is elsewhere. But if you return to Pune, anytime, you know where to look for me."

I nodded, ignorant of the tears already gathering in my eyes.

"Don't be sad. Every man has his own journey to make. We can help each other for a while, be companions for the time being, but none of us can be with anybody forever. That's the truth. And that's life! Learn to accept it gracefully and proceed, wherever you are destined to," Anand preached.

There was little to say against what Anand said. I hugged him one last time before turning my face to the mountains and proceeding towards Nepal.

For the first few days I was put up in The Snugl Hotel, Kathmandu. The very air of Nepal felt gratifying on my parched skin.

A week later I shifted to a small, inexpensive lodge, about 5 kilometers away from Swayambhunath temple. The temple was famous for its hoard of monkeys, which the local people considered sacred. For some reason, I couldn't consider those naughty mammals, incarnation of the divine and hence could not treat them with respect.

"It's okay, if you don't like them, God will not punish you. Only if you take this little one," said a Nepali boy, stretching before me his thin hand, on which there was a little puppy. The puppy was just born.

I was touched; seeing that helpless little one snuggling on his inexpert hands.

"That's cute," I observed.

"You want? You can take it," he offered.

"And what you want me to give you in return?" I asked.

"Anything," the boy shrugged his fragile shoulders.

"Will you bring me people, if I read for them?" I placed my request.

"You read what?" he asked.

"Cards," I replied.

"Read what?"

Two days later, he brought me my first client for card reading. Words spread, and gradually I was getting a persistent trickle of people, both locals and tourists, who arrived at my door either for card or face or palm reading. Money started to flow in steadily.

One of my clients, an ardent Buddhist and a follower of Karmapa Lama, informed me that the Lama was there in the temple.

"You want to meet?" he offered.

Meeting with a Lama, I thought. The idea struck a chord within me, and not long after I climbed up the little hill where the temple was. The entire stretch I could hear Tibetan chants rippling down towards us in soft spells.

At long last when I finally reached the temple, Karmapa Lama was already there, sitting on a throne like structure, and all the Tibetan men who were musicians, playing long horns and drums at the tune of Buddhist chants. It appeared to me as though I had landed into a magical world where music, chants, incense and peace were flowing in one synchronized whole.

Karmapa Lama's face reflected a state of calm that

was unruffled and unearthly. Divine! He looked at my face and smiled in the gentlest way. He blessed me. And I felt just the same. Blessed.

When I returned, and narrated my experience to the lodge manager, he pointed that I was very lucky to have been blessed by the Lama. "Few people get that," he observed.

Lucky? Well, I was not certain, but I was at the right place at the right time. Moving in the right direction, as Anand might have said.

That night Karmapa Lama's face kept returning to me. Also, what Anand had said while crossing the border; *every man has his own journey to make; none of us can be with anybody forever, that's the truth*. If Anand was right, why so many people marry, have children, have a family? Why do people cling to one another? Why do lovers meet and fall in love? Why do we promise each other that we will be there, forever? I had no answer.

For a long time, I kept looking into the distant snowcapped mountains that shone like diamonds in the dark. The Tibetan chants kept whirring in my mind, thrusting on me a reflective serenity. That was when I heard the melancholic music of flute reaching my ears from somewhere not too far.

I came out of my room and discovered a gentleman with brown eyes and curly brunette hair, playing the flute in the balcony. He had a few audiences too, listening to him, enthralled. I joined the listeners.

The music was divine. And the flutist, beautiful. For, when he played, I found it impossible to look anywhere other than his face. After the recital, I receded into my room.

Next day I met him again, sitting alone in the balcony, mindfully observing a yellow bird on the railing.

"You play lovely," I said, smiling.

"Thanks," he replied, looking at me. His eyes were dreamy, I noticed. "Am Arthur Moreau," he introduced himself.

"Am Sona," I said. "From India."

"You don't look Indian," he observed.

"No, am American. But I have come here from India," I elaborated.

"You have lovely eyes," he said, now smiling.

Was he flirting with me? I wondered, standing there, nearly blushing.

"Don't expect a thank you in return," I blurted out.

"I wouldn't mind a walk, down that road," Arthur said pointing the hill road that reached a pinnacle I was yet to see.

And a new journey began; Arthur and me. Every day, for about an hour we walked, once in the morning; a second time in the evening, after our tea, when the sun would set.

We walked that same mountain up and down, again and again, until we knew each other well, until our legs pained so much that we could barely walk, until there was nothing more to tell, to share. At times I thought of Osho's warnings. *No more relationship,* he had admonished. I did not even hold Arthur's hand, and yet there were moments when I felt guilty of disregarding him.

Arthur would play the flute, every night, sitting in the balcony. He said he was the only child of a Parisian businessman, but he considered himself a musician, who was trying to pursue his passion. Arthur was about a decade younger than me.

He'd bring me hilly flowers, and small presents every now and then. Very soon we ended up talking the entire night away, sitting in that chilly balcony.

One day Arthur procured local pineapple rum and brought it to my room. The drink was strong, for soon we were quite tipsy. For a long time, we sat next to each other, when gradually I felt Arthur inching towards me. One thing led to another; soon we landed in the bed, making love like two lost lovers. It could be the effect of alcohol that we swigged an hour ago. Maybe Arthur had real feelings for me. Or perhaps after all my time in Pune as a celibate, I too was beginning to yearn for sex. I did not know. The only thing I remembered was, when I opened my eyes it was 8.30 am, next day.

After a quick shower we went to Yeing-Yang café for breakfast. The moment we took a seat, an American woman came towards me in brisk steps and said, "Do you mind if I sit down here?"

"Have we met before?" I said, trying to place her lost looks and sad eyes, against the battalion of foreign faces I had met in Pune.

"No, but I have this feeling you can help me!"

I looked at her, puzzled, wondering if she had escaped from an asylum.

The American lady introduced herself as Erica Jones. She said the Nepali police had sent her a telegram stating that her sister, Eva had a horrible death in Kathmandu. Hearing the news her mother had gone insane. Erica, along with her husband, Smith Jones had come to Kathmandu to find out the details. They were put up in a room above the café and wanted me to read cards to her and tell her where her sister could be found.

I did not know why but I felt a strong urge to help Erica. In some way she reminded me of the helplessness I had felt when Nina died. The sudden shock that had left me momentarily paralyzed.

I entered the room with her. Arthur accompanied me. Smith was inside the room. Looking at his face I could say that his eye sight would not last long. And that, encased in an impossible and incurable darkness, perhaps one day he would lose his sanity too. But I said nothing to Erica.

Anyway, a short while later, I entered into a trance to see things for myself. It was a dangerous act, I knew it even then, but a part of me wanted to help Erica. And I saw everything… in that trance, as clearly as I saw everything in that room.

"There were three people involved in the crime. Two men and a woman. The men were not westerners but Orientals. The woman was from a western nation. Your sister's body was mutilated before death," I said.

The effect was nauseating, both the experience and the revelation. Erica thanked me profusely, willing to pay me whatever I wanted. I declined.

"But you deserve a payment," she insisted.

"I did it for your mother," I said and closed the door.

Arthur did not say a word. Seeing me in trance, he was so shocked that he could hardly speak. He held my hands strongly all through the return journey. It was a life-saving gesture, because, had he not held my hands that day I would have collapsed somewhere on the road.

Later I came to know at that time in Nepal, there were three people, two men and one woman who were serial killers. One man was half Nepali and half Indian, the other, a Vietnamese. The woman was French. Together they had killed a lot of people in Thailand, Nepal and India. They were back-packer types, who moved from place to place, killing people after robbing or raping them. After death, they'd burn the bodies of the victims in forests. That group had killed Eva.

I was beside myself at the news. Nevertheless, that incident made me instantly famous; a celebrity of sorts. And on top of everything, there was Arthur, who was always there by my side, loving me, or making love to me. And playing the flute when he was in the mood.

Chapter 25

I I have a surprise for you," Arthur said one night, after one round of passionate love making and three consecutive rounds of pineapple rum.

"What?" I said suddenly sitting up, startled at the mere thought of surprise.

"Am planning to return to Paris, but with you," he began and then paused.

The incurable romantic that Arthur was, nothing was impossible. But a trip to Paris with him was the last thing on my mind.

"You are planning or already decided?" I asked with a naughty smile.

"Decided," Arthur said planting a wet kiss on my mouth.

A week later we packed our bags and flew to Paris saying our final goodbyes to Yeing-Yang café, our lodge and to Kathmandu. Many of my clients, some of them who became friends by then were inconsolably sad at the news. They bought little farewell gifts; a gesture that touched me profoundly. It was thus, a metal Buddha, a *Thangka* scroll, a red pashmina scarf, a necklace made of glass beads, and a small but real Nepali *Khukuri* would find a permanent home in my travel bag.

Given the nomadic nature of my bearing and the perpetual run that I had embarked on, it was doubtful if I would ever have a proper house where I would settle in, giving those trinkets of love all the respect they deserved. Road became my home, and those talismans my family. Wherever I went after Nepal, I always made it a point to keep those knickknacks on my window sill, on bedside tables, or even on the altar at times, when space was a constraint. And I'd stare at them for hours together, when melancholy would overwhelm me.

Paris was a big city. Another world! Millions of galaxies away from the place we flew from. We were put up in an apartment rented by Arthur. It was a small studio flat on the 6th floor of a building near Concorde. After living in India for some time, surrounded by people who were mainly into meditations, followed by the simple and good-natured Nepali population, Parisian folks jostled me with awe.

Not long after we landed, Arthur took me to a party where he introduced me to his circle of friends. Some such people whose face and form, facts and figures I could never forget for the rest of my life. All were alcoholics, most drug addicts. Some were gay, a few transvestites, and remarkably few, outrageously straight. So straight that they could have had sex with a Tom Brando or Ryan Van Dijk or Hatsumi Yamamoto or Chepkirui Otieno, whoever came first. I sensed, they exchanged partners and had orgies too on a regular basis.

One woman had blue hair and another one, a shocking pink. One of them was with a clean-shaven head, and it took me a long time to realize that he was not he, but she.

Some were in their expensive looking inner garments that didn't quite keep the promise of concealment. Nipples were straight on the face. Men didn't even consider it necessary to cover their privates. Balls were hanging like balloons in birthday parties. A few were in biker clothes with purple lipstick and knee length boots. My head did not take much time to go dizzy.

The party night went on and on... much longer than I had anticipated. Arthur went out for a walk after a while and did not return until 2.30 am. All the while I was alone, I sat in one corner with a bottle of French wine, and some hash. After spending more than a decade as a bar girl in America, I was witnessing the wildest party I could ever imagine. Many a time, people, both men and to my surprise women, made subtle advances towards me. I declined. Sex in public, especially orgies made me uncomfortable. I might have had sex with scores of men, but I had never slept with two men at the same time, and in the same room. Sexuality was not an art to be displayed in an exhibition. Sex was a private affair, and sexuality, an intimate proposition.

Anyway, after Arthur returned from his walk, we left the party, utterly spent. It was while climbing those never-ending stairs of his apartment that I had my first attack of breathlessness. I was overcome by a strange fatigue, and my chest tightened into an uncomfortable clutch, forcing me to stop at each landing for a long time before I could drag myself up to the next level.

Arthur sat with me on the stairs.

"You need to check up with a doc," he said looking worried.

"Am ok," I replied. But something within me was not quite ok, and I felt it in my bones.

Of course, I did not realize it at that time what was wrong with me. The ailment got detected much later in my life, at a time when nothing could be done.

When Arthur realized that climbing those flight of stairs on a regular basis was quite a herculean task for me, we shifted to his parent's palatial house in upcountry Paris. Arthur's mother Marylyn was a lot younger than I had anticipated. She was a few years older than me. With her clear complexion and wrinkleless face, she looked a lot younger than I was. Marylyn could be called a beauty by any given standard. With well-rounded breasts and gentle curves, she stood tall and firm, with a cascade of dark brunette hair. She believed in makeups and remained decked up round the clock.

Marylyn didn't seem too pleased to see me, next to her son.

"D'où t'as trouvé cette pute? Elle t'as baisé? Ah bah jén suis sûr," she said looking at Arthur.

Arthur did not reply.

I didn't understand a word of what she said but was certain that she said something derogatory. For that I needed no translator service, which Arthur had been providing me until then. I noticed Arthur turning red in his ears, too embarrassed to speak or look up. Rest of the days, Marylyn's disapproving glances and smug indifference made me understand my position without much effort.

His father, Adrean had a no nonsenses face with a well-kept white beard. He wasn't too excited about me either. Both the parents made it clear and in no uncertain terms that I was a short time guest, who could not linger in their fabulously furnished mansion for too long.

An American woman, who was 14 years older

than their son and with an Indian guru, was an idea they somehow couldn't appreciate. And when they discovered that I had married multiple times and had three children, they literally looked scared, as if I was an American ghost who landed in Paris to nibble on their French son's flesh using *Tantric* techniques. Promptly they made it their primary task to unhook their son from the dangerous addiction called Sona.

Initially, Arthur ignored them, sighting that he loved me. It was all that mattered. And I was touched. We'd go for long walks in the city, visit parks and churches, spend a lot of time chatting, sitting near the Seine. Arthur was a good conversationalist, apart from a flutist.

"You my one girl friend whom, I speak English," he confessed in his broken English one rosy evening sitting near the Sacred Heart Church.

"Your English is good," I said somewhat elated at his proclamation. "You learnt it in school?"

Arthur shook his head. "After school," he said. "More from passion. Maybe I know one day I meet American lover!"

I blushed, unable to reply.

I noticed a middle-aged man crossed us. Quickly he returned and looked intently at me. I was surprised at his bizarre reaction.

"How long have you been here, from India?" he said pointing his finger at me.

I was so taken aback by his comment that it took me a while to understand what he said.

"Excuse me?"

The man repeated.

"Short time," I replied.

I noticed Arthur looked at him in a way as if he was seeing a ghost.

"How long have you been a vegetarian?" he asked next.

I did not know what to reply.

He looked at his feet mindfully for a while, as I kept looking at his face trying to remember if I had met him somewhere.

"Take one aspirin every day," he said in a grave tone.

"What has that got to do with vegetarianism?" I said, unable to place his comment.

He ignored my question.

"You read cards, don't you?" he said, with a broad grin.

I nodded. "How did you know?" I asked, knitting my brows.

"Never mind! Lucien Bernard, that's your man. You should meet him," he said adjusting his cap.

Before I could ask him a question, he walked away. That was when I noticed a mild limp in his left leg.

"You know him?" I asked Arthur, pointing the man.

"I thought you know," he replied, surprised.

"Strange guy! Who is this, Lucian Bernard?"

Arthur told me that Lucian was a famous tarot reader in Paris. A part of me immediately revolted.

"You knew about him but didn't take me to him?" I protested in rage.

"I do not believe in all that," he added impatiently.

"It's not about your belief. It's about mine," I said, got up and started marching. I didn't wait for him to reply. When I reached some distance, I turned my head slightly to see if he was following me. I saw him looking at the church, his mind already preoccupied with something else.

That I reckon was our first fight. I was unhappy with Arthur, unhappy for not telling me about Lucian; unhappy for being so casual about it. Unhappy for all the cold shoulders that his parents showered on me.

That night, for the first time ever since we landed in Paris, Arthur and I went to bed without making love. We never got intimate again.

Nevertheless, Arthur took me to Lucien the following day. Lucien stayed in Brittany, that was about 5 hours' drive from Paris. By the time we reached him, it was well past noon.

Lucian was eighty-four years old, with an ancient but handsome face, speckled hands and kind eyes. One look into those eyes and I could tell that he was a wise man. He spoke in French and did not understand a word of English.

"*Je savais que tu venais* (I knew you were coming)," he said softly, followed by a smile.

I was taken aback at his comment.

"*Ouiiii* (How)?" I asked.

"*Je le savais,* (I just knew)," he said.

Arthur translated back and forth.

Lucian said that he did a lot of card readings during the war for refugees, helping them find their families. Also, for people who got out of the concentration camps.

"*Mais il y a long temps que ça c'est passé* (But that was long time ago)," he reminisced with nostalgia.

Now he fed birds. They were his companions; he referred, not once but a few times. I wondered if his bird feeding was an act of compassion or an act rooted in senility. I wondered if he realized he was repeating himself a ridiculous number of times.

Lucian could no longer read cards because of his frail health and weak eyes, but he was still interested in anything related to it. When he learnt that I came from India, he started saying...

"*India est belle... India est belle.*"

I left his house happy and Arthur visibly irritated. The entire journey he blamed me for making him drive that long for seeing an old haggard of a man. He could have enjoyed his parties instead. Arthur dropped me home and then vanished for the next three days. I was alone and clueless.

Our relationship was beginning to rupture. On the fourth night, when he returned, he was drunk and so hopelessly stoned that it took him another couple of days to resume normalcy. He refused to disclose where he was.

Often, I'd notice him peeing on himself, totally unconscious of the act. At times he would fondle his private parts as if it was a flute. The entire day he would lie in his bed, stark naked. Arthur refused to say a word.

Initially I blamed drugs for his pathetic state. He must have had something that destroyed his nerves, I inferred. But when days rolled into weeks and then an entire month passed and Arthur did not recover, I feared that perhaps it could be a case of depression. Arthur's parents accused me of the condition that his son was in.

Although I was not well conversant with French but their looks and body language told me everything I needed to know. I was beginning to grow uncomfortable with them and decided to leave Paris and return to India.

The day I revealed my plan to Arthur, he did not stop me. He kept looking at me absentmindedly. That was when I realized that his love for me had expired. The emotion that had once tied us slowly faded until there was none. At the end of it, there was neither love nor care. Once again, I felt alone and completely drained. I thought of Anand's proclamation, that we are all alone in our respective journeys. Perhaps he was right. It was useless to seek solace in a partner.

A week later I took my flight to Bombay. I remembered Lucian all the way back. His wrinkled face, his wisdom, his love for birds and cards; things he had said to me in French, which Arthur translated. His life!

"You don't belong here," he had said.

"Where?" I had asked with a hand gesture. Lucian understood without being translated.

"Paris," he replied immediately, pointing the floor with his index finger.

Lucian proclaimed that I did not belong to Paris, and that I wouldn't linger there for long. Although the city was full of love but the tempo would burn me out. And that I'd soon begin to dislike it. Was he referring to Arthur when he said that? I now wondered. For, no sooner did we return from his place, Arthur and I diverged.

What struck me most was the precision of his prediction. I was there only for a while and spent about twenty minutes. Even in those twenty minutes, we barely had a conversation. He did not understand English and I could not speak French. Whatever he had said, I understood only after Arthur had translated them. How could he be so accurate?

For, whatever he had said was true. However, I had loved Paris deeply during the first few weeks of my stay, but very soon I got bored of it. The beauty, the silence of its countryside's, the extravagant Parisian people, those wild parties, Arthur's aimlessness, his parent's snobbish indifferences... everything was beginning to crush me from inside. I had a constant feeling of estrangement, and it increased with every breath that I took.

Paris was not home. It was a foreign city and it remained foreign. It was definitely not a place where I could belong.

Suddenly, a quick thought crossed my mind.

'Where do I belong? Or do I really belong anywhere? If I am American, why am I sitting in an India bound flight? I could have taken a flight back to the US. If nothing, I still have my children there. If I intend to go to India, what is the motivation? Whom do I want to meet? And why?'

Despite all the rooms and shelters I had taken refuge in multiple places, home was a concept I had never embraced. What people called home, was an idea which always eluded me.

It was like those fireflies I had often noticed inside the Osho ashram, which I always wanted to catch. But the moment I thought I had caught one, and opened my palm to check, it would be gone. Only to appear a while later in another dark corner, blinking, prompting me to look at it, breeding in me a desire it catch it all over again.

Chapter 26

I reached Bombay with a broken heart, a bundle of cash, and a bad attack of amoebic dysentery.

I felt so emaciated that from airport I went to a cheap lodge in Church Gate to put up for the night. As night wore on, my condition deteriorated, so much so that towards morning I found it difficult to lift my head from the pillow.

A doctor was called by the manager, who advised me a series of tests and a long list of medicines.

"This medicine will cure you for the time being, but get those tests done," said the Parsi doctor, with pink face and round spectacles.

I nodded, not knowing whether to take them or skip. Because the money I had with me would not permit me the luxury of having elaborate tests and treatments.

A mistake! What I forgot to consider at that point of time, was that I was no longer a woman in her twenties, with a body strong enough to endure anything. I was aging, and my body was bound to give up. In that crazy journey I had embarked on, the first casualty was my health.

When I was younger and sexually active, I had abused

the feminine side of my body. Multiple children, when I was not fit enough to bear even one; a string of abortions that nearly killed me, not once but several times in a row. Few and futile suicide attempts that I had made, I admit quite foolishly, had left me hollow from inside. Added to all that, my faithful relationship with alcohol and drugs, which progressively nibbled away what little remained.

On top of everything, the psychological cataclysms that I had suffered from, throughout my life, jumping from one relationship to another, had left me emotionally vacant. If at all I had a spirit inside me, it was so crushed that often I had a feeling of being a walking corpse .

Realization came to me the day I went to a local hospital in Bombay for the tests. There was a lady sitting in front of a stretcher, thumping her chest repeatedly and crying, as she looked at her seven- year old dead son. Her cries were piercingly loud and so heart wrenching that I could not bear to linger there a moment longer.

The scene was excruciatingly shocking. And yet, my eyes were dry. However sad I must have felt for that woman, tears did not come to my eyes. I found it impossible to shed a drop.

In the end I escaped from the hospital without taking the pathological tests. I walked and walked and landed up at the Gateway of India. There I stood for a long time, peering into the briny blue. I must have crossed countless buildings, bumped upon and elbowed through scores of people, crossed numerous roads, being honked upon or shouted at, but I had absolutely no recollections. For all I knew, it was like a long tunnel that I had walked through, with no one by my side and no destination ahead of me, with nothing to hold me back, and not a soul to adhere to.

Memories of my children flashed into my mind. I realized that I had not thought about them for a long time. What they might have turned into? How each one of them looked? What were they doing? Where was Harrison? In the haul of my life, in the absolute vagary of it, I had given up my children. Motherhood is a blessing totally wasted on me. I couldn't help but reflect. And with that reflection, finally came an unstoppable gush of tears.

A part of me wanted to go back to America right at that moment, embrace them and not let them go until my last breath. But that would also mean returning to Stephen and the impossible cogwheel of domesticity. That would mean giving up on the freedom I had begun to love so ardently.

In a way it was wise to be where I was, to do what I was doing; moving forward, I decided. "Life is meant to be lived forward," Anand always said, I recollected.

Anand! Again, that name popped up in my mind. Should I go to Pune? I knocked myself. I think I should, I told myself, convinced that it was Anand, who could heal my wounds. And yet travelling to Pune did not happen immediately, as I had desired. Destiny had another plan in place. For, after returning to the lodge that night, my stomach pain increased in leaps and bounds, so much so that I fainted.

When I opened my eyes next, I was in a hospital bed. Several tests were done. The reports declared that I had cancer in the sigmoid colon. The world around me crumpled down into a mass of black ash. What remained behind was a strange hum inside my head that forbade me to hear the outside noise. It was as if a pair of bees got inside my head and lost their way out. There, they hummed and hummed driving me crazy.

"It's just the beginning …," the doctor said, when he noticed tears dripping down my face.

"I understand," I said, nodding my head.

I left the hospital a few days later. I walked and walked the entire day, where I did not know; smoked one cigarette after another. When fatigue began to settle in, I sat on a deserted part of a beach and cried.

Grief is physically exhausting. For, soon I fell into a deep sleep right on the beach, my body soaking up the brine. When I woke up, an ink like darkness had encompassed the sky, the sea and the sand. There was no one in the vicinity, only waves lashed on the shore incessantly and kept me company.

The few days that followed were the longest ones of my life. And yet I had no memory of them. Days went on and on with annoying monotony; then nights descended with its lulling calm, as I lay motionless in my bed, looking up at the ceiling, wondering. Wondering what? I had no clue.

Not too long after that I took a train to Pune.

Chapter 27

My first job after returning to Pune was to find Anand. It was a challenge, because the address that Anand gave me was lost, and I no longer remembered the name of the street. I had no details of him other than his name.

But as destiny had it, the challenge was easily overcome. Two days after my return to Pune, I met Anand on MG Road. I was in an auto-rickshaw and he was walking on the footpath. My eyes fell on him and I shouted his name. He must have been absorbed into something else, but his feet stopped at once and he looked my side.

"You heard me?" I asked.

"How could I miss your voice?" he replied. His happiness reflected through his jingly voice, and the sparkle of his dark eyes. There were quite a few grey strands on his temples, I noticed, but his face was unusually wrinkle free.

"Ahh," I said smiling.

"When did you come to Pune?" he asked.

"Two days ago," I paused, "was looking for you. I lost your contact details," I added sheepishly.

"Oh Sona, you are just the same!"

"I am sorry… but" I began.

"Just forget it. Come let's sit and have some *chai*," he said pulling my hands and taking me inside a dirty looking café on MG Road.

We spoke for a long time, sitting in that café. Anand swigged three glasses *chai* in the process and two plates of *bun-maska*. I told him about my Nepal odyssey, and then the trip to Paris. At last, when there was nothing more to be said, I told him about my ailment. Anand stretched his eyes wide in shock. He took a long time to speak.

"So that's the reason you returned to Pune," Anand pointed after absorbing and assimilating my information.

"In a way, yes," I added candidly.

"Body is a delicate machine, Sona. If you abuse it too much, it's bound to give up," he said as we got into an auto rickshaw.

I nodded, looking outside, seeing the soothing beauty of a falling evening.

"Where are you put up?" he asked.

"At a lodge near the station," I said.

"And then?" he persisted.

"I don't know Anand. Honestly, I have come to meet you."

"That sounds so you," he opined.

I smiled, unable to dig out a reply.

"Let's do something. Come with me. I have rented a house on Prabhat Road, you could stay there for a while," he offered.

"Are you sure? I can stay there?" I asked uncertainly.

"Absolutely!"

Promptly I quit the lodge, and in that same auto-rickshaw we went to Anand's house.

The house was small, barely suitable for one, and yet Anand welcomed me with all the warmth of the world. Only at night, when he began to make a bed on the floor, I started feeling uneasy.

"What's that for?" I said pointing the blanket on the floor.

"Me," he replied, too busy to look up.

"We are a couple as per the marriage certificate, so you could very well sleep next to me on the bed," I added jokingly.

"That paper proves nothing," he replied in a serious tone.

His statement hurt me. It was as if he was nurturing a grudge against me.

"Okay, then allow me to sleep on the floor," I proposed.

"Impossible. You are my guest, you will get the bed," he said.

"But I will not be able to sleep in peace, knowing that I have taken your bed," I argued.

"You look exhausted Sona, I doubt you will be able to keep your eyes open for long," he said as he lay down.

And Anand was right! For, the moment I put my head on the pillow, I fell asleep, and did not open my eyes until eleven the next day. Anand had left for work, but he had kept a plate full of food on the table. Toasted bread, scrambled eggs, two bananas, a small bowl of strawberries and a bottle of jam. After ages, I ate, without brushing my teeth or taking a shower. After ages I ate a breakfast not prepared by myself. After ages I ate a proper breakfast.

Anand had a furniture store on Rasta Peth, where he worked from morning till early evening. He also had a second hand book store in Appa Balwant Chowk, where he sat from evening till the shop closed. Anand said that his parents died in a bus accident on their way to Rishikesh, and hence he lived alone in that house on Prabhat Road, while the remaining of his family members stayed in his ancestral house in Bhonsle Nagar. The furniture store was opened by his grandfather, a Kutchi businessman, whose ancestors made ships. The store was still the primary source of income for the entire family. Anand had a penchant for books, and hence invested in a book store. He said his living expenses were met out by selling books. And his life was made by reading them.

"So, you wish to grow old making furniture and selling books," I inferred, after he briefed me about his family and personal history.

"No," he said, putting his feet on the railing in the small balcony that overlooked the tree lined road.

"Then?"

"I am planning to make a farm house, somewhere, a little removed from the city. It will have lots of trees and a square of land for agriculture, orchard, farming, a pond may be. There will be shaded places for meditation. People could come and stay for a while, basic facilities, a room and wash room, nothing fancy," he added emotionally.

I kept looking at his soft face as he went on adding romantic details to his dream project. Unlike me, where I could not see clearly what was to happen tomorrow, Anand could visualize a project he might start ten years later.

Incredible! I thought. No wonder my life seemed such a waste to him.

"Mango Grove," he said suddenly and stopped.

"What's that?"

"I'll name it Mango Grove," he said.

I smiled, taking in the expression of his face, the dream in his eyes, the gentle smile that glistened his lips.

"But I fear for you Sona," he stated.

"Fear? Why?"

"What will you do? Regarding your treatment, I mean," he said.

I fell silent.

"Look, don't get me wrong. You could stay here for as long as you want, but I think for the moment, you should go back to your country, get treated, then come back," he opined.

"I don't know Anand," I replied helplessly.

"How long will you not know? How long will you escape?" he said with urgency. "A day will come when this disease eats you up, if you are not cautious now."

"I understand Anand what you are saying is right, but I don't feel like returning to America," I said candidly.

"Who is telling you to return? Get treated, then come back. Plus, your visa has also expired. You need to fix that too. How long will you linger here like an illegal immigrant?" Anand said.

Like every other question pertaining to my life, I had no answer.

That night Anand convinced me to return to America. He was a man of reason and logic, some such things, I had absolutely no connection with. Yet, I stood convinced.

Once again, he helped me with all the visa formalities and came with me to Bombay to see me off. Standing at the airport, I had a *deja vu*, as Anand held my hands, as he moved forward to embrace me. His hug was warm, all-encompassing as I snuggled myself deep inside his girdle. There was some magic in his touch, in his embrace that sparked within me a sincere longing.

"Life is very precious Sona, don't waste it in vagary," he preached.

I nodded looking at my sandaled feet. The life I was living; had lived so far, Anand would reckon as absolute waste. The blessing was wasted on me, the way motherhood was, I reflected in silence. He made every moment of his life useful, fecund, while I was just walking the earth, spending my time.

"Would you give me a place in your Mango Groove?" I asked.

"All yours," he added, smiling.

That night I took a flight to New York, then another one to Santa Cruz, California. A doctor by the name of Nicholas operated on my sigmoid colon.

I was admitted to a hospital and the surgery was done in a few weeks' time. Pain was unbearable; the entire time I'd be on morphine. Initially I considered calling Stephen, but then thought better of it. I was away from him for so long and had practically not been in touch with him, so calling him now in the hours of need would look shallow, I decided. Wisdom was in taking up the battle alone. If I would survive, I could go and pay them a visit.

After the surgery, it took me a while to recuperate. I was nearly unconscious the entire time. When the pain abated, and I was beginning to regain my strength, I was released from the hospital.

Nicholas arranged for a studio apartment for me to stay, until I was fit enough to be on my own. Living alone in that strange house in America made me uncomfortable. I missed India, I missed Pune. I longed to meet Anand.

With one thing leading to another, I met with another disaster. Tests revealed that I had developed a series of cysts in my uterus that needed to be removed.

"The earlier the better," the doctor added taking an extended glance at my reports.

He said that two surgeries could not be done in one go, and hence a period was given to me, for recuperating. I was supposed to get back to the hospital after a span of two months and then undergo hysterectomy.

I did, as instructed. There wasn't an option. I was thirty-eight then and was about to get a vital feminine part of my body permanently removed. I was aware that from then on, I would have to live with that short coming for the rest of my life. Who was to be blamed? I wondered lying in the hospital bed.

I had abused my body so much and to such an impossible extent that at times it seemed no short of a miracle that I was still alive. For months I had lived on bare minimum food, just enough to satiate my cravings. I had smoked like a chimney and fucked like a prostitute. I had gallons of alcohol from the age of twelve, perhaps thirteen.

I had been on drugs, on and off - hashish, marijuana, lsd, heroine, what not. I had delivered three children, countless abortions that I no longer remembered. As though that was not enough, I had attempted two suicides; both futile, both shockingly painful.

People often point to destiny against any debacle they encounter. But I blamed none, other than myself. Because by then, I had seen enough to realize that my life, whatever it added up to, was my own craft. I was the sole architect of everything that had happened. I had none to point my fingers at.

Chapter 28

After the surgeries and a recuperation time of nearly six months, when I was bored stiff by relaxing all day long, I decided to visit Stephen and my children. I did not know what compelled me to take the decision; only that I did, after some contemplation and extended pondering. But once I made up my mind, I lost no time to travel to Biddeford where I presumed Stephen would be.

Nearly a decade had passed since my last visit. I had not contacted him in any way. I wondered if Stephen married again, and that after my hours of travel I'd end up meeting the other woman in his house. Wouldn't that be disappointing? Of course, Stephen was free to marry, and if he did, I would be the other woman and not she. But the thought of Stephen marrying another woman unsettled me. Suddenly, I discovered myself feeling envious of that unknown and perhaps non-existent being.

I thought about my children too. How old they would be now? Bella would be 16 and Bill 14. Would they recognize me? What were they doing with their lives? I sensed a staunch disciplinarian in Stephen. Had he infused the trait into his children? Or did he turn out to be an indulgent father, pampering and spoiling them? I could not imagine further. Neither of them; nor their lives that must have gone on despite me.

Biddeford welcomed me once again, exactly the way it did the last time. And yet, the context had suffered what one would call a paradigm shift. Stephen was still there in that same little house up on the hills. Doing that same job in that same hotel, Swamp Fox. Even his furniture did not change. For a moment it felt intriguing to realize that in the last decade when I had changed home and a place to sleep in at a rate, which could not be exactly called normal, Stephen had slept on that same bed, under that same roof.

"Ahh Sona," he said. There was not a drop of surprise in his eyes, I noticed. He appeared as though he knew that I'd come.

"Hi," I said and stopped, not being able to fish out the right word to strike up a conversation. Standing at the door, I kept looking at him in speechless silence.

Stephen was barely fifty and yet his face had wrinkled. He looked frail, and thin. His back was bent as if he was eighty. His once lustrous eyes had hardened, having lost their sparkle. I observed with dismay. I wondered what could be the reason behind that uncalled for calcification.

"Are you going to say bye from here?" Stephen said, sensing my dilemma in entering his house.

I blushed.

It felt odd to meet an ex-spouse. The effect was disorienting. Memories, both good and bad, were abundant, so many moments of expired love - of arguments - of mutual hatred - of a time when we were a lot younger and much less wise.

Stephen said he had suffered one major heart attack

and two minor strokes. His blood sugar was mostly high, and his knees were bothering him. He was turning a lot more forgetful than he should.

"Doctors suspecting Alzheimer," he said in a depressing voice.

I listened mindfully, taking in all the disastrous effects that were written all over his face and frame.

"I have survived," he declared at last, after his long chronicle of ill-health.

How I wished I could recount all the big and small ways I had survived over the last decade.

"You have changed," Stephen observed.

"We all have, in some way," I replied.

"Certainly, we did. But you have changed for better," he pointed.

"Better? How?"

"I don't know," he shrugged his shoulders. "But you did."

Stephen refused to divulge. I refused to nudge. It was highly probable that the obvious and visible upshots of recovering from two major surgeries were perhaps written all over me that Stephen read as easily as I had read his, hours ago. Or perhaps, the serenity of age was beginning to settle in me of which he was earlier not privy to. Maybe the countless hours of meditation I had in the Osho ashram tuned me into someone more matured and tranquil.

Nevertheless, I could say that he was admiring that version of me. The expression of his face changed, softened when he spoke to me. He did not resent or grudge against my sudden arrival. He welcomed me with outstretched arms, like a mature husband, exactly the way I had expected. He made coffee for me and then sat next to me, almost touching my thigh. Was he saying something through the touch? I wondered.

Stephen said that Bill would join the army. He was in a boarding school. He came home occasionally. I recollected our last meeting.

"He asks about me?"

"Who?"

"Bill."

Stephen did not reply. Without saying a word, he answered me.

Then he gently placed his palm on mine and said, "It's okay Sona."

"No, I deserve it, totally. Cannot blame him," I said feeling a surge of tears.

"Children have their own ways of interpreting things," he observed.

"Does he even remember me?" I asked impulsively.

"He does, but does not say," he said.

"How do you know?"

"I know. He is a boy. Boys are like that."

Stephen's reply saddened me, noting how well he understood my child, while I am a mother, perhaps would not even recognize him in a crowd.

"Problem is with Bella," Stephen said, perhaps to divert the topic.

"What's with her?"

Stephen said that her heart was weak and had been operated thrice in the last few years. She had developed diabetes too and her kidneys were nearly non-functional. If her kidneys were not transplanted at the earliest, her life could extinguish any moment.

"What is keeping you from the transplant?" I asked stupidly.

"Money, what else," he said gloomily. "My income goes away in maintaining this house."

The news rattled me so much, that for a long time I could not speak. I did not even remember thinking anything. I was just there, sitting next to Stephen, holding his hand, feeling miserable.

"Is there a way I can help?" I volunteered after a long while.

"I understand your sentiments Sona, but it won't be easy," he said.

"It had not been easy for you too. But you did. Now it's my turn," I added emotionally.

"Still, think about it. By the way, you have any news about Anna?"

I shook my head.

"I think you should call her once."

"You have her phone number?"

Stephen nodded and gave me a phone number. I called Anna from his place and spoke, for a long time.

Initially Anna refused to say a word, then after much coaxing when she finally opened her mouth and told her story; I wished I hadn't heard it in the first place.

Anna said that Mama was at an old age home now, in San Jose, totally senile and partially blind. Uncle Earl had died in a car crash that broke his spine and twisted his head. His body was beyond recognition. Anna said, she had no information about Larry, where he was and what he was doing. Charles was in New York now and had married a New Yorker, Kate. Both opened a fast-food joint that was doing well. Cindy ran away from home when she was about sixteen. Since then, there had been no news from her. Lola was the 3rd wife of a rich Texas based businessman, who was an alcoholic and a wife beater. She had suffered three major and seven minor fractures over the last five years of her married life.

"And what are you up to?" I said finally, noting that she was not saying anything about her life.

Anna fell silent, but I could still hear her heavy breathing.

"Am good," she said at last.

"But I feel all is not good," I said tentatively.

Anna laughed. When her laughter subsided, she started to cry. Noise of her wails made my eyes watery.

"What is it, Anna? Is there a thing you are hiding from me?"

"You know me so well," Anna replied.

Anna said at 18 she had fled from home with Bosco, a Vietnamese guy, intending to marry him and live happily ever after. But her love story went downhill when Bosco sold her into prostitution and married another girl. For some years Anna had worked as a prostitute in Las Vegas, until she was diagnosed with AIDS, two years back. Now she was forced to quit the trade and accept life of a destitute.

There was nothing left for her to do other than waiting for death to release her from the terrible pain she was in.

"Pain? Where?" I asked, gulping phlegm.

"This life," she replied philosophically.

"Whose number is this?"

"It's a home, for people like us," Anna replied dispassionately.

I stopped and did not have the heart to ask any further; for, the truth was, I could not comprehend what kind of life she was forced to embrace. So carried away was I in an unspeakable grief that, I did not notice when Anna had hung up from the other side. I sat like that with the receiver pressed to my ears, as tears accumulated on my lap.

That night, I thought about my own death. When would it be my turn? At what age? Which country I would be in? How would I accept it? Bravely like a soldier, or fearfully, like any other human being. Anna was a lot younger than me and was standing on the threshold of life and death. Was she afraid? Or was she happy to secure her release from a life, which I gathered to be hopelessly tragic? I felt inconsolably sorrowful at her revelations.

"Look who's here!" Stephen suddenly exclaimed, elated.

A moment's pause.

"What am I supposed to do?"

I heard in a woman's voice. Quickly I banged the phone and turned. It was Bella.

"That's rude," Stephen said in a futile effort to hush her comment.

"You get back what you give," Bella replied and moved towards the refrigerator. She brought out a carton of milk, poured some into a tall glass and started sipping, sitting on a chair in the kitchen.

Bella was sixteen, thin to the point of looking sick, with two small mounds for breasts. The only mammoth part of her body were her feet, that were oddly swollen. I felt sad for her, taking in the disfigurement.

"I'll be back in a moment," Stephen escaped from the sight, perhaps giving us space and time to know each other.

Bella observed Stephen without any visible emotion, as he moved out of the house.

"Hi Bella," I began uncertainly.

Bella lifted her middle finger up and said nothing.

I swallowed the insult.

"I am sorry Bella," I started again. This time more gently.

"Look man, don't pretend. For God's sake don't pretend. It doesn't suit you," Bella barked on my face.

"I am sorry Bella... for," I said again.

"Oh! You are sorry, are you?" she added sarcastically.

"I mean it," I said trying to sound as genuine as I was feeling.

"I don't give a fuck," she barked yet again. "You did what you had to do."

"I understand your anger," I said looking at my feet.

"Do you?"

Having said those two words, Bella once again

showed me her middle finger and walked out of the house. I saw the slow pace of her movements, the way she was walking, as if each step was causing her pain. As if each step was more effortful than the previous one.

Bella was wearing a white, almost transparent knee length dress. She wasn't wearing any undergarments. Her body was visible through the dress to the extent of looking vulgar. I wondered if that was the way she always dressed. Why had Stephen never objected to it?

The door closed with a loud thud and a part of my world crumpled down into splinters. I broke into a violent stream of tears that refused to stop for a long time.

"It's her ill health that makes her lose temper, Sona, don't take it to your heart. She is sweet otherwise," Stephen said, stroking my head.

"It's all because of me," I said impulsively. "I shouldn't have left them."

"Things happen the way they ought to happen. We cannot blame each other," he consoled.

"That's your goodness speaking."

I stayed back with Stephen that night. As night wore on, Stephen told me the entire story about Bella. He said my departure had impacted her a lot, although she was not always vocal about it

"May be, she was in the wrong age," Stephen said.

After seeing me off in that bus, Bella returned home and cried for days together. She entered into depression and had been under medication for a long time. When she began menstruating, at the age of eleven, she developed diabetes. Her cardiac ailment also returned. One thing leading to another, her kidneys started getting effected and were malfunctioning. Since then, she had turned cranky with severe mood swings and temper issues.

"Lemme arrange for some money so that we can take care of her transplant," I said.

"It's a huge sum Sona. From where will you get?" Stephen said.

"I don't have all the answers now, but will find a way," I added uncertainly.

The next few days I thought about all the different ways I could earn money and get Bella treated. But before that I had to go to LA to meet Anna and then to San Jose to meet Mama. I thought of Anand, over and over again, for having somewhat forced me to return to America. Or else I wouldn't have known all those details.

As a gesture of gratitude and remembrance, I wrote Anand a long letter, first thanking him for suggesting me to return. Then giving him a detailed report of my surgeries and my current health, which was not so bad after all. Finally telling him all that I had gathered, first from Stephen, then from Anna. Tears dripped from my eyes and dropped on the paper, smudging a few words here and there. I was sure Anand would read that too.

The few days that I stayed in Biddeford, I made several attempts to talk to Bella, to make amends for my past error. But she remained resolutely detached. She refused to even look at my face, let alone speak to me. I realized with painful certainty that I had broken her so much that perhaps it would be impossible to reconcile. Fault was mine and I accepted it with humility. I did not blame her a drop for the disagreeable way she behaved with me.

Most of the time, when Stephen was out, Bella would roam around in the house stark naked. To annoy me, I suspected, but did not comment. I wondered if she remained nude in front of Stephen too. It was disconcerting to see a grown-up daughter standing naked in front of one's eyes, with half grown breasts and ill formed nipples, and a skinny body that vaguely resembled a woman. Perhaps that was her way of showing *I don't care*; her way of rebelling against a mother who had left her at a crucial age. I felt sorry for her; and more than that, I felt sorry for myself.

I swore to Stephen that I would arrange funds for her surgery. That was perhaps the only way I could make amends for my errors.

Three days later, I made my way, first to LA, to meet Anna and then to San Jose, to meet Mama.

Encounter with Anna was as sad and devastating, as I had anticipated. Yet, I could not come to terms with the pathetic state of health I discovered her to be in. Anna was thinner than a stick without a dash of flesh on her body. Even her breasts had shrunk up like raisins. Her face had turned dark, and her eyes were bulging out of the sockets.

During conversation, her eyes drifted from my face to nowhere. Not once, but quite a few times. She turned delusional. Time and again, a name popped up, Harry. When I asked her, who Harry was, she couldn't reply. Anna wetted on herself, sitting in the bed, I noticed. But she didn't seem to be bothered. I wondered if she still could feel her body, or already she had begun to lose control. If she could see me properly or was only guessing that it was me.

"Good you came. Was thinking a lot about you," Anna said, weakly.

"About me?"

"Yes. When you know your time is up, you like to meet loved ones," she said taking her eyes away from my face. Something in her told me that I was probably seeing her for the last time.

I broke into a fresh bout of tears, thinking about all the days and months, when Anna had helped me during Bill's delivery. She herself was a child then, and yet looked after Bella.

"You had cared for us, when we were little. In a way, you had been our mother," Anna said with a wry smile on her nearly absent lips.

"And what an adorable sister you had been," I replied, remembering the good old days.

"Everything will remain the same, only I won't be there!" A drop leaked from Anna's eyes.

"Hey," I said cupping her hand with my palm.

Anna embraced me and howled on my shoulder. I could feel every bone of her emaciated body. I did not ask about her life, I mean the one before she had contracted aids, convinced that it would be another chronicle of pain and sufferings, perhaps too gruesome to hear. I could not even pretend to comprehend her life as a prostitute, what she must have been through, day after day, night after night.

When she unhooked from my girdle, she looked visibly calm. Perhaps, it was the composure of resignation, when one is aware that she is powerless to fight any longer; and that surrender is the best defense.

After a while, she fell asleep tucking a pillow close to her chest. Anna looked like a baby. I sat next to her for some more time, sensing that could be our last meeting. An hour later, I left, kissing her on the forehead.

Anna's ghastly image haunted me the entire journey from Los Angeles to San Jose. I wept like a lost child, wondering how many more deaths I would witness before it would be my turn.

I remembered Anna's birth, how Martin drove her and Nina home. I did not visit the hospital to welcome them. And yet, when the twins arrived, they completely encompassed our lives. Encompassed my life! Anna's cries kept me sleepless at nights, Anna's giggles made my day. I had held her and cuddled her, changed her diapers and given her a bath. There were even times, when I had held her at Mama's leaking nipples, when she was overcome with melancholy.

Anna was my stepsister, and yet, I had always loved her as my own. I did not know why, but that day, seeing Anna's pathetic state, I thought about Martin's cruel assaults on me. His rape attempts! The cunning insults that he had piled on me, until the moment I fled from the house and married Galvin. Was Anna paying for her father's sins? I wondered.

Sad as I might have been seeing Anna, but a part of me was happy for her. For, the kind of darkness she was cloistered into, death was the only escape. It did bring me comfort realizing that her suffering would end soon. Anna's sight brought into my mind the image of Bella. If we failed to acquire money for her surgery, she too would lose her life. It was just a thought that caught me unawares and yet, I could feel my chest tightening, my heart beating unreasonably fast.

"I need to arrange for funds, by hook or by crook," I reminded myself time and again, all through the journey.

Meeting Mama was in a way less melodramatic than Anna's, for, Mama appeared to be a member of another galaxy now, unknown and undecipherable to me.

"Mama…I am Sona," I said touching her hands.

Mama looked up and kept looking at my face with an uncomprehending gaze. It was difficult to ascertain the extent of her recognition.

"Who?" she said after a long time, in a voice that was barely audible.

"Sona," I added with emphasis.

Another spell of silence followed. We kept looking at each other. Mother's eyes lacked vision; I could tell; her face lacked an expression. If memory did not betray me, she had been a beauty once, and yet nothing of that remained. The old lady who sat in front of me had practically no resemblance with the mother I had grown up with.

The house doctor informed me that Mama had forgotten everything. There were days when instead of walking she'd crawl on all her fours, and they would be forced to tether her to the bed. At times, she would play with her own excrements, and smear it on her stomach and neck.

All the information and experience rattled me so much that for a long time I forgot the rest of the world. I kept on thinking and thinking, about our lives, individually and collectively. Evening brought me melancholy, a thousand times more than I could handle, so much so that I ended up visiting a pub.

Although Anand had warned me against alcohol, and not totally fit to swig down bottles, still I ended up drinking; making myself comfortably numb under its spell.

"Old habits die hard," I heard a voice from the behind.

I turned my dizzy head and saw Andrew Smith, standing behind me, perhaps watching me for some time.

Andrew was the owner of two pubs and had a huge name in the world of hashish smuggling. I had worked for one of his pubs ages ago, that's when we got to know each other. Andrew was blind by his left eye and had a deep scar that ran across the left side of his face. Many said his boss had taken the eyeball out with a knife for a breach of contract. He was also the one who had made that malevolent looking cut on his face, so that every time Andrew would look into the mirror, he'd be reminded of the incident. Andrew never made a second mistake.

"Hey Andrew!" I said, trying to stand up. My feet faltered, that's when he strode forward and held me by my shoulders.

"You need not get up. Long time. Where have you been?" he said sitting opposite to me.

I told him about my travels to India and Paris, and then back to America.

"How is Anna?" he suddenly asked.

"How come you know her?" Surprised, I questioned.

"I met her in Vegas once."

I wondered if he had met her as a client or was the meeting a chance encounter.

Andrew stopped suddenly, somewhere mid-sentence. I sensed that he was unaware of her current status. I told him about Anna, then about Mama, and finally about Bella. He listened to my entire story, sipping Vodka Martini.

"So, what will you do now?" he asked, looking worried.

"I don't know, let's see. Maybe, I should start reading cards here, for some time," I added uncertainly.

"Look Sona, don't get me wrong, but the kind of money you need right now, your card reading could not fetch," he said and paused, perhaps trying to read my expression. "Come, let's sit in my chamber," he said getting up.

I followed him with faltering steps into a small chamber at the mezzanine floor of the pub.

Once we settled ourselves in, he brought a stiff peg of Bourbon on the rocks and placed before me, with a proposition.

"All you must do is take a hash with you and deliver in Holland. You will visit the country as a tourist, and your travel expenses and visa costs are one me. Plus, you will get whatever money you want, for the job," he said, then lit a cigar and began smoking. The room gradually turned smoky. My eyes burned. I felt dizzier.

"Why me?" I asked after he finished briefing me the plan.

Andrew thought for a while.

"Because you are the best person for this kind of job. I know you are a smart woman, who could handle people and emergency situations," he said.

And I thought about my last experience of smuggling marijuana in Mexico, the jail sentence that followed and then the long and disagreeable case that I had fought. The shitty mess I was into for months. A part of me immediately wanted to run away from that room and never return. But then, thought better of it. For, Bella's image was still fresh in my memory, and I could go to any extent to rescue her from death.

"And what if I get caught?" I asked.

"Let's assume you won't. But in case you do, I will take you out. You need not worry," Andrew assured.

Andrew sounded genuine, and was indeed a genuine person, for all I knew, although he dealt with drugs and pubs. But I found it difficult to accept him at face value.

Men of his trade were only good as long as the deals went smoothly. The moment crisis popped up its head; they'd be the first ones to take their hands off. And if possible, kick you in the butt. It would not be too difficult for Andrew to wipe me off from the world, if I messed with him or with his deal.

"I need time to think," I said avoiding his eyes.

"Trust me Sona, nothing's going to go wrong," Andrew assured, in a mellowed down voice.

"I have to cross international boundary. Risk is huge, if I get caught, hope you understand. I could be imprisoned for life," I argued.

"If you get caught, I'd know right away. But hang on... why are you talking about getting caught? Is there anything that's disturbing you?"

"Why me? Why a woman? You must be having hundreds of men who could do the job," I argued.

"Because they don't generally suspect women as smugglers. Plus, you already have a track record of travelling. Your chances are slim," he opined.

"But I have a criminal record too," I said.

That was when I divulged him about my experience of smuggling marijuana in Mexico. And then, my imprisonment. He gave me a patient hearing, but something about his expression said that he knew all those details long before I opened my mouth.

"Don't worry about that. I knew Henry. He was a bastard! You are going to be fine. I guarantee," he said, taking his feet up on the table.

"I need time to think. Please," I requested.

"Okay… as you please," he said.

That night I was put up in a motel not too far from Andrew's pub. I took a long dip in the bath tub. Lying naked in the bed, I thought about the terrible things I had witnessed after my return from India. My personal wrangles and health issues appeared too insignificant against the ghastly stories I had heard and seen.

I needed money to treat Bella. That was true. Perhaps the biggest truth of the hour. But could it justify the risk I would put myself into, smuggling hash from America to Holland? I had no answer. And yet, I knew if I could do the job, I'd earn enough money that would buy my daughter recovered health, perhaps a good life.

Having made up my mind, I went to meet Andrew next morning.

"Am ready!" I said, the moment our eyes met.

"That's my girl," he said patting my arm.

Two weeks later I flew to Amsterdam via Zurich. The only instruction that Andrew gave me was to dress like a tourist and behave like one. He bought me four sets of tourist-looking clothes, travel bags and snickers. A big hat and a gaudy handbag.

"Don't ever look panicky, whatever happens," he reminded for the hundredth time, dropping me at the airport.

The hashish was in my suitcase that surprisingly

went through all the procedures. I landed in Zurich, bought myself a small bottle of vodka from duty free shop, swigged it down in one shot. And then, waited at my terminal to board the next flight to Amsterdam. I retained a calm look, while my heart jumped like a marble ball on a glass floor.

I landed in Amsterdam and stood at the conveyer belt to collect my suitcase, when I noticed one man and two women marching towards me. Their walk was a straight spine march, I observed.

"Pick up your suitcase, put it in the cart and come with us," said one of the women in a hushed but confident tone.

I knew that I was caught. The world around me crumpled down before my blinking eyes.

Without creating a stir in the air, I went ahead with them and got inside a cab that was waiting outside the airport.

It so happened that a huge consignment of drugs was getting transported from America to Amsterdam. A team of ten people were carrying with them a stipulated amount, in red colored suitcases. That raised suspicion in the Airport authority people and in the process of checking those ten identical looking suitcases they decided to check all the suitcases that arrived by the same flight. My arrest was an accidental by-product of the search.

Police kept me in a small prison the first night. The following morning, they shifted me to an all- women's prison with a term of three months. The shock was so profound that the initial few days I did not know what to do. Whom should I speak to? Thursdays were especially painful, when all the other inmates had guests visiting them, I had none. Alone and silent, I suffered in the dark, unable to speak their language, unable to convey my emotions.

Then one Thursday, suddenly I had a visitor. I rushed to the gate and discovered Andrew, standing with a hat and a beard that made him look so different that it took me a while to recognize.

"You, alright?" he asked gently.

"See I told you," I said controlling my anger. "The thing is gone."

"That okay," he said sadly. I could see that the financial loss had impacted him more than I had anticipated. "Listen, Babes, they are going to keep you here, for three months, and then hand you over to the American Government. Most likely you will be taken to New York and shift you to another jail, till the time the case is put up and bail is granted. Don't worry about the bail money. I'll take care of it. You just keep your lips tight. Please."

I nodded my head, unable to speak, contemplating the length of time I'd be in prison. Of course, Andrew did not force the job on me, he had given me a choice; he had given me time to think. It was my decision. And yet, I felt a deep rage against him. My innards began to tremble, so much so that I blurted out, "Oh yea... keep your fucking advice to yourself!"

Andrew did not reply. Perhaps he understood my rage. Perhaps that was the moment he was looking forward to, to make his escape from my sight. I did not know. For, few seconds later, he was gone.

"You take care," he said and left.

I was thrown back to my solitude once again.

In prison, boundaries between yesterday, today and tomorrow blur into one indistinguishable whole. What people reckon as now, lasts and lasts, shrouded by memories, laden with regrets. The only job I was left back with, was to think, to recollect, to regret. And I thought, about Bella, about Anna, about Mama. About all the people I had met so far, crossed paths with, had helped, being helped by, married, made friendship with... the list was endless.

I realized that there are moments in one's life when one pauses, looks back, reflects; when one is forced to contemplate the path she had taken, to arrive where she has arrived. A path strewn with follies and errors; precious moments lost to vagaries. And yet, see to it that has made her what she is today. In a way, those errors have shaped her present, and perhaps, will shape her future too.

I too did the same. Had made mistakes, erred, hurt others... and in the process hurt myself a thousand times over, knowingly, and unknowingly. I too did things that made me shudder. But where exactly did I go wrong to deserve imprisonment? True, I needed money. But I needed it to save my daughter from death. Perhaps the mother in me was dominant when I had decided to deliver the consignment. The more I thought, the more confused I grew. The rigid demarcation between right and wrong got increasingly muddled up, pulling one into the domain of the other.

Thankfully, there were works in the prison that kept me busy and mind preoccupied. Or else, I could have lost my mind too. I cleaned garments for the entire floor. I did not know why, but cleaning garments, washing off the stains gave me a bizarre satisfaction. I felt as though I was washing off my own sins. The joy was indescribable. The effect delightful! During my free time, I made little handicraft products for sale.

Three months passed in an eerie silence. Eventually

one day, an officer came into my cell and announced that it was time to go. They brought me back to the airport; I boarded a flight and landed in New York. From there, I was taken into another flight that landed me in Austin, Texas. From the airport I was hand cuffed and taken to the county jail.

There, like hundred other seasoned criminals I was given an orange dress to wear. I stayed in that jail for a while, until Andrews gave the bail money and arranged a lawyer to fight my case.

The day I was released from prison, Andrew was there to receive me. We drove all the way back to San Jose in his car. It was a pleasant drive. But at the end of it, I was so exhausted that once I hit the bed, I slept for 48 hours straight, dead to the world, dead to everything between heaven and the earth, dead to the fact that I had to make a few urgent phone calls.

Two days later, finally when I woke up, for some time, I felt like having landed from another galaxy. It took me a while to regain my bearing.

I called Anna. An unknown lady informed me that she was no more. Anna had left her last breath two months ago.

I knew Anna wouldn't be there for long, and yet the news of her death rattled me more than I had anticipated. I tried to recollect what I was doing, when she had left her body. I remembered our last conversation to in painstaking detail. Back in my room, I lit a candle and said a prayer in her name. That was when I realized I hadn't told Anna how much I loved her. I prayed for her eternal release, if belatedly. That was the least I could do for my little sister.

Chapter 29

Calling Mama, I discovered that she was in that same state.

"No improvement," the house doctor lamented over phone.

I sighed and hung up, wondering where my other siblings were. Did they know about Mama, or Anna? Did they care at all?

When it was time to call Stephen, to inquire after Bella, my hands trembled, so much, that I ended up making two wrong numbers in the process.

"Hello," Stephen said.

Even after all the years that separated us, I felt a stir inside me.

"It's me," I said, feeling perspiration all over me.

"Ah… Sona. How have you been?"

"Am okay… good!" I lied. "How is Bella?" My heart beat so fast that for a moment I could not hear a thing.

"She is okay, the same," he said in a sad voice.

"Look I am sorry, I am still working for the money," I fumbled for a speech.

"That's okay. I understand. Things take time to happen. You are trying, that's important," he consoled.

"Does she understand?" I said and stopped.

Stephen fell silent, I got my answer.

"Anyway, it's all my doing… this hatred. I deserve no better. I can't ask for more," I said.

"She is suffering, Sona. If possible, forgive her," he pleaded. "She is still a child and does not understand much."

"I know… but."

Our conversation trailed off. In the end I did not tell Stephen that I had just come out of jail, knowing that the information would add no happiness to him.

I did not know why but I felt a desire to call Anand and speak. Hospitalization and then imprisonment had left within me a terrible loneliness that made me feel hollow from the inside.

Anand gave me an emergency contact number. I bought a calling card and dialed.

"Don't blame yourself for everything," Anand said, after hearing my side of the story. "There are things in your hand which you can do. And there are things that are beyond you. Learn to accept it," he opined. "But you should not have accepted that drug consignment."

"I need money Anand, and lots. So, I accepted it. Getting caught was my ill fate. Luck was not on my side," I argued feebly.

"That's nonsense," he spat. "You accepted it because

you wanted easy money, less labor more money. If that's the way you think you are going to earn, then jail is the obvious place you land up."

I fell silent, having nothing to say in my defense. For, it was true that I wanted easy money; less labor and more money. I wanted a quick bypass and not the long road. Perhaps it was the myopic desire of wanting everything easily and hastily, that had propelled me into the quicksand of trouble.

"Are you even realizing Sona, these repeated cases and imprisonments are putting you on the wrong side? You could be treated as a criminal for the rest of your life," Anand said, enraged.

Anand was thousands of miles away, yet I could feel anger in his voice. Rarely did Anand use harsh words in his speech or raise his voice against me.

"Am sorry Sona, I shouldn't have shouted at you," he said moments later.

"I liked it," I replied.

"Sona!"

"Yes?"

"Nothing."

"I am feeling so sad Anand… about everything," I burst into fresh tears.

"Sitting in your room and crying may be comforting, but it will not bring you happiness. If you want to be happy, work. And if possible, work for others. Make another soul happy, you will be happy forever."

That was the last thing he said before hanging up.

The next few days I kept on pondering what Anand

had said. For some reason his words and thoughts always left me thinking. There was something powerful about him that always overwhelmed me. Anand was a common man, yet I could feel he was an enlightened soul. He held within him a goodness that was beyond comprehension.

Andrew and I met a few times, at his pub mostly, where he kept on insisting that I join his pub and work. His lawyers were getting my papers ready. After everything that had happened, Andrew remained faithful to his words. Perhaps the slit on his face and his lost eye had taught him lessons of a life time. He could have taken his hands off the minute I got caught. Had he wanted, he could not have come all the way to Amsterdam to meet me. And yet, he did every little thing that was within his capacity to console me, to help me come out of the prison and eventually help me fight the case. That made him a friend.

"Work will keep your mind engaged," Andrew insisted.

I kept looking at my feet, wondering what to say. Anand insisted that I work, so that I could make another soul happy. But working in a pub and pouring beer into a drunkard's glass was certainly not a road to happiness.

"If you don't want to work full time, work for a few hours. At least that way you will keep yourself productive," Andrew negotiated.

"Okay," I budged after a long negotiation. "But will work from 8 to 12 in the evening, four hours a day, if that's okay for you."

"Perfect!" he said elated.

So once again I dived into the world of pubs and bars. It was while returning from the pub one evening, my eyes fell on a rest home at the crossing of Merritt St and

Blackie Road. On an impulse I entered. To my horror, I discovered there were about eighty old people living under its shelter. Nearly everybody had bedsore, a few appeared to be impervious to the pathetic situation they were in, most were emaciated and desperately needed care, and a handful appeared to be on the brink of death. I was beside myself at the sight.

"All they need is a dash of care and a lot of love," a lady whispered into my ears.

Her name was Kate Williams. She worked there, full time. Kate was twenty-two, daughter of a rich Newark based businessman. She was unusually fat for a woman her age. Kate had been a drug addict once and was in a rehabilitation center a couple of times. Once cured of the addiction, she entered into a bout of depression that ended up making her hopelessly suicidal. Kate said that her psychiatrist had told her to come to that place once a week. That was five years back. Kate had been coming there ever since, not missing a single day.

"I have discovered the purpose of my life," Kate added smiling, at the end of her story. There was a twinkle in her eyes and a smile on her lips that defied all metaphor.

I fell in love with her smile; I fell in love with her story. I fell in love with her.

Kate was young enough to be my daughter and had already discovered the purpose of her life. I marveled at the conviction with which she made that statement. The intent in her eyes was appealing, inspiring. And there was I, sitting next to her, nearly twice her age, but clueless about her life. I squirmed with guilt and ignorance. I squirmed at the purposeless demeanor of my life.

Promptly, I joined the home and began working from

morning till evening, until it was time to go to Andrew's pub and pour drinks to guests. That was of course to keep Andrew happy and earn myself a living. Real happiness came from the day job, where I toiled like a donkey at a salary that could not buy me two square meals a day.

Every morning, I changed sheets of all the eighty beds, and then gave bath to about twenty-five of the inmates, washed their sores with Betadine, combed their hair and brushed their teeth, clipped their nails when there was a need, feed the ones who could not get up from the bed, cleaned their pee and wiped their buttocks. In short did everything possible to ease their suffering, to make their life bearable.

"As you sow, so shall you reap," a wrinkly lady in her late eighties with a fractured femur bone and a dysfunctional retina said every day, while I gave her a sponge bath. She repeated it so many times that one day I asked her, "Why you say that every day?"

She smiled a toothless smile.

"Because all of it is my making," she whispered in a wobbly tone.

"I couldn't get you," I said, rubbing her fractured leg carefully. Her skin was freckled with black spots that made her look as if somebody had sprinkled ink on her.

She said her name was Agnes, and she was the daughter of a Nebraska farmer who bred and raised cattle. She used to take care of the cows ever since she was a child; feeding them and bathing them. But there was this one cow that always gave the best quality of milk but would kick Agnes every time she touched her udder. One day the kick landed straight on her right eye and she lost her vision. Doctor said that her retina got irreparably damaged. Being possessed by a severe rage at her unfortunate blindness, Agnes had ground glass and fed it to the cow. A day later the cow died. At that time Agnes had felt victorious, not realizing what she had done. She grew up into a young woman and then turned old. Years passed but the memory of her evil deed remained inside, like that ugly scar on her face. Like her dysfunctional retina.

"I am suffering because of that," Agnes lamented.

"You were a child then Agnes, too young to understand things," I consoled.

"I have taken a life," she added ruefully. "There is no greater sin."

I told Agnes that whatever had happened, was several decades ago, and that there was no point in remembering it now; she should take all those negative thoughts out of her mind. That was the only way she could relieve herself of the unreasonable burden she had been carrying inside.

"Easier said than done," Agnes observed.

"True, but for once, forgive yourself. It won't pain you anymore," I advised.

Agnes turned her head to the other side. She did not speak another word that day. I sensed that she wanted me to stop preaching. Quietly, I left her bed and attended another one.

Next morning, when I reached her bed to give her a bath, her bed was empty. Agnes was no more. She had died in her sleep. The lady next to her bed, Martha said that Agnes smiled and hummed a tune for a long time that night.

"Agnes was happy, I could tell, even though I had not seen her face in the dark," Martha said.

I patted Martha's head and smiled. It was intriguing that smile came up effortlessly, without me having to try. Perhaps that was what real happiness was all about; *making another soul happy,* as Anand had opined.

Martha was a patient of multiple sclerosis and was there forever, but very few treated her with kindness. I suspected people held her differently because of her dark skin. Martha's ancestors were from Grain Coast, West Africa, who were bought into the country. Her forefathers had first battled slavery, and then apartheid.

"Multiple sclerosis is like fighting against a cat, in comparison," Martha said proudly.

I kept looking at her beautiful dark eyes, incapable of comprehending the strength needed to make that proclamation. Martha was given high dosage of morphine every night, to make her fall asleep, so that she could be kept comfortably cushioned from pain. And yet, people said that she cried in her sleep, every single night.

"You are beautiful," I said.

"Not much of that beauty is left," Martha lamented. "But you have sad eyes," she observed.

"Is it?" I replied, surprised at her perceptive power.

"I am two times your age. You cannot hide anything from me."

I couldn't say a word. Not that I lacked speech, but against the incredible stories that she had told me about her family. My life and struggles seemed shallow in comparison.

"I have a friend. Her name is Lita Russel. Meet her once. I don't know where she is now, but her office used to be on 8th Street, on top of The Book Junction," she said slowly.

"Office, what kind?".

"You will know. Take my name," Martha said. "She is a wonder woman."

"Okay, will go, if you insist," I said.

That evening I skipped my work at the pub and went to meet Lita. Across the canvas of my life, if ever there had been an occasion when a soul, totally disparate and unrelated to me had shown me the real direction of my life, it was her.

I did not know what Martha read in my eyes that day, why she asked me to visit Lita, why she insisted with so much of conviction. And yet, I marched to The Book Junction that very evening. Perhaps that was what destiny was all about; unwittingly connecting with people who would bring out the magic.

By the time I reached Lita's chamber it was dark. She occupied a room on the second floor of The Book Junction. Her cabin was small, barely fitting two straight back chairs and a small table. Yet that was one of the most spectacularly creative places I had ever seen. The walls had shelves lined with hundreds of miniature shoes. Tiny shoes of all design and color one could imagine.

"Martha has sent me," I started.

"Ah Martha... how is she?" Lita asked softly. There was a big candle that glowed on the table next to her. That was the only source of light in the room.

Lita had an oval face with a skin as radiant as a translucent membrane. Her eyes were divine. She was wearing a white top and a wine-colored skirt. A pair of bright pearls adorned her ears.

"Not much of improvement," I said looking at her

walls, taking in the intriguing collection.

"That's my collection," she said reading my distracted look.

"Interesting!" I said admiringly. "But why shoes, if I may ask?" I added after a short while.

Lita laughed. There was something marvelous about her smile that instantly brought my attention from those tiny shoes to her face. Either it was the beauty of her pearly white teeth or the child like jingle in her laughter. Perhaps both.

"They are for all the tiny tots who had lost their lives," Lita said.

And I thought about the string of abortions I had done in my life.

"They are beautiful!"

"Now do as I say," she instructed.

Lita told me to sit straight and close my eyes and relax. I did. For some time, we kept quiet. I inhaled a faint fragrance of sandalwood. Was it from the candle? I wondered. Or did she spray something. Perhaps a room freshener. It was interesting that while I was talking to her, I did not notice the fragrance.

Then something strange happened. I could feel strong currents of energies in the room, all over me, rotating and revolving in crazed orbits. Unable to withhold my curiosity, I suddenly opened my eyes and discovered that Lita was sitting in front of me with her eyes closed, but there were lights all around her. She glowed from the inside with a unique brilliance. The glow was soothing, stunning.

"Close your eyes Sona," she said gently, without

opening her eyes.

I shut down my lids immediately, but then a quick thought crossed my mind. How did she know my name? I had not told her anything about me, so far. In fact, other than taking Martha's name, I had not said anything. Did Martha tell her that I'd come? But how?

"Don't keep your thought tap running," she instructed.

Quickly I tried to stop thinking. But it was impossible. A million and one thoughts fought for my attention.

"I can't," I blurted out after some time, feeling vulnerable.

"Try," she said.

I fell silent, this time trying my best to keep my mind on track.

"Am trying," I said.

"And now?" she said after a while.

The moment Lita said those two words, my mind went blank. For some time, I felt like floating in a sound proof darkness. I could not see, feel, hear, smell, or even touch anything. The rock-hard chair below my bottom and the ground below my feet suddenly evaporated. And yet, I was not scared. On the contrary I felt ripples of happiness all over me. I lost my grip on time. The experience went on and on.

"You may open your eyes now," she said after some time. How long, I had no idea.

I opened my eyes and looked at a wall clock on her rear. If memory did not betray me only ten minutes had passed. The light around her that I had seen earlier was gone.

She started speaking, very gently, in a voice that seemed different. For the next ten or perhaps twenty minutes she spoke without a break. My past, my present, my future! Some such details that were beyond my comprehension. And many more things that I did not even know existed. By the time I came out of her cabin, I felt dizzy with information and joy. It was new to me, something sublime.

That night, I had my first transcendental experience. Lying in my bed I looked outside the window, when suddenly a face appeared. The face was round and glowed with a brightness akin to the one that I had noticed in Lita. The face came bubbling through the window and stood near me. Looking at it I could not say whether it was a man or a woman. I kept looking at it with wonder in my eyes, trying my best to make sense of everything I was beholding. Then it revolved around me thrice and before I could blink next, it dissolved, making a crackling sound in the process.

I did not exactly remember falling asleep, or even losing my consciousness. But my next moment of total awareness was the following day. It was morning and I was lying in my bed, flat on my back. I could remember every detail of the previous night but I was no longer sure whether it was real or a dream.

I felt extremely weak, so much so that raising my head from the pillow seemed to be an effort. I lingered in my bed for some more time, anticipating a change, perhaps a surprising renewal of energy. Before too long I drifted into a sleep so deep that when I woke up next, it was well past noon, and I had missed my day at the home.

Unable to resist myself, I visited Lita again the following day. She was wearing those same pearl earrings with a black, knee length gown. Lita heard me patiently while I narrated her, my experience.

"Is the face a known one?" she asked when I stopped talking.

I pondered.

"Am unable to place," I confessed.

"That's okay. Don't be bothered about it."

Lita said that such experiences were natural and I shouldn't be touched by it. She predicted that I was to have many more experiences in the coming days.

"Experiences like?" I said looking worried.

"It's difficult to project them now, sitting in this room. But I sense, they would be of various types," she said.

"But why me?"

"Because you are more vulnerable, more sensitive than many. May be, due to your varied experiences. Perhaps the effect of drugs that you had taken, or due to alcohol," she predicted.

Lita again took me by surprise. For, I never really confessed to her that I had taken drugs. And yet, she spoke to me about it in a way as if she knew everything about me.

"And what I am supposed to do?" I asked.

"You need not do a thing. Just sit back and enjoy, the way you see cinema."

Lita did not divulge more but I suspected that she knew a lot more than she was willing to divulge. I too didn't pester her too much, fearing that it could annoy her.

That evening I returned to the pub and did not leave it until the next day. It was the Christmas of 1982 and the pub was unusually crowded.

The following morning, I came to the home when Martha asked, "You met her?"

"Oh yea," I said, but for some reason I was reluctant to reveal her my experiences.

"She's lovely, isn't it?" Martha said.

"Yes, she is."

"Have you seen those shoes?"

"Yes, interesting," I observed but cryptically.

"She told you about them?"

"Not exactly."

"It's for her lost children," Martha said looking at the ceiling.

"How so?" I asked, taken aback by her statement.

"All her children had died," she replied in a sad voice.

"How many?"

Martha said that Lita gave birth to a dozen children but not one survived. All her children had died after birth. Those numerous deaths had turned her into a living dead, until she became a psychic reader and a healer. Many said that she could see each of her child's spirit roaming around her, and hence she kept those shoes for them.

My eyes watered at her story. For a mother, there is nothing sadder than losing a child. I too had lost many, sometimes voluntarily, at times inadvertently. And yet I could not imagine her sorrow. That she was alive was nothing short of a miracle.

"How do you know her?" I asked.

"She has been my friend for a long, long time," Martha reminisced with nostalgia.

A week later, while I was sitting in the Alum Park,

I met a strange phenomenon. It was dark and there was no one in the vicinity. Suddenly a large herd of bats came from nowhere and flapped their wings over my head. They made strange hooting sounds that chilled my spine. I was so overcome by terror that momentarily I lost my mind, got up from the place and started running with all the energy I could muster. In an effort to escape from the place hastily, I did not even turn and look back.

By the time I returned to my studio apartment, I was drenched with perspiration, from head to toe. There was a crushing pain in my chest. I was out of breath. I dropped in the bed with a thud and lost my consciousness.

That night I had my first heart attack. I did not realize it for a long time that the strange sensation in my chest that kept me writhing in pain, was not due to that I had experienced in the park. Neither was it due to the long run I had taken at insane speed. It was due to a series of small but significant attacks that my heart had nudged through. I had survived, without having any notion, how I did.

Chapter 30

Martha died a month later, on the first week of February, 1983. That entire week I did not visit the home, because of my ill health. My heart was beating abnormally fast, and my blood pressure was jumping up and down to the point of throwing me into unconscious spells, a greater number of times. Doctor advised me to rest, and I rested. By the time I returned to the job, Martha was no more.

In my career as a caregiver in that home, I had spoken to her only a couple of times. Yet hearing about her death made me sad, so much that I could not work for the rest of the day. It was difficult for me to look at the empty bed.

I returned to my apartment and cried, as though I had lost a friend. I contemplated visiting Lita and informing her about the death but could not gather the strength to do so. When tears dried up, I fell into a deep sleep. The following day when I visited the home again, I discovered a strange sight.

A new lady occupied Martha's bed. She was not aged but strangely wrinkled, to the extent of looking astonishingly old. Her expression was vacant; her eyes were stiff, like a pair of brown pebbles.

"Her name is Cindy," Kate pointed. "Drug abuse!"

The name fell into my ears like a thunderclap; I ran towards her bed. Yes, she was Cindy, my long-lost sister, but so pathetically transformed that her face was practically beyond recognition. Last time I had met her at Mama's place, when Cindy was a girl of 14. I tried to remember the year but couldn't. I tried to remember how she looked back then. That, I could do with some effort.

Kate said that Cindy was found on a footpath in San Jose, near the 10th Street and E Taylor Street crossing; in rags and totally out of her senses. The house doctor had suspected that she was a typical case of long-standing drug abuse.

"Chances of recovery?" I asked impulsively, taking in the information.

Cindy was a devastating sight! Yet I found it difficult to take my eyes off her face.

Kate shook her head with an upturned curve of her lips. I got my answer.

Cindy was nearly thirty, emaciated to the point of being skin and bones. Her face was speckled, the facial skin was calcified (an effect of uncontrolled heroine intake, I knew) and her hair was frizzed like a thin bunch of unruly mops. Cindy could speak but her speech was slurry, as though she had swigged down bottles. Not one word came out of her tongue straight. She couldn't recognize me. I was beside myself with grief.

I touched the crown of her head; her frail body shook violently, then she turned motionless. She looked at me with a dramatic frown. But her gaze lacked recognition.

"You haven't forgotten my touch!" I said gently, putting in a sincere effort to smile.

Cindy looked into my eyes. She smiled. But her smile was joyless.

"You...?" her voice trailed off.

"Sona," I said.

She did not talk further, only kept looking at my face, until she fell asleep.

Looking at her, taking care of her I wondered where Larry was. Although Larry was older, but he and Cindy had been inseparable, once. Did she know about Anna? And Mama? It was difficult to gauge.

Over a period, Cindy's condition improved, so to say, she could speak a little, but her hands and feet were still non-functional. Drugs impaired her CNS so much that it was a task to make her sit straight. It was impossible to estimate the degree of her recovery.

"I want to take her home," I told Kate one afternoon, while having lunch.

"Honestly speaking, I don't think it's a great idea," Kate opined.

"She is my sister, Kate, I can't let her die here, like a destitute," I argued.

"Look, I understand your sentiments, but here, she is under constant supervision. Once you take her home, she will be alone. And these people could be dangerous when left alone," she added sensibly.

"But look at her, she cannot turn her back without help, how would she get drugs? She can't even speak decently. I am her sister, I am having problem understanding her," I argued.

"Just think about it! If you ask me, she is good here.

You will come and see her every day. You are taking care of her anyway."

Perhaps Kate was right, her arguments rational. Her years of dealing with derelicts had left in her a solid experience. But the sudden outburst of emotion took better control of me, disregarding the obvious fact that I still needed money to pay for Bella's surgeries. I had a serious drug smuggling case on my head for which Andrew's lawyers were still fighting. I needed time to settle myself in America again, after years of travelling like a nomad.

The result was a terrible blunder. I brought Cindy home underestimating her caliber. She was incapable of moving a thread, how the hell would she procure drugs? Plus, she did not have a penny. I kept on reminding and comforting myself, while Cindy continued taking drugs beyond my knowledge.

Bringing Cindy home brought me another box full of shocking stories. I listened to them, with astonished eyes and rasping pants. Her speech grew well well enough to make sense of what she was trying to convey.

Cindy said when she was about 18, Rumi, her boyfriend introduced her to the world of drugs. She left home with Rumi and shifted to Los Angeles, where both lived in a rented apartment for some time. Rumi was a small-time peddler and Cindy became a part time hooker; just to earn enough money to buy her drugs.

"I'd go from one car to the next, and when there would be enough money, I'd stop seeing customer and do drugs."

The year was 1976, she recounted. I wondered where I was around that time. India? Nepal? Paris?

Life like that continued for some time, until police

arrested Rumi and Cindy was left alone to make for her living. It was thus, her downfall began, of health and emotion, of life. When she could no longer pay for her rent, she was thrown out of the apartment. Drugs by then had dissipated her faculties so much that prostitution was no longer an avenue for survival.

"I met Larry once," Cindy reminisced looking outside the window.

I was uncertain if she was telling the truth or cooking up some kind of story.

"Where?"

"In jail," she replied.

"You went to jail?"

"I went to meet Rumi, and he said Larry was there."

"And?"

"Larry was convicted of murder. I met him a few times after that," she said.

"And Mama? You were in touch with her?" I asked, feigning innocence.

"Don't talk about her!" Cindy barked. "You know what she is? A bitch … a fucking bitch ..."

Perhaps there was no reason to solicit for Mama, knowing the kind of life she had lived, and forced us to live. But a part of me felt sad for her; and sadder for Cindy, for saying that. Realizing the brutal fact that what Cindy said was true. I wondered if Bella would say the same about me; think of me the way Cindy now thought, because my life as a mother was not too different from the mother we shared.

"She is a mother too," I argued feebly.

"Mother, my fucking ass!" Cindy exclaimed heatedly. "All her children were products of her violent sex."

Something in her attitude told me that perhaps Cindy still did not recognize me. And my doubt got clarified with her next question.

"But who are you? Why are you trying to defend my mother?"

I sighed.

"I am Sona, you remember, your elder sister, the oldest one.

Cindy thought for a while.

"Yes, I remember," she said smiling faintly.

But I could say that my existence had been wiped out of her mind. Not only mine, but Anna's, Nina's and Lola's too, for, she never spoke a word about them. The only name that surfaced time and again was Larry.

I explained to Cindy that it was easy to judge Mama, but she was a woman too, with her own desires and longings. And that, as a child it would be convenient to judge parents and dig out mistakes in them.

Still, what Cindy said, argued, was right, and bang on the spot. She had a point. Because my experience with Mama was not too different from hers. I too was convinced that it was her folly that had dragged us from one hole of misery to the next. And that, it was entirely her callousness that at an age of ten, I was sexually abused; first by my own father, and then, by my stepfather. As a child, or even as a young adult, my only complaint against Mama was exactly the same.

Yet, I did not know why when Cindy accused Mama,

I had an impulse to defend her and not join Cindy in the allegation. Perhaps the mother in me was defending the woman in Mama. Or the woman in me was defending the mother in Mama. Maybe, in the very act of defending Mama, I was, in my own way, legitimizing my follies that weren't too removed from that of Mama's. Had Bella been there, she might have said that same, if not more, derogatory things.

"You can say all these because you are good," Cindy said hoarsely.

"I can say all these, because I am a mother," I replied calmly, at the same time wondering, *am I?*

Cindy did not appear to hear. And even if she did, she chose not to reply. She fell back into an eerie silence from which she never recovered.

Two days later, one night I returned from the pub to discover her lifeless body in the bath tub. She was lying there, naked, with her legs parted into a 'V'. Her left hand was on her groin. There was foam in her mouth. Post mortem report said Cindy died of drug overdose.

I had no idea from where those drugs came, who bought it for her, or from where she got the money. I did not know when she took it, just the way I was oblivious to her existence all those years.

Cindy came to my home, stayed for a while and then, not too long after, she died, leaving within me a vacuum that sucked up every bit of my energy. For days after her death, I remained motionless in my bed, overcome by a melancholy that was unspeakably sad.

A month later, I had a heart attack and was shifted to a hospital.

Chapter 31

When I opened my eyes, I discovered myself lying in a steely hospital room, tethered to all kinds of instruments. Stephen and Bella were there.

"Thank God you are okay," Stephen said coming closer.

I smiled, feeling too weak to speak. Bella seemed unperturbed. She remained seated, chewing her bubble gum in a way as if she had come for a movie show. She was wearing a dress so short, that I could see her sky blue under garment.

"How are you?" I asked feebly, looking at Bella.

She did not reply.

"See I told you. She just wants attention," Bella said coldly to Stephen and left.

"Ignore her," Stephen said, putting on his best consoling face.

"It's all my making," I replied, smiling sarcastically, remembering Cindy.

"Just relax." Stephen patted on my head.

"Who told you about me?" I asked.

"A lady named Kate. I gather she is your friend," Stephen said.

"Yes, she is," I said feeling thankful.

"Doctor says your breathing is uneven," he said.

"Why am I even alive?" I said in a remorseful tone.

"That is not for us to decide!"

Stephen said that Bella's condition deteriorated in the past few months. That was the reason behind her sour behavior. She was having troubled vision and her diet had been reduced to basics. Bella was unable to digest food. And my already broken heart broke down to a few more pieces.

"I am sorry, I could not arrange funds," I said on the verge of tears.

"That's okay Sona, don't think about it too much. Will make some arrangement," he consoled.

I wondered if his consolation was genuine, or if that was solely meant to comfort me.

"Why don't you stay with us for a while," Stephen proposed after some time.

"Let me think," I said. "Thank you but..."

Stephen smiled.

"I understand we are no longer husband and wife, but we are still parents," he added.

"But Bella?" I asked uncertainly.

"She will learn to understand," he said. "Leave it to me."

A week after my release from the hospital I travelled to Maine to stay with Bella and Stephen. Bella was visibly upset and Stephen was genuinely pleased.

I was allotted the guest room with Bella's room on my right and Stephen's room on my left. The strangeness of living once again with him was so unsettling that it took me a while to adjust myself in the new settings. Thanks to the pills I had to gulp in dozens, that made me doze off around eight in the evening.

Living with Bella was quite a feat, and I realized it immediately, right from the first moment. She was an adult now and quite beyond my reach. It was too late to make a beginning. She hated me with her entire being and it was all too obvious. Bella lacked pretention. More often than necessary, she reminded me what a poor mother I was, and that I was never there for her when she needed me. I nodded, accepted her charges, knowing the truth hidden in her remarks.

"You are a pathetic mother," Bella spat.

"Maybe I am, but you must also realize the first seven... no eight years of your life I was there with you," I argued but gently.

"See, there you are! You do not even know how many years you spent with me," she mocked.

I fell silent, unable to find a response.

"You drop from the sky one day, suddenly and say you are getting money for my surgery. You don't even do that. You vanish for months... only to appear again with this new drama... heart attack. Ha ha ha... I find all of it a fucking joke," Bella barked.

"I am sorry Bella, having failed you," I said trying to touch her hand.

"Don't touch me, you whore..." she blurted and left the house, shutting the door with a loud thud.

You whore rang in my ears for some time, before I could regain normalcy.

That evening I realized for the first time, the length, breadth and depth of the damage that I had done. I understood and not without regret that I had lost Bella, perhaps, forever. After what she had said, it was clear whatever I'd say in my defense would only add insult to injury. I could not win her back even if I invest the rest of my life.

I got up from the seat, went into my room, and cried. In the futile effort of discovering freedom for myself, and happiness for my spirit, I had deprived myself the most basic emotions of all; love. I felt poorest of the poor, a hundred thousand times more indigent than the destitutes I had once cared for.

"Open the door, Sona, please!"

It was Stephen, knocking on my door. Although he spoke loudly but his voice lacked cheer. For some reason I felt sad for him, having to endure that bottomless misery, alone for all those years.

I opened the door, fell upon his shoulder and cried; heard a few of his sniffles too. More than what Bella had said, perhaps, it was the crushing fear of losing her, and our collective inability to do anything about it.

Bella did not return home that night.

"She is at Vivian's place. I know," Stephen said. "Vivian is marrying this fall. May be Bella is thinking..."

Quickly I put my palm on his lips.

"Bella is going to live long," I said.

Three days later Bella returned, with high fever, crimson eyes and a pair of infected feet. She was delirious and cried out in the middle of her sleep. But every time I wanted to touch her body; she shoved my hand with an unkind gruff. Even in moments of unconsciousness, she resented me.

"I don't see a reason why I should be here," I told Stephen one evening, after dinner.

"I don't see a reason why you should leave," he replied.

I looked into his eyes, mindfully absorbed those words of desperate wanting. Stephen wanted me to linger there for some more time. Loneliness was making him despondent. Stephen was craving for company. Perhaps it was the need of his age, where a woman by his side would fill him with emotional comfort. He wanted me to give time to Bella so that our relationship improved. His anxiety over the uncertainty of my future was genuine, for, during my stay he asked me a hundred times, what I had been doing all those years, alone and unprotected, without a steady income or a partner.

"I'll return only when I have money," I said.

"But how will you get it? Who will give you?" Stephen asked looking worried.

"I don't have all the answers right now. But I will find a way," I replied.

"Don't do anything stupid," he said, trying to make a funny face that somehow did not suit him.

"I will not," I said averting his eyes.

Stephen fell silent, but there was sadness in his eyes. Perhaps there was fear too, fear of losing me yet another time.

"I have not been a good mother, I understand. I accept it. Okay, I have had relationships with men, have slept with them. But I cannot accept that she calls me a *whore*. This is the only way I could buy her back, by curing her. This is the only way I could mend our relationship. Please give me a chance." I said and left the room.

That night I decided what I'd do next. But I said none of it to Stephen. I left Maine the following day leaving behind a note for Bella.

"When she is gets better, give her this," I handed the sealed envelope to Stephen.

Stephen drove me to the bus terminus in melancholic silence. The ride brought into my mind one more journey like that, years ago, when our children were sitting in the back seat, and I was about to embark on a journey alone, eager and frantic to live my life my way, to set out into the world, free. Had I known that day, the terrible price I would pay against that momentary breath of freedom, I would have reconsidered my choice.

"Call me from time to time, wherever you are," Stephen said moments before I was to board.

"Take care of Bella..." I said, and then, "and yourself."

Stephen smiled: his eyes glistened with unshed tears.

I turned my back, not wanting to look at him. I was sure he was looking at me with deep longing. Did Stephen change over the years, or I did? What was it that I now saw in him, which I couldn't see earlier? They say, *if you love a soul set it free*. Did Stephen love me so much as to set me free? Or in the very act of giving me freedom he secured his own freedom too; freedom to do whatever he pleased.

I kept on wondering, as the bus glided out of the terminus.

Love is an illusion of the moment. It expires once the moment deceases.

I dug out a little diary from my hand bag and wrote those two lines.

Perhaps that was the truth of the moment, my truth of the moment. Because, as the bus moved away, those thoughts too receded from my mind. So much so that after a while I was no longer thinking about Stephen and his uncertain, perhaps expired love. I was apprehensive of the future, eager to embrace my new mission, ready to jump into the world of crime that I was certain would bring me quick cash to rescue Bella from her terrible illness.

Dear Isabella,

By the time you read this letter, I will be gone, a hundred thousand miles away from you. I know what you must be thinking: what's new? I don't blame you Bella, for the hatred I have noticed in your eyes. It's all my doing and not yours, am aware. I am the one who is guilty and not you. Never you!

I may be away from your world but know that you are never removed from mine. I carry your image with me, within me, wherever I go.

It gives me tremendous joy in saying that in you I see a faint reflection of myself, the exact woman I had been, when I was your age. That same attitude, same loveliness, those same eyes… that same anger on mother. I admit, I had often judged my mother for the kind of woman she was, the kind of life she had lived and forced us to live. I had once held her guilty for follies that could not be called follies.

I am a mother now, has been ever since you were born. Much before that (You have an elder brother, Harrison, but will talk about him another time). I know what it takes to be a mother, and I judge her no more. I see her with kindness, if belatedly, I see her as another woman, like you and I, full of vices but also, full of love.

Today you are a woman, Bella. One day you will become a mother, which I pray you do. Perhaps that day you will understand me a lot better and judge me no more. Perhaps that day you will love me as a daughter must.

I wish you good health, happiness and loads of love.

Your mother,

Sona.

Chapter 32

"I need money," I pleaded to Andrew, a day after I joined the pub.

"Are you sure?" Andrew asked, looking carefully at me.

I nodded.

"What's the matter Sona?" he asked gently, taking in my hassled look.

"I am in desperate need of money. I cannot see Bella dying," I said on the verge of tears.

"Okay! I understand," Andrew pondered. "Are you sure, you want to do it again?"

"I don't have a choice," I said helplessly.

"Are you sure?" he repeated.

I nodded. "But I want more money this time," I added with urgency.

Andrew agreed. "You will get whatever you want!"

And we began to prepare. To Ginza, Tokyo, this time.

"Why Japan?" I asked. "I don't know the language," I said.

"Because Americans don't need a visa there. Plus, you are going there as a tourist. An American tourist in Japan, this time of the year is a perfect thing," Andrew rationalized.

I was convinced. The desperation in me was so ardent that had Andrew asked me to go to Mexico again, I would have dived headlong.

The following week I travelled to Japan with 10 pounds of hashish. I was nervous almost to the point of a fresh heart attack. Tokyo airport was cold, yet I perspired continuously.

"You are, okay?" a fellow traveler observed, standing beside me in the baggage counter.

"Am okay," I replied, averting her eyes.

"I am Eveline," she said, extending her hand. "First time in Japan?"

I nodded. "I am Eva... Eva Gardner," I lied.

Eveline smiled. "You have a pretty face."

Perhaps Eveline was casually chatting with me, the good-natured conversation one stranger had with another in a foreign country. But I began to grow tensed and annoyed at her unwarranted probing. And to move away from her as quick as I could, I picked up a wrong suitcase and proceeded towards the customs. The gentleman at the customs granted me a clean entry.

I smiled, first at him, then to myself. It was not until I reached the hotel that I realized the blunder I had made. After a shower when I wanted to get myself into a fresh set of clothes, I discovered to my horror that the suitcase was not mine, and the keys won't work. Getting into the old set of clothes, I rushed to the main desk and told them about the mishap.

It took me nearly thirty more minutes to reach the airport gate where a gentleman was supposed to be standing with my suitcase. And there he was, standing erect in a navy suit and a hat. He introduced himself as Martin Russell. As I stood there, shaking hands with him, I thought of another Martin I had interacted with, ages ago.

I had absolutely no idea how Martin escaped from customs, and neither did I have the courage to ask. I thanked him and then got inside the taxi that was waiting for me. In my desperate attempt to escape from the sight, I did not even offer Martin a ride.

I returned to the hotel, took another shower, got into a fresh set of clothes, made a phone call to a nameless person and delivered the consignment.

I had to remain in Japan for three more days, to justify my travel as a tourist. The following two days I roamed around the beautiful city, did little bit of sight-seeing, ate loads of sushi and drank *sake*, all the while worrying about the money that was in my room unattended. Remembering what Stephen had told me, I called him.

"That same," he replied, when I asked after Bella. "How are you?"

"I am good," I said, wondering if I should tell him I was calling from Japan.

"Where are you calling from?" he asked.

I cut the line without replying. I couldn't tell him the truth, and it would be a terrible injustice, if I lied. It was wise to shut my mouth and evaporate from the scene. He was more used to that attitude of mine; I rationalized standing in the telephone booth.

A few days later I returned to America. Andrew picked me up from the airport. He gave me my commission immediately. I transferred the money to Stephen without delay, and then, a day later called him again.

"How did you get the money?" he asked.

"I got it. Don't bother," I replied.

"Of course, I will be bothered Sona... you are my..." he fell silent.

"Do it immediately," I said referring to Bella.

"I will, but will you not come?"

"It's better if I stay away," I said remembering all Bella had said to me, the last time.

"But you are paying for it," he protested.

"Tell her you arranged it," I said.

"If she asks how?"

"Then tell her you sold some property, something..."

"That would be a lie," he said.

"Not bigger than my life."

I said and hung up.

Returning to the pub, I thanked Andrew for giving me the opportunity to earn the money.

"Anytime," he replied good-naturedly.

A day later I returned home with the intention of resuming my job but found it difficult to move my feet after a couple of hours of working. Perhaps my heart was getting weaker; or my increasing age was wearing me down; or perhaps the overwhelming experiences I was having, one after the other, was burning me down from inside. Not too long after that I decided to quit.

"Will miss you," Kate said hugging me.

"You are doing a great job," I said.

"I have taken in more," she said looking at the rows of beds occupied by ailing souls.

"Yes," I nodded. "There isn't a better place."

"What did you learn from them?" Kate asked.

"Value of life!" I said and walked out.

I never returned to that home again, but the memories resided within me. That place was like a rest house, where travelers rambled in, and then, after a while, drifted out. Kate was perhaps the only one who lingered, until she was diagnosed with brain cancer and forced to quit.

We exchanged letters for some time, when Kate informed me about her disease. I was appalled. Yet, I could read no sadness in her, for suffering such a life-threatening disease. Kate was about to die and she knew it, accepted the inevitable, the way she might have accepted her doom. Kate battled for a few years, bravely, like a warrior, and then, one day her letters stopped coming. I sensed she was gone.

I went to meet Lita after I recovered from a prolonged bout of influenza. The thought came to me abruptly, one evening, while I was sipping coffee. It was as if an irresistible force tugged at my feet to visit her. An hour later, I discovered myself sitting in front of her, in that room with beautiful shoes.

"Have you heard of Cassadaga?" Lita asked.

That voice again! I felt ripples of peace all around me. I shook my head.

"That's where you should be," she said.

"What's there?"

"Go and find out."

Located in Volusia County, Florida, Cassadaga is the psychic capital of the world. It's a small spiritual town where people visited for card and psychic readings.

I took off from Andrew's pub and visited Cassadaga, intending to be there for a week. I stayed there for the next three years of my life.

Chapter 33

Cassadaga was good and meaningful, but only for a while. Soon I got bored with the dreary monotony. Similar kind of settings wearied me down. Perhaps it was in my genes, that routine and predictability did not go down well with me. I liked to live my life on the edge, even if that meant one meal a day, and rock-hard wooden bench to sleep on. Even if that meant not knowing from which end the next sun would rise from. It wouldn't be a terrible lie if I said I thrived on the pleasure of that perpetual shuffle of my surroundings, the ever-changing demeanor of the walls and ceiling that encompassed me. Forever was a word that did not exist in my dictionary. Somehow, it did not fit inside my orbit. It was nothing forever; whether it was maintaining a relation, or a profession, or staying in a city, or following a passion. I hopped and skipped and jumped from one destination to the next, from one man to another, from one profession to a new one, at such a ridiculous pace that one might have considered me imbalanced.

"Don't you get bored seeing the same things again and again?" I had asked Anand once.

He laughed; the one that gave his face an instant rebate on his age.

"Life is about seeing the same thing with new eyes," Anand had philosophized. "Observing the slow and steady change in yourself. Being a new you!"

I thought about it now, sitting inside my room, sipping wine. Anand had a point I could not disregard. Anand talked less, but every little word he said, made sense. Yet his maturity and wisdom were lost on me.

After staying in Cassadaga for nearly three years, I finally called it a quit.

It was somewhere in the middle of my last week in Cassadaga, one day, Anand called me.

"Is everything okay?" I said feeling pleasantly surprised at his unexpected call.

"Can't I call you?" he replied. "Happy New Year!"

"Of course, you can. But…"

"Couldn't sleep last night, remembering you," he said.

"That's nice," I said happily.

"What's nice?"

"Remembering me," I said, blushing.

"When are you coming to India again?"

"I don't know."

"Make a trip, if possible."

Having said that, Anand hung up. I kept on pondering on what he said. His longing seemed genuine, sincere. Was he insisting that I visit him? It had been more than a decade since we met.

Promptly I booked my ticket to India. The day I boarded the flight from Florida, I was uncertain of the purpose of my visit. Even when I landed in Bombay airport and took a cab to Pune, I was unaware of the real reason behind my impulsive visit.

18th January, 1990 was the day when I finally reached Pune and then to Anand's residence. He was beside himself with joy. He embraced me and did not let me slip out of his grasp for a long time. Standing there, in the warmth of his embrace I felt as though I had returned home. I was somewhat convinced of the purpose of my visit.

However, the reason revealed itself the following day, when Anand informed me that Osho had left his body. Tears streamed down my face at the news. I couldn't speak to him for a long while.

Anand and I went to the ashram in Koregaon Park, where his body was kept for a short time. Subsequently his body was taken to the burning ghat on Lane E. When it was time to touch the pyre with fire, I felt a chocking sensation in my throat. Perhaps it was because of the thick crowd that surrounded me, crushing me from all the sides. Or the deluge of thoughts and emotions that overwhelmed me from inside. I did not know. What I knew, was I did not linger there for long. I saw fire catching the pyre, and then I turned my back and started walking. Anand followed me.

We returned home walking, all the way from Koregaon Park. It took us nearly two and a half hours to reach home. We did not speak to each other the entire journey.

Anand showered and got some *pav bhaji* from outside. A peculiar hunger took charge of me. I ate and ate, as if I was hungry since the last century.

After dinner, Anand made his bed on the floor and fell asleep. I remained awake for some time, sitting next to the window observing the gentle night sky.

When I could sit no longer, I got up, and kissed Anand on his lips. He woke up with a start but did not stop me. He surrendered to my touch. He surrendered to me!

That night, for the first time, we made love. And yet, making love to Anand was ironic. He entered my body after all the vital feminine parts were removed. He entered my body, when I no longer looked at men through the lens of carnality. He entered my body, when nothing but a vacant shell remained of me.

"What was that?" Anand asked after some time.

"Love," I replied.

"Is it?"

"Perhaps," I said in a hushed tone, wondering, *was it*?

"Whatever it was, it was terrific," Anand complimented in an exhilarated tone that revealed his deep contentment.

I fell silent, not willing to take the conversation further. Not that I lacked a speech, but that I was happy with the here and now. I was happy with the newly discovered ecstasy that overwhelmed me. I was not too keen to look beyond the visible fringes of time.

Anand fell into a deep sleep. I kept looking at his reposed face in the shallow darkness of his modest room. He rested his hand gently on my bare belly, perhaps not wanting to lose the warmth of my touch. I did not know what was on his mind. Perhaps he was dreaming of a future with me. Perhaps not. Perhaps like me, he too was happy with the present, not desiring to complicate our relationship by getting into the complex web of matrimony.

"That was the most beautiful night I ever had," Anand said, first thing next morning.

I smiled with my eyes closed; not wishing to open them for the fear of breaking the delicious spell I was in.

"How did you manage visa in such a short time?" Anand asked, few days later.

I dug out that fake certificate from my purse and wagged it. "This."

"I can't believe this Sona," he said looking shocked. "And what did you say?"

"I said my husband is in India. And he is not well. I want to visit him," I replied sheepishly.

Anand laughed.

"My God! You are one woman," he observed.

"How am I supposed to take it?" I said defensively.

"I admire your wit Sona, but you should not have lied," Anand philosophized.

"Had I not lied, I wouldn't have been granted an entry," I said heatedly.

"Aha... nothing like that."

"Yes, it is. Many are red listed, and aren't allowed to get in. I know about all these, hence did not take a chance. Plus, when I have an alternate, why not use it for the right purpose?" I argued.

Anand stopped and did not probe further. Whatever he said that evening, either in my offence or defense, I was sure of one thing. That, Anand was happy I was there with him, in his house.

I stayed with him for about a month, and then returned to America. For the first time, I noticed tears in his eyes, as he came to see me off.

"Will wait for another surprise," he said with a long face.

"Good bye," I said and turned my back, not wanting to show him the stream of tears that now ran down my face.

Returning from India, I went to Biddeford again, to visit Stephen and Bella.

Bella had recovered and appeared healthier. I could see she had sobered down, significantly. She came with Stephen to receive me from the bus depot.

"Are you considering my proposition?" Stephen asked me that night.

"Which one?"

"Of staying here," he hinted and then paused, "forever."

I thought for a while. Saying *no* right on his face seemed blunt, after all he had done for Bella, after all he was still doing, to accommodate me in his house. And yet, saying *yes* would be a cruel lie; given I was not actually considering him.

"I need time," I said at long last.

Stephen smiled.

"Bella has changed," I observed.

He nodded. "I gave her your letter."

"Is it?"

"Yes, but after the surgery."

"How did you know I would send the money?" I asked, surprised at his confidence.

"I knew," he shrugged his shoulders.

I observed him, taking in his changed look. Stephen had aged a lot, perhaps more than his due. And yet one could see that once he had been a handsome man; a possessor of beauty. Had I continued my relationship with him, perhaps my life would have been smooth sailing, if not a totally happy one, I pondered.

"Bill is coming with his family, here, for a day," Stephen said.

"That's nice," I said, wondering what he and his wife would make of me.

"Bella had told him you arranged the money for her surgery," he said.

"And you told her?" I said raising my brows, remembering my phone call, clearly instructing him not to tell her.

"Of course, I had to. There are things both our children had seen when they were little. Now both have grown up. There are things they should know, understand. They like it or not, appreciate it or not, I don't care. I can make no pretense of it," he added heatedly.

"Thank you," I said feeling a ball of phlegm in my throat.

"But from where did you get all that money?" he asked, looking intently into my eyes.

"Let it be with me," I pleaded.

"Let's hope you haven't done anything you shouldn't do," he reminded.

"I am eager to meet Bill," I said, quickly drifting from the topic.

Bill's name brought into my mind, thoughts of

Harrison. I wondered where he was. What he could be doing, professionally? He was the one who made me a mother, for the first time. Now, we were two galaxies apart. I wondered what Galvin had told him. Did Harrison remember me at all?

Two days later Bill arrived with his wife Nichole. Bill was a faint reflection of Stephen when the later was young; uptight with strong manners and less of a smile. His eyes sparkled with brilliance. Nichole had a face that was immediately appealing.

"I heard you read cards?" Nichole said, with a sweet smile and a small frown.

Heard from whom, I wondered, *Bill, Stephen, Bella?*

"At times I do," I nodded with a thin smile.

"Can you really see the future? That way?" she persisted.

I noticed that Bill was observing us from the dining table, sipping his beer. He had not spoken to me ever since he came. It was Nichole, who was doing all the talking.

"Not entirely," I confessed, "but certain aspects, we can see and predict."

"Can you read for me?" Nichole requested.

"What you want to know?" I asked.

Nichole thought for a moment, pursing her thin lips. I could say that she was considering something, something grave. There was a small frown on her forehead. Quickly, she looked at Bill, as if to seek his permission. Bill nodded, slightly, making effort to keep the gesture as subtle, as possible.

"I want to know when I will have children," Nichole

said at last, peering into my eyes. There was honesty in her looks, in her way of saying what she lacked, perhaps wanted.

I heard what Nichole said, took in her expectant look, and then, fell mum.

Nichole said she loved children and desperately wanted to become a mother. But she was unable to conceive. I felt sad at her inability.

"When its time, you will," I consoled.

"When will be the time?" she added immediately, eagerly. "Could you please tell me?"

I declined, politely. I told her that I never read for my children. It would be difficult for me to predict hard truths, even harder, to see something ugly and not speak. Nichole was disappointed.

"But that's the challenge Sona, to read for a person keeping your emotions away," she argued.

"You are a physician, right? Can you operate on him?" I said pointing Bill, without turning my head.

Nichole looked at him; she smiled and then turned her head and replied, "I think I could do."

"And what if, you have a child, someday. Could you do the same?" I asked.

Nichole thought for a while, looking at her beautiful feet.

"I think I would do," she said, "You see Sona, I have been trained to look at things objectively, and not emotionally, when I am in the OT. I have operated on people who are my friends," she justified.

"In that case I must say you are a brave heart!" I complimented.

"Am I? Braveheart or not, I don't know, a professional for sure," she said gleefully.

I liked Nichole. Something about her appealed to me. During the process of conversation, she told me about her life. Her estranged parents, her long dead sister, her years of delusion and wandering, her meeting Bill and falling in love, their marriage... everything! I admired the honesty in her bearing. The candid way she spoke about her parent's wrangles and their eventual parting in the bitterest way imaginable.

Although she was a child to me, I was beginning to feel small in her presence. Had she asked me where the money came from, for Bella's surgery, would I have told her as honestly? I wondered. I doubted.

That night I reflected on what Nichole had said. *Can you really see the future?* She had asked me more than once, perhaps convinced that it was difficult to see the future. And yet, I had seen people's future, often predicted details with shocking accuracy. What had propelled me to make those prophecies I still didn't know. What I saw in a person's face, how I could read their cards, what I felt in those moments when I concentrated with my entire mind, nobody knew.

Many opined it was drugs that spoke through my lips; many said it was the alcohol. And yet, every time I read cards, I felt strangely detached from everything that I reckoned to be me. Even there were times when I discovered myself hanging from the ceiling, when my physical body sat in front of my clients. To an outsider it might appear meaningless, but nobody knew the truth but me.

"You turned out good," I told Bill, the following morning, moments before their departure.

Bill nodded, he smiled. Yet I could see that his smile was superficial. It lacked glee.

"I am sorry," I added, when moments drifted and he did not reply. "I fell short."

"It's okay Mama," Bill said. "You tried."

"I could have been better," I confessed.

"It takes a lot to face the truth. You are gutsy!"

"Nichole is intelligent. You chose well. She'll make you happy," I added, smiling.

"Thanks," he said getting inside the car.

Moments later Bill and Nichole were gone.

The thought came to me sometimes later, and quite abruptly. That, those brief exchange of dialogues was my first conversation with my grown-up son. When I had left him with Stephen decades ago, he was a child of six, small, immature and without a mind of his own. I did not even remember speaking to him then, other than giving him instructions.

And yet, when Bill spoke today, he appeared strangely formal; a million yards away from me, a thousand miles distant than a stranger. Although he complimented me, but something inside him was still spiteful. I could feel it in my marrow.

The few days that I was there, Bella spoke to me, but always from a distance, and in a tone which could not exactly be called warm. She neither hugged me, nor asked after my health. She neither asked me where I came from, nor did she inquire where I would go from there. She did not call me Mom. Bella retained her passivity in anything that was related to me. It was as if she now punished me with silence of the entire world.

Chapter 34

From Biddeford, I returned to San Jose and resumed my job in Andrew's pub. During the day, I read cards for people. Although not totally, but my health improved. Over the years, I made a few more trips to Biddeford. Stephen too at times came to San Jose, perhaps to convince me to reunite with him.

Then, one day I got a call from Nichole. She informed me that she was expecting.

"This is the best news I have had in a while," I said elated.

The joy was indescribable. I was about to become a grandmother. In due course, the baby was born; a girl child. On Nichole's insistence, I named her Nina.

Four years later, Nichole conceived again. I felt delirious with happiness, remembering what she had told me the first time I met her. Nichole was into her fifth month, when one day she called me to inform that she was suffering from a peculiar restlessness.

"I don't know Sona, I am not feeling good," she said over phone, sounding slightly hoarse and hugely worried.

"Don't worry my dear, everything is going to be fine," I said to calm her.

That was the last time I spoke to her.

For, exactly seven days later, I lost Bill, Nichole and Nina along with a few thousand other fellow Americans in the terrorist attacks, which the world would reckon as 9/11.

"Did you check the news?" one of my clients, John said first thing, after he took his seat in my cabin. "It's devastating!"

"Why? What happened?" I asked, stupidly.

"Open your TV!" John said.

I switched on the television; and couldn't believe my eyes, as I witnessed the towers crumbling down, like pillars of sand. The broadcast was running in an endless loop. I was beside myself with horror, when I noticed men jumping out of the windows.

How much more terrible, intimidating the inside could be, that men thought it wise to jump off the windows? What it took to make oneself believe that the phenomenal dive would be a more efficient way to die than getting strangled in that impossible smoke? How long it would have taken to hit the ground? Was it a free fall? Of course, it was! Only gravity was at play; gravity, in collaboration with one's willingness to escape from the harrowing death that could possibly haunt them until the end of time.

I was jostled back to my senses by the loud ring of telephone. It was Stephen.

"You, okay?" he inquired.

"Kind of," I said trying my best to take my eyes off the television screen. Impossible, I thought. One had to be blind to look elsewhere.

"I can understand," he said.

A pause. I wondered what to say next. He cleared my dilemma.

"I called to find out, if you are okay," he admitted unabashedly.

"Thank you," I said.

Stephen hung up without saying another word. Was he inquiring if I was alive? Was he afraid to lose me? Did he care for me still, after all these years of absence?

Couple of hours later Stephen called again. This time not to inquire after me, but to give me the news that instantly thrust me into a kind of benumbing oblivion. He said that Nina, Bill and Nichole had lost their lives in the attack. Nichole had a meeting with his investment manager there, that morning on the 75th floor. Since she was expecting, Bill had accompanied her.

"And Nina?" I asked.

"She was with Bill," Stephen said hoarsely.

I did not know what Stephen said after that. He must have said something, many things but I heard none. Hundreds of miles of static absorbed every bit of his words. What remained behind was a cold blank darkness that seeped through my ear and settled inside my chest. A kind of emptiness that would take one million years to fill.

I did not remember what I had done next, if at all I had done anything that day or the next day. I did not remember eating, drinking, peeing or even thinking anything for about a week. I lay in my bed, listless and kept looking at the ceiling, as if Bill, Nina and Nichole would emerge from it.

Out of all the losses I had suffered from, in my life, this one seemed to be the most devastating. Death of a child is something a mother should not see. I wished I had died before hearing the news.

Can you really see the future? Nichole had asked, and what I sensed, quite inquisitively. Being a doctor, perhaps she refused to believe in the rubrics of psychic prophesying. And yet, she wanted me to read her cards that night, insisted a few times, which I had declined, sighting that my reading could be interfered with emotions I felt for her. Had I read her cards that night, could I have seen the unforeseen? Could I have predicted that she'd lose her life in a few years' time? Could I have foretold her that she'd become a mother one day, only to lose her child? I would not know.

"You need a break Sona," Andrew opined seeing my miserable state of mind and body.

"Death is all I need," I replied looking up, as tears rolled down my cheeks.

"It's not in our hands," Andrew said.

"Wish I could read my own card and predict my time."

Andrew laughed.

"Listen Sona, I am going to Australia for a meeting. Why don't you accompany me? We could be there for a while, say a couple of weeks, and then return," he said after his laughter subsided.

I pondered.

"Meeting with?" I said with suspicion.

"A friend," he said, taking a long drag from his cigarette.

"Your gay friend?" I joked.

"Could be."

I agreed to his proposal without giving it a thought. At that point of time, I did not know what exactly his plan was. I did not even know whether Andrew was speaking the truth. Or what lay ahead of me when I boarded the flight with Andrew. I did not know that the vacation, which I intended to take for two weeks would last for four long and arduous years, at the end of which I'd be so exhausted and beaten up that, I would have a feeling of being a hundred years old.

The stopover in Singapore was five hours. Andrew and I had a couple of drinks in the airport and then, boarded the next flight for Sydney.

The baggage claim at Sydney airport was long, and while we stood, I noticed a man advancing towards me with confident strides. He had brown skin and dark hair, medium build. Something about his body language told me that he was a man of authority.

"Are you visiting friends here?" the man whispered into my ears, coming dangerously close.

I looked up and signaled Andrew to come. He did not notice.

"You like India, don't you?" he said.

And I knew right at that moment that something was wrong. Within seconds, fifteen men clad in uniform surrounded us. We were taken to a glass room where our luggage was already opened on a table.

"You can't do this to me," I protested as they tied my hands and shoved me in. My jaws dropped at the sight.

"Oh yea…," said a lady.

"You both are under arrest," said a gentleman, nearly twice my height and exceptionally beefy.

"On what charges?" I asked heatedly. My heart was hammering so loud that for some time every sound around me appeared muted.

"For smuggling opium," somebody replied.

"Opium?" I gasped.

"Yes, we have found 8 pounds of opium from your suitcase, and 10 from his."

I looked at Andrew. He was standing there, looking mindfully at the floor, disregarding my piercing gaze. If I had a gun in my hand, I would have killed Andrew that very moment, and then fired a bullet into my mouth.

"But I … but I…," I fumbled for a speech, wondering how the hell that opium got inside my suitcase.

And then I remembered the moment when Andrew came to my apartment to pick me up. He insisted on having a cup of coffee before we started. The time when I made his coffee, he had opened my suitcase and stuffed those packets of opium.

I closed my eyes briefly, realizing the mess I was in, yet another time.

From the airport they put us into a van, hand cuffed and guarded by armed men.

"I thought of you, as a friend," I said to Andrew.

He didn't reply. He didn't even look into my eyes all through the journey.

The van dropped me at a high security prison for women and took Andrew away.

When those metal doors clanged behind, one after the other, it was like a scene from a movie. I felt like sinking inside a dark pit, the depth of which was beyond me. After walking an interminable length, when I finally entered a cell and turned around, I saw a couple of women locking the gate with a loud bang. The blackness of the night swallowed me. Hopelessness crushed me yet another time.

I crumpled down on the floor and cried like a lost child. Something about the prison reminded me of morgues. It was the lifeless cold of the room, or the grey color that threatened to engulf me from all sides. Perhaps it was the absolute silence, or the sudden loneliness. I did not know.

The first thought that struck me was *how am I going to last in that hole*? And yet, I had survived, in that bone chilling cold for nearly a year; till the time I was taken to the city court for my trial and sentenced for 4 years for the alleged crime I had committed.

It was the beginning of a new life. The setting was alien, and people, unfriendly. Of course, one could not expect many good-natured people hanging out inside a prison. If anything, the very thought of being sentenced, whether for a month or a year or for life, turned most women hostile. Some were dangerous, beyond doubt, and I could feel their hostility even if we crossed path for a second. But most of them were pathetic products of society, who had committed crime out of sheer desperation. My heart went out to them, to those frail souls wandering in that desperate place.

There was a Eurasian lady, Kendall, who had killed her cousin, because the later was after her boyfriend.

"And you killed her just for that?" I asked while doing the laundry.

"It's not easy," Kendall said, avoiding my eyes.

Kendall was in her late twenties and was there for two years. Rigorous prison life and her inner morose had aged her nearly three times.

"I was on drugs when I stabbed her. Was not in my senses," she confessed with teary eyes.

Kendall said she did not remember the argument that turned into a wrangle in which, Kendall had struck her. The incident had happened years ago, but the guilt had never really left her.

"You know this cousin of mine," Kendall paused, "we were inseparable from childhood."

I couldn't understand her point. Why had she killed a woman, who had been her companion since childhood? It was difficult to understand criminals anyway. Why is it that a man turns violent and kills another man? Kendall confessed that she was on drugs. That was the trigger behind her violence. But every murder was not committed under the spell of drugs. Perhaps, human mind was like that, I was forced to conclude. What a person does at the spur of a moment is beyond comprehension.

"Why you do laundry here? It's quite strenuous for a woman of your age," Kendall observed.

"I like cleaning things…" I replied.

"You could work in the kitchen," she said.

"May be some day!"

There was a horde of other activities that kept me creatively busy, apart from my daily laundry job. I'd sculpture, make small things like incense holder and sell them to the correctional officers. That helped me buy a few essentials like toothbrush and toothpaste, comb and shampoo. The very act of keeping myself engaged took loads off my mind.

After the initial shock of getting arrested, life gradually settled into something sober, if not totally smooth. I was alone for most of the time, doing my work and keeping to myself, yet friendship with a handful of inmates made each of my days bearable. Their stories shook me and stirred me, but in the end, consoled me. Because they made me realize that I was not the only one who had suffered a cruel fate. There had been countless others, equally battered, equally luckless.

My roommate, Willimina, was the most troubled soul I had ever come across. She was nearly 200 pounds, with a mop of unruly hair that she never cared to brush. Willimina smelled like rotten eggs. Living with her in the same room was the closest I had come to living in a pigsty.

But that was not what troubled me. Willimina would speak loudly at night, often changing her voice into a male one; that scared me down to my bones.

"Yes, there, you… that you… sick man, you think I don't know who the fuck are you?" Willimina would scream one moment.

"Ah… delicious, this is the best pie I ever had," she'd say the next moment, in a male voice.

And the conversation continued… Sometimes, she would get up from the bed and walk with her arms folded and continue talking. At times, she'd come close to my part of the room, sit and tap my feet with her dirty fingers, perhaps with an intention of conversing with me.

I'd listen to her, lying tight in my bed, pretending to be asleep. It took me a while to realize that Willimina was suffering from schizophrenia. The day I understood her malady I couldn't waste a minute without taking an action.

"There should be only 2 people per cell, right?" I asked Mr. Blake, the correctional officer.

"That's right," Blake said, nodding his head, without looking up. He was writing some report.

"But there are 3 in my cell," I said.

"That's impossible!" he exclaimed.

"Of course, it's possible," I protested.

"I keep a record of each cell," he said, taking off his spectacles.

"I know you do. But you don't know that this lady... this lady... Willimina, with whom I am sharing my cell, she is schizophrenic."

Blake looked up in visible alarm.

"She is what?" he asked making a frown.

"Schizophrenic... she is schizophrenic. She has two different personalities. She talks all night, sometimes she walks and talks and I am scared. She gets violent at times," I said in one breath.

"What took you so long to come to me?"

That evening, Willimina was taken to an asylum, from where she never returned. A week later, Blake called me and informed that she was no more.

"Willimina killed herself," he lamented.

"What!"

"Good you told us about her. She could have taken your life," Blake added.

I returned to my cell with a heavy heart. I had never spoken to Willimina, and neither did she. Other than her name, I did not know a thing about her. I had only observed her, most of the time pretending not too. Yet, her death saddened me.

That night, and the few nights that followed, I could not sleep. I was alone, and thanks to Willimina's absence, there was no smell either, to bother me. But sleep refused to accommodate me. I twisted and turned the night away; thought about her repeatedly, exhausting details that I had picked up from her.

A week later, an Albanian inmate, Afrodita, told me that Willimina had killed her husband. The male voice she'd speak at times was her husband's. She was serving a life sentence.

"Good, she had committed suicide. It's kind of escape," Afrodita opined.

"Killing oneself is no escape," I said, wondering what was on her mind when she took her life away.

"Of course, it is. That's the best solution," Afrodita insisted, convinced that taking one's life in an adverse situation was the only solution.

I did not refute Afrodita, but that night, I contemplated about my own death. I was an American, in a prison in Australia against serious charges, practically devoid of a family; I did not know when my trail would be due? How many years of imprisonment would I get? If at all I'd return to America after serving my time? My health was giving up in bits and pieces. I was unable to walk more than ten steps at a time. I was suffering from acute chest pain, more often than I was willing to admit. And a breathlessness that often left me exhausted for days together. The ulcer in my stomach was getting worse by the day. I was unable to keep my mind off my body. And on top of everything, I was doing an unreasonable amount of physical labor.

Would it be all right, if I took my life? This body is mine, and I had an absolute right to own or disown it; I argued silently. I was answerable to none. And to be honest, I was aged enough that anything could happen anyway. I could close my eyes and not open it again. Why would I endure all of it, when I could finish everything with one small slit of my wrist?

And so, for the next few days I framed and reframed all the different ways I could kill myself. Would the Australian Government give my body back to the American Government? Or would they bury me here like a moth ridden pig? Would Stephen ever know where I had been, the finishing few days of my life? Perhaps not. Never! It would be beyond his imagination to seek me in a prison in Australia.

Those thoughts were hauntingly unsettling, so much so that one night I felt my entire body bust into a bout of cold sweat. I suffered another heart attack, which of course got detected twelve days later, when I was barely able to move a step, and was taken to a hospital.

The doctor was beside himself with shock when he saw my report.

"How the hell did you manage to survive?" he exclaimed.

I had no answer. I kept looking at his face with blinking eyes, not knowing what to reply.

"Perhaps that's what destiny is all about," I said after a long time.

The doctor looked into my eyes, deeply.

"You don't look like a criminal," he observed.

"What do I look like?"

"I don't know… But there is something in your eyes, that's different," he opined.

The doctor moved to the next patient, a woman in her seventies with a huge bandage on her head. I observed him for some time, the compassionate way he treated his patients; held them with respect, although they were serving sentences. I thought of Nichole. Had she been alive, she would have done the same. Silently, I mourned for her death, and the death of my unborn grandchild.

I thought of writing to Stephen, about my frail health, and the fact that anything could happen. That he should be prepared to meet the obvious, but then, thought better of it. Writing to him would mean revealing my unfortunate address, which I was not sure how he would take. It was better to remain silent rather than create chaos with unnecessary information.

I returned from the hospital a few days later with a long list of medicines and some advice to take as much rest as possible. That of course was not possible.

Chapter 35

A month after my return from the hospital, one morning around 5 o'clock an officer came, woke me up and took me inside a van. We drove in silence through what I gathered to be a forest. I wondered where I was going. Exhaustion of the previous day had numbed my senses, so much so that I dozed off in the moving van and bumped my head several times against the window.

It was the day of my trial. I sensed the moment we reached the court. The drive exhausted me so much that by the time I stood in the witness box, I had not a shred of energy left inside me. I saw Andrew, standing in the corner, his hands cuffed. He looked at me and nodded his head.

The day was 1st April, I noted. Of all the days in a year, it had to this, I thought behind my pursed lips.

"3 over 4," the judge announced, after what appeared to be an interminable length of time.

"What does that mean?" I whispered to my lawyer.

"It means you must do 3 years, and if you misbehave then it would be 4 years. No time out for good behavior," he whispered back. "You are lucky," he said as an afterthought.

"How so?"

"One could get 25 years for smuggling opium," he informed.

I let out a big sigh of relief. Immediately I thought of Andrew.

"And how much would he get?" I said pointing to Andrew.

"We are yet to see," he said.

But I was not permitted to linger a moment after my sentence was declared. Immediately I was brought back into the van. The entire return journey I tried to envision the next three years that I was destined to suffer in that prison. I couldn't. Something was constantly preventing me from anticipating my future.

What it could be, I wondered. Would I die before I completed my term? Was death knocking on my door? How many years would Andrew get? Could it so happen that he would be released without a charge? Thoughts swarmed and whirled in my mind.

A few days later I was shifted to Emu Plains, a low security prison. Almost immediately, I started planning for my escape. The very thought of staying in that foreign land for three years terrified me. I never grew accustomed to the settings. If anything, it made me feel alien. It bred in me a constant sense of foreignness. I was on a perpetual look out for opportunities; measuring distances, calculating height of the wall, noting the time of the day, the day of the week, when it could be easy to escape without creating a stir.

Then one evening, I jumped off the wall and ran. The very act of climbing a wall and then jumping on the other side at the age I was in, would have been enough of an ambition to make another woman embrace prison life with gratitude. But I was different, and hence, did the reverse. I gambled on my life, took advantage of the light security and fled.

One had to lose freedom to value its worth. In those dark cells, often I had felt the unbearable pain of losing my freedom. I understood its worth. The naked vulnerability! But stealing freedom from a prison and then running for life was an adventure not everybody could relish. I did. The joy was overwhelming. The sense of freedom was so overpowering that I had disregarded every other thought, like how would I survive without a penny in my pocket? How on earth would I manage to get my passport? What would I wear? Because all I now had on me was a set of ill-fitting prison clothes. I could be caught any moment. The police would not even have to try.

Obviously, I thought none of those. I ran in the direction which I thought would lead me somewhere, anywhere. A drug store, a food shop, a departmental store, a restaurant. I could do a job, get some money, fix myself with a set of clothes, a plate of food, and then perhaps some sleep. I was wrong. I ran through miles and miles of darkness, with nothing in the vicinity.

When my breath took control of me, so much so that I could barely inhale, when my feet turned stiff with pain, when my body felt heavier than 500 pounds, I stopped, looked around, and then crumpled down on the road with a callous thud. Moments later, I fell asleep; or perhaps, lost consciousness.

A sharp chill woke me up. I discovered myself lying on a road that ran through a vast field. I was in the middle of nowhere. For a moment I reconsidered my idea of escaping. Should I go back to the prison? Because I could not possibly survive on the run with the little energy that I had. But then, which way to go was the next big question? Both sides looked the same and interminable. I was no longer sure which direction would lead me where?

Following my instincts, I staggered in the forward direction. One, two, three... hours and hours of walking at a speed that would put tortoises to shame. After three more days on the road, I finally reached what appeared to be a rudimentary square. There were outlets, a food joint, a pawn shop, a bakery and a rustic looking bar. My stomach rumbled at the picture of a chocolate cake that hung outside the bakery. I lingered at the entrance.

"You want anything?" a voice came from inside.

"Umm... I am looking for some kind of job," I said fumbling, as I walked inside the bakery with tentative steps.

The lady, possibly the owner looked at me with lingering eyes, first from top to bottom, then, from bottom to top, until I grew embarrassed. She was nearly my age with a white face and golden hair but a build that was nearly triple my size.

"You know how to bake?" she asked.

"No, but I can scrub utensils, mop floors, do cleaning and stuff," I confessed.

"Is that your dress?" she pointed with her index finger.

I was at a fix. Should I tell her the truth? I argued with myself. But then, she would immediately call the cops and hand me over.

"Kind of," I said avoiding her eyes.

"Mopping the floor won't pay you much," she said.

"Would it pay me a bite?" I said, "One meal a day?" I added as an afterthought.

"I am afraid not. There is a bar there, in the corner, you could work there, if you are interested to earn something decent," she said, as she loaded muffins on a tray.

I looked at the tray with hungry eyes.

The smell provoked my stomach a little somersault. Forcefully ignoring the loaded tray, I looked outside into the direction pointed, considering the proposal. The thought of entering a bar suddenly terrified me. What if I met a cop? Bars are cops favorite hangouts; I knew.

"I can't stand the smell," I lied. "Low salary is better."

"Come on in," she said.

Her name was Margarette, widow of a pilot, who had died in a plane, crashed into the Tasman Sea, on its way from Queenstown.

"How old were you then?" I asked, scrubbing a set of greasy pots.

"Twenty-three," she said, putting icing on a two storied wedding cake. "I was sleeping, when they called."

I tried to imagine the scene. A woman sleeping soundly in her home, when a telephone rings and break her sleep, only to tell a story that would perennially alter the course of her life. I thought about the phone call Stephen had made, telling me about Bill and Nichole. The grave after shock!

"I am sorry," I said.

"That's okay. That was years ago. Are you hungry??" she offered.

I was feeling so ravenous that it would have been a

terrible offence to my empty stomach, had I refused. I tilted my head in the forward direction, without a speech. I could see that Margarette was a brave woman. I felt shallow in her comparison.

She gave me a plate of cinnamon rolls, a slice of pineapple cake, and a mound of dark chocolate soufflé. A cup of hot coffee. That plate could cost me my three days wages, I calculated before stuffing them into my mouth. But Margarette did not mention about the cost. Perhaps she intended to give it to me in charity. I should have felt thankful to her for that shred of unasked for benevolence, but I felt guilty, for cheating the woman who was being kind to me. For denying her the most basic truth of my current life: that I was a convict, who had fled from the prison.

"Any children?" I asked, as I polished the last crumb off my plate. I thought of taking my tongue out and licking the three fat lines of chocolate mousse from the plate, but then controlled my impulse.

"Boy, a cop now," she said looking at her cake in progress.

Immediately I felt like puking. All the cakes and pineapple, cinnamon and mousse rumbled inside my stomach with such an ominous ferocity that I feared Margarette would hear them.

"Where do you live?" she asked.

I pretended not to hear the question. Opening the faucet, I started scrubbing all the pans and dishes intently, wondering what I should do now. Should I escape? Or wait for the night to descend, for the shop to close. I thought and thought the rest of the time, under the wholesome pretense of working mindfully. Until it was time to close the shop.

Margarette handed me a note.

"For today," she said with a warm smile.

I sensed it was my wage for the day.

"I fled from the prison," I blurted out, looking at a spot on the floor.

"I knew it the moment you entered," she said in a flat tone. The evenness of her tone, and her attitude surprised me. She behaved as though she met criminals every day. "Where are you from?" she asked.

"America, am convicted here, in Australia for smuggling opium," I elaborated, this time looking into her eyes.

Margarette closed her eyes. She inhaled and then exhaled deeply.

"And you have nowhere to go," she said without drama.

I nodded, feeling helpless, restless and embarrassed.

"Come with me," Margarette said, closing the door.

We got into her car and drove to her house. A double storied house with elegant furnishing.

"That's him, my husband," Margarette said, pointing to a framed photograph of a good-looking man in uniform.

"I need a shower and a change of clothes, if possible," I requested.

Margarette took one protracted look at me, and then vanished inside a bedroom. Minutes later she emerged with a T-shirt and a track pant. Men's clothing! I wondered whose they were, her cop son's or her dead husband's?

"Bathroom is that way," she pointed towards the stairs.

I soaked inside a tub of soapy warm water, leaving behind every worry. Something about Margarette told me she would not call the cops right away. When was the last time I had such a luxurious bath? The day I left home. I remembered and regretted with towering hopelessness.

Getting up from the tub I stood in front of the mirror. A blur ... that I rubbed with my flat palm to peer at the woman I had now morphed into. Skinny down to the bones, pair of breasts hanging like two over squeezed mangoes, face buried under a mesh of wrinkles, eyes dry and impervious. And once men called me beautiful! Years and years of abuse were shrieking right into my ears.

By the time I came down, Margarette was done with the cooking. Two plates were on the table, waiting to be filled, a bottle of red wine in between. I took a seat. A huge chunk of beef steak, succulent and delicious looking, a bundle of baked potatoes and an assortment of stir-fried vegies. My mouth watered at the sight.

Margarette smiled.

"Feeling fresh now?"

I nodded.

"What's your name?" she inquired.

"Sona," I replied looking at my plate.

"Sona, you want some wine?" she offered.

I nodded again.

Margarette poured me a glass. I felt thankful.

"Sona, once you run from a prison, you have to run forever," Margarette said slowly, looking into my eyes.

"It was not my fault, not this time. I did not even know I had opium inside my case," I grumbled.

"That's not the point. You have been convicted, given a sentence..." here she paused. "How many years?"

"Three on four," I replied, cutting a chunk of steak and thrusting it into my mouth.

"Let's take three," she said.

"But it's pathetic," I protested feebly.

"Running is more! Plus, how long will you run? You don't have a penny. I don't find you in great health. They have your passport; you cannot leave the country, unless you manage a false one, for which you don't have the money..." Margarette paused for a moment.

She had a point. I fell silent.

"Who are there in your family?"

I said I had a daughter Isabella, fighting diabetes, and recovering from a kidney transplant. A son, Bill, who had lost his life in 9/11, along with his wife Nichole and daughter, Nina.

"And husband?"

"Ex-husband, Stephen," I said, wondering if I should add a line about Harrison. But then, he was out of my galaxy for so many years now, that I stopped wondering about him. "Stephen and Bella are together."

"Does he know you are here?"

I shook my head.

"He married again?"

"No."

"You are in relationship with another man?"

I thought of Anand, and then said, "no".

That was lie of course, because I loved Anand, perhaps more than I was willing to accept.

"You love him?" she said suddenly.

"Whom?" I asked, getting immediately conscious of myself.

"Your Ex-husband?"

"I don't know," I shrugged off my shoulders.

"He loves you?"

"I think so…," I said wondering if he really loved me. Of course, he did. Hadn't he requested me to reconsider our marital status? There was urgency in his voice, a tone of desperation, a sincere wanting. "Yes, he loves me," I said after a while.

Margarette smiled.

"Have you even wondered if something happens to you here, your family will never know?"

"I have thought about it," I confessed.

"And what have you done? Decided to jump off the prison wall and run!" she mocked.

I felt my ears burning.

"See, there you are!"

We ate rest of the dinner in silence.

"You knew I escaped from prison?" I asked tentatively, after we settled ourselves on the couch.

She nodded.

"How?"

"From your dress. My son is a cop," she replied taking a long sip from her glass.

"Then why didn't you call the cops right away?"

"Because I want you to understand the consequence of what you have done and then surrender."

Tears dripped down my eyes, realizing that I would eventually have to return to the prison.

"Tomorrow you call the cops," Margarette said, looking into my face. That was when she noticed my watery face and bloodshot eyes. "Okay, tomorrow you rest. Call the day after."

"Is it important?" I said, somehow reluctant to lose hope.

"It is. And if you don't, I will," she said in a rigid tone.

When the bottle was finished, she got up from the couch.

"That door is open," she said pointing the door. "You are free to escape this minute. I leave the decision to you. But remember, if you run from here, you will run forever."

Having said that she vanished inside a room and then closed the doors, leaving the entire space to me. I marveled the uptight way she said those words. The personality of her bearing. Her purposeful life!

I did not run out of the door that night. For, I realized that Margarette was right. If I fled from there, I'd have to flee for the rest of my life.

"I will surrender now," I said the following morning, over coffee.

"You can do it tomorrow. Relax today," Margarette said.

"If I have to get back, why not today? Why not this minute?" I said getting up from the chair and moving towards the telephone. "Number?"

Margarette parroted a number. I dialed. Did she memorize the number last night or she remembered it? I wondered, as I held the telephone against my ears, listening to the ring. There was amazement in her eyes, I noticed. A smile of contentment on her lips.

"Get a shower quick, before they come. Let me fix you a breakfast," she said getting up from the chair at once.

Showered and shampooed, morally and physically chastened, I sat before a sumptuous breakfast spread. Two poached eggs, four bacon strips, two buttered toasts, a bowl of fruit yogurt, a chunk of pepper jack cheese, a giant mug of coffee. A feast!

I gobbled down the food as fast as I could, even though I was not particularly hungry. Life had offered me very little luxury like that.

"You are very generous," I said with the coffee mug in my hand.

"And you are very good," Margarette replied, smiling.

"I am not sure," I said.

"Eyes cannot see its own beauty," she said.

"I want to hug you before it is too late," I said.

"It's never too late to make a beginning. Come," Margarette said with outstretched arms. She smiled. There was something electric about her smile that I could not disregard.

I rose from my seat and embraced her. Right at that moment there was a knock on the door; and I knew that my time was up. It was a matter of seconds now. The door would open and they'd rush in, handcuff me and take me back to the prison.

"Will write you letters," was the last line I heard from Margarette.

I nodded, unable to speak. Tears gathered in my eyes, not at the thought of going back to the prison, but at the thought of losing a friend, as warm and lovely, as Margarette.

Having fled from Emu Plains prison once, I was brought into a high security prison, where I had been earlier, before my trial. The thought was so demotivating that my blood pressure suffered a major fall. I was unable to get up from my bed for the first couple of days. And then, I was put through another trial for my escape.

"Why did you escape?" the judge demanded.

"In search of freedom," I replied.

"You could not wait until your release?" he said, annoyed.

"I thought I was going to die. I don't want to die in a prison. I don't want to die in this country. Your country is beautiful, people are great, but I would love to return to my country," I blurted out, half emotionally, half in a desperate attempt to save myself from a severe punishment.

"Then why did you come back? I heard you called the officers."

"I did," I confessed looking at the floor.

"Why? You could have fled."

"Yes, I could have. But then I realized, once I escape from a prison, I am a fugitive forever. I cannot run for the rest of my life. I am too old for that," I said, putting my words to Margarette's thoughts.

The judge was silenced.

"I wish you all the best in life," he said signing some papers.

Later I was told that the judge gave me an extra three months as punishment, which was bare minimum. People could get as long as 8 years.

I felt thankful for the slim moment when I mustered the courage to speak the truth that was pertinent to my existence; a truth that saved me in the end. Perhaps that was the power of truth, I contemplated, lying inside my room that night.

Chapter 36

The rest of my term passed uneventfully. Or it could so happen that my perceptions turned blunt, and my senses numb. I was just there, barely existing, passing the time, oblivious to my surroundings.

Margarette wrote many letters, which I always replied. Her letters were laden with the fragrance of love. Love, that was so little in my life. I inhaled lungful, reading and rereading them one hundred times. In her, I discovered a friend that I never had. I had met her only once, stayed with her for a day, and yet, she touched my heart in a way nobody could.

During those lonely nights, I thought of Anand too. How was he? What was he doing? Countless times I toyed with the idea of writing to him, but then write what? That, I was locked in a high security prison in Australia, charged for smuggling opium? The news could only make him sad. I rejected the idea.

Nearly four years later, one day, I was taken back to the airport and then, made to board a plane that promised to take me to San Francisco. I nearly jumped with joy, contemplating my impending freedom. As the plane made its noisy ascent into the blue sky, I let out a long sigh of relief. I had never felt so happy.

"At last," I told to myself, but at what cost? I had lost four years of my life. Survived one major and two minor heart attacks. My body was more fragile than ever. My limbs turned weak, barely capable of sustaining my weight. My hair was thinning at an alarming rate. I was just a bag of brittle bones, breathing with difficulty. To an onlooker I might have looked a hundred years old, although I was barely sixty.

They left me at San Francisco airport.

Finally, I was alone, without supervision, to mend my way into the world. And yet, the thought brought me no joy. The burden of being alone sunk inside me like a mass of wet cement. Gradually it solidified, turned heavy, so much so that for a long time I discovered myself sitting in a chair, incapable of taking a step. Where? In which direction, I thought again.

America had changed post 9/11, and I could see it the moment I landed. People looked at each other suspiciously. Security became tighter than I had anticipated. Queues appeared like long serpents with inexhaustible tails. It took me a while to absorb the surroundings, and their newness. My eyes burned at the glare of lights.

I thought of Mama, after a long time. Was she alive? I had no way of knowing, because, by then I had lost all the telephone numbers. The only number that somehow, I managed to retain was Stephen's. Should I call him? Moments passed in that single thought.

After much deliberation, and when I could no longer remain in the airport, I called Stephen.

"Hello," he said. That familiar voice!

"It's me, Sona," I said.

"Hey... how are you? Where have you been?" he started shouting.

"Am in San Francisco," I said and paused.

"San Francisco... not bad! But how long have you been there?"

I had no answer. Should I tell him the truth, I knocked myself.

"How is Bella?' I asked after a while.

"She is good. She is dating someone," Stephen added with some enthusiasm.

"That's nice. You met him?"

"No," he paused. "Why don't you come over, for a few days?"

What a relief! I sighed.

"Are you sure?"

"Absolutely!" he said and hung up.

I booked the next flight to Maine that was scheduled to depart seven hours later. It was a long wait and I had nowhere to go.

I thought of all the people I had crossed paths with, the string of cities I dwelled in, the countless beds I had slept in, the spectacular number of meals I had gorged upon, the innumerable nights I went to bed, hungry but not thirsty, the thousands of miles I had travelled, by plane, car, train or by bus, the hundreds of thousands of hours I had spent doing nothing but simply waiting... waiting for my turn to come, whether it was time to board a flight or time to stand up in the witness box, whether it was time to get released from a prison, or time to reunite with an old mate.

Dear Anand,

How long it has been since we met? Seven years? Perhaps more. I have lost the count, all the days, months and years that I have lived not with you, but with your memories. Only your memories. I have spent a greater number of years in your absence than with you by my side. Yet, I have kept you alive in my memory. Being apart from you is always a mixed feeling – the agonies terrible, the memories delicious.

Despite everything, I always like to think of you as my longest companion. Ah... companion! This word itself stirs within me a deep longing that I have seldom felt for any man. I always look back at the time when we met first, here in California. So many years have passed since then; so many events, so many happenings, so many things that one could easily lose track of how everything started. I guess that is how all stories start. At least the ones that endure.

And then our meeting in Pune, eventually snaking our way to Delhi, where you miraculously procured that marriage certificate. A paper attesting us, husband and wife. I have kept that certificate with me ever since. It still sits somewhere inside my handbag, carefully folded and thrust into a plastic bag, as though it is a treasure.

Really, you have done so much for me that I probably need another life time to thank you. And thank you enough!

In any relationship, the early memories are generally the most pleasing. But in our case, I feel it is the reverse. The last one is of course the best. Do I have to tell you why?

Our love has a life of its own. And I trust, one day it would outlive us. I remember Anand, once you had told me that marriage is not the union of two bodies but that of the minds. I now know, what you meant when you said that. What you and I share is beyond anything one could ever imagine or even comprehend. So, let's leave it here, this journey – the one that we made – you and I, beyond the periphery of rationality.

As for me, I am returning to Stephen, intending to be there for a while. He is the father of my children, and I admit, he has been good at it, even though he wasn't a great husband all the time.

But now, we, I mean Stephen and I have entered an age when anything is possible. My health is fragile, and if instincts do not betray me, his too. It would be wise to forget our old bitterness and look at life with new eyes.

Wishing you happiness of the entire world.

Love,
Sona.

While writing the letter, many times my mind flew back to him, to his beautiful house on Prabhat Road, aware that it would perhaps be my last communication with him. Purposely, I did not inscribe any address. Of course, I had none. But I wanted nothing from him in return, not even a line from his part of the world.

I stood in front of Stephen's door exactly fifteen hours after that call. It felt weird to come back to him after so many years. It was like completing one full circle and standing at a point where everything began. But Stephen did not seem to mind.

"Welcome home!" he said with a broad grin, as he opened the door for me.

I smiled, moved forward, and then, on an impulse, hugged him. Stephen obliged.

"Look at you!" he exclaimed, after a minute, taking in my lean frame and haggard look. "What the hell happened to you?"

"Nothing, it's the exhaustion," I lied, as I placed myself on the couch.

"Coffee or beer?" he offered.

"Coffee would be good."

Stephen brought two mugs full of piping hot coffee. Sipping at the cup I remembered the last time I had such wonderful coffee was at Margarette's place. Should write her a letter, first thing tomorrow, I made a mental note.

"Where have you been?" Stephen said.

"Was here only," I lied again, looking away.

The weight of the truth was crushing me. Perhaps the effort of lying was showing on my face, for he quickly said, "You look distracted. Is everything okay?"

"Am tired. Need a shower," I said.

Stephen guided me to the guest bedroom which appeared ready to welcome me. The curtains looked clean, the bed sheet and comforter, new. A pair of towels hung in the washroom panel; a bottle of un-opened shampoo, a bar of soap. Did he arrange all these? Or was it, Bella? I wanted to ask.

Although I hardly had any clothes with me now, but the closet was empty, I noticed. Perhaps Stephen wanted me to stay there for a while. I needed some clothes, a sweater and jacket, anticipating the winter that was to settle in a few weeks.

After the shower I got into a fresh set of pants and T-shirt. Those were Bella's. It felt odd to wear my daughter's clothes, but I had no choice.

"Need to pick up a few stuffs," I told Stephen that evening, after a supper of minestrone soup, garlic bread and pork loin.

"We can go tomorrow," he said.

"Where is Bella?" I inquired.

"Went to Boston for a week, with her friend... this guy... Wilson," Stephen said with a hint of smile.

"Ahh... that guy you were talking about?"

Stephen nodded.

"What's he like?" I asked.

"He is a scientist, good chap, measured, decent," his voice trailed off.

"He loves Bella?"

"I think so."

"Intending to marry?"

"Bella doesn't want. She says she can't handle marriage," Stephen said.

Can't handle marriage. That same thought! I wondered if Bella had inherited that notion from me, if my life had set before her, a wrong example.

"And what does Wilson say?" I asked.

"He is okay with it. Quite an accommodative guy," Stephen claimed.

"Does Bella know I am here?"

"I told her yesterday that you called, and I invited you."

I looked at Stephen, taking in his altered appearance; the absolute honesty of his bearing. The unpretentiousness of his conversations. His concern!

"Can't we be a couple again?" he asked holding my hands. There were tears dripping from his eyes.

"It will look odd," I said.

"Does it matter?" he questioned.

Of course, it did not. And yet, I could not reply to him with a conviction that I perceived in him. My tongue felt heavy when I tried to open my mouth and answer, the truth that was still burning in my heart. The truth that was like a hidden volcano, foaming and frothing within me, ready to explode.

That night Stephen and I slept in the same bed, exactly 42 years after our marriage. The last time we had spent a night together, he was a man, burning with desire. And I, a woman bubbling with life. But today, he was old, beaten down by age, bowed down by obligations. And I, hammered by… well, what not.

He held my hand all along, as though I would slip away from him, never to return. It felt strange to be so close to him. When he was young, he had drifted away from me, perhaps repelled by my over sexuality. I too had moved away from him, even though he was my legally wedded husband. And now, in the autumn of his life, he was seeking me out with an urgency that defied comprehension. He felt satiated with my touch, the pleasure of holding my hand, just my hand, not wishing for more. Not even a hug or a kiss, as I had anticipated, perhaps expected. Desire seemed to have drained from him, as blood drains away from a cut. I couldn't help but notice.

I did not know the moment when tiredness gave way and I closed my eyes, but when I opened them, it was another day. A new beginning! Stephen was wide awake, looking at me, blinking. His face appeared peaceful, sublime.

"Good morning!" he greeted.

I looked at him. I smiled.

Epilogue

A decade later, one morning Anand came to Osho ashram for a session of meditation and a leisurely walk in the garden. He had not been to this part of Pune for a long time. It reminded him of Sona. He had read and re-read her last letter, but did not bother to reply, assuming that she must have reunited with Stephen and was living happily ever after.

As for him, he had built the Mango Grove, his dream project. It was a modern version of an ancient hermitage. All the rooms remained booked round the year. All the rooms, except one, that was locked ever since it was made. That room was for Sona, he liked to think of it that way.

While walking in the garden, Anand noticed an old lady sitting on a bench, entranced in meditation. Although his eye sight had weakened over the years, something about her posture intrigued him. She held a striking similarity with someone he knew. Gradually, he walked towards the bench and then, suddenly paused. His heart missed a beat.

"Sona!" he exclaimed.

Sona looked up, slowly, smiling as she did.

Acknowledgements

Sona is not a work of fiction. It is the true story of an American woman, who, by virtue of her destiny, and at times, out of her own volition, travels across the globe, meets new and interesting people, makes friends with them; and in the process, makes her life utterly bewitching, and her life story, dangerously thrilling. However, all the names of people mentioned here are fictive, altered mindfully to respect their privacy and retain confidentiality; except for Osho, with whom Sona did meet in his ashram in Pune. Most of the geographical references made, whether of a country, state, or city, or even the prisons, do have real existences, although we have taken creative liberty to portray them embellished with imaginative inputs. We tried our best not to hurt the religious, cultural, and political sentiments of any particular nation, community, group, or individual. If our scribble feels hurtful, however remotely, it is entirely unintentional. Our singular intention in writing this book is to present before the world, the breathtakingly fascinating life of Sona.

My heartfelt gratitude goes to my beloved friend Sona, who trusted me with her life stories and crazy adventures.

She inspired me to write this book, although she left this world without seeing it completed. It was a great pleasure spending time with you, my dear friend!

Most of all, I would like to thank my amazing husband Joy Basu, for his contribution, expert notes, and invaluable support. This accomplishment is as much his as it is mine.

My special thanks go to my family and Tia Adélia for her love, support, and encouragement.

I am beyond grateful for my dear friend and co-author Sudipta Mukherjee. I could not have created this book without her continual support and vision.

I am thankful to Shraddha Hadnoorkar and Ragini Kashyap, who painstakingly undertook the transcription process while pursuing college degrees.

My sincerest gratitude goes to Black Eagle Books, to Mr. Satya Pattanaik for accepting our manuscript, to Col Partha Roy and Ms. Aparna Sen, who edited this book with enormous skill, warmth, and precision.

Last but never least, this undertaking could not have been completed without the participation of so many people whose names cannot be enumerated. Their contributions are sincerely appreciated and gratefully acknowledged.

- Ihina D. Basu

My sincere gratitude goes to the publisher, Black Eagle Books, especially Mr. Satya Pattanaik for accepting the manuscript and transforming it into a wonderful book.

I would like to extend my heartfelt thanks to my friend, Ihina D. Basu, also a co-author of this book. **Sona** was originally her idea that we worked together to make our shared dream. Many thanks to her, for all the different ways she has helped me in framing this story.

My bottomless gratitude goes to my mentor, Mr. Randhir Khare, for patiently hearing the first draft. His observations and inputs are of inestimable value in the making of this book.

My thanks go to my friend, Pooja Borele, for her inputs on the art and craft of face reading.

I am grateful to my husband, Amit Kumar Bhattacharya, and my daughter, Ananya Bhattacharya for being my twin towers of strength and support. You are my home and my world!

I extend my sincerest gratitude to my parents, Samir Kumar Mukherjee and Neena Mukherjee, for their unconditional love towards me. I wish them eternal peace.

I thank my brother, Sandip Mukherjee, for his unflinching support.

To all those people – friends, and relatives, who willingly came forward to help me in shaping this book, I owe you an immense and very special debt of gratitude.

Last but not the least, my heartfelt thanks go to the readers who have picked up this book from countless others.

- **Sudipta Mukherjee**

Ihina D. Basu
To know more about her, do visit her website:
www.soultherapyheal.com

Sudipta Mukherjee
To know more about her, do visit her website:
www.authorsudipta.com

Black Eagle Books

www.blackeaglebooks.org
info@blackeaglebooks.org

Black Eagle Books, an independent publisher, was founded
as a nonprofit organization in April, 2019. It is our mission
to connect and engage the Indian diaspora and the world at
large with the best of works of world literature published
on a collaborative platform, with special emphasis on
foregrounding Contemporary Classics and New Writing.

www.ingramcontent.com/pod-product-compliance
Lightning Source LLC
Chambersburg PA
CBHW030238120726
47903CB00005B/1538